## Praise for The Ahriman Legacy Series

"It is a fast-paced read that is powered by non-stop action and a taut, emotional narrative, elevating the story beyond the usual hijinks of the genre novels. It is sure to entertain and please spy thriller fans."
— **RECOMMENDED by the US Review of Books**

"Most thriller writers depend on reference books and the Internet to do their research for their novels. But Puja Guha has 'been there, done that.' She's traveled throughout the world from remote poverty-stricken nations to the boardrooms of high finance in the world's richest cities, and it shows in this excellent novel. Fans of high-paced and action-filled thrillers won't be disappointed."
— **Brendan DuBois, bestselling mystery author, three-time Edgar Award nominee and James Patterson collaborator**

"Resurgence of the Hunt is both a gripping thriller and a nuanced character study. Puja Guha writes with real authority and authenticity."
— **Lou Berney, Edgar Award-winning author of November Road**

"Taut, pacy thriller, with well-drawn characters, believable relationships, and a satisfying plot."
— **Cathy Ace, award-winning author of The Cait Morgan Mysteries, and The WISE Enquiries Agency Mysteries**

# Battle for the Veiled City

## Puja Guha

Book V of The Ahriman Legacy

**Battle for the Veiled City**
**Puja Guha**
www.pujaguha.com
pujaguha@pujaguha.com

Copyright 2024 Puja Guha All rights reserved.

*License Notes*
This book is licensed for your personal enjoyment only. This book may not be re-sold or given away to other people. If you would like to share this book with another person, please purchase an additional copy for each recipient. If you're reading this book and did not purchase it, or it was not purchased for your enjoyment only, then please return to amazon.com or your favorite retailer and purchase your own copy. Thank you for respecting the hard work of this author.

Print Edition ISBN: 978-0-9905930-7-2
Ebook Edition ISBN: 978-0-9905930-6-5

*DEDICATION.*

*For the city of Tehran,
the place that inspired this book.*

*One of my deepest regrets is that I will probably never be able to visit.*

## Also by Puja Guha
## Spy Thriller Suspense Series:

The Ahriman Legacy Book I —
*Ahriman: The Spirit of Destruction*

The Ahriman Legacy Book II —
*Road to Redemption*

The Ahriman Legacy Book III —
*Resurgence of the Hunt*

The Ahriman Legacy Book IV —
*Reckoning from the Shadows*

The Ahriman Legacy Book V —
*Battle for the Veiled City*

## Historical Thriller / Domestic Suspense
*Sirens of Memory*

## Contemporary Indian Family Drama / Woman's Fiction:
*The Confluence*

**Find out more by joining Puja's mailing list at:**
http://smarturl.it/PujaList

# Prologue

*Tehran, Iran – May, 2024*

Farah Nassiri strutted toward the audience, feeling the weight of her six-inch heels with each step. The hoots from the assembled crowd sounded like inconsequential background noise. She had executed the routine countless times, and despite the tiny camera hidden at her shoulder strap, tonight was just like any other show—capture the crowd's attention, dance, spin, and earn an individual lap dance. A specific lap dance that would give her access to her target, Reza Tavakoli, the son of prominent businessman Azim Tavakoli.

*Just get his attention. The rest will follow,* she thought, flashing a smile as she walked forward. She scanned the crowd and spotted Reza to her left, close to the stripper pole on that side of the platform, just like usual. He was already looking at her with hungry eyes, and she met his gaze as she paraded to the other end of the platform before making her way back toward him. She tossed her head back and flipped her hair over her shoulder, at the same time easing the zipper down on her jacket. The jacket covered the sequined bikini she was wearing underneath. After a few more steps, she shook the jacket off and tossed it into the crowd, then grabbed the steel-finished pole with both hands. She took a few steps to start her spin, then took off into a standing pencil spin, watching Reza for a full revolution before flipping into an invert with her legs spread wide. Hooking her right leg over the pole, Farah released her hands and allowed herself to slide down as her spin slowed, then climbed over her leg. Right side up, she swung her other leg wide before bringing it back to the pole, sliding all the way down in a fireman's spin. She landed effortlessly on her feet and turned to face Reza at the edge of the platform.

"Join me again tonight?" he whispered as he slid a hundred-dollar bill into her bikini string.

She paused and gave him a seductive smile. "Of course." She offered him her hand and stepped down to the main floor.

\* \* \* \* \* \*

Fifteen minutes later, Farah emerged from the curtained room where she had left Reza and smiled to herself. As with their previous encounters, she had invited two other girls into the booth, and had this time captured a number of compromising pictures, which would be useful if her handlers required more persuasion to get him to cooperate. Farah had retained most of his attention as planned and played the contact carefully; she had remained slightly aloof, and the tactic worked. He still seemed completely enamored with her, having returned to the club weekly since she'd started dancing for him three weeks earlier. She'd gotten him even more drunk that night—she probably could have stolen his wallet right out of his hands. Instead, she approached closely, seductively slid his jacket off and played with the top two buttons of his shirt before stepping aside for one of the other girls. After that, it had been easy enough to hold his jacket pocket against the cloning device hidden in her other bra strap to replicate his phone and transmit all the data to the receiver she had installed on her phone.

The rest of the night passed quickly; a couple more dances on the main platform. She was about to step into the hallway leading back to the dressing room when she passed the last draped booth in the main stage area. In her peripheral vision, she caught a glimpse through the crack between the two curtain panels.

*It can't be.*

She stopped mid-step, almost face-planting because of her heels. She backpedaled a couple of steps and paused at the gap, squinting past another dancer. The two younger men slightly obscured her view. One was fanning out bills, with the other seated behind him, but she could make out the older man in the back well enough. A weight descended upon her chest, and her breathing grew heavier. It couldn't be, but it was.

She would recognize that face anywhere. It had been burned into her retinas from her days working in the military brothel. Another life, long ago left behind, but his memory was one of the few things that had stayed with her. He was scum—arrogant, odious scum—but far more intelligent than any of the targets she'd gone after since being recruited by MI6. This man had orchestrated a major terrorist plot, killing hundreds at the Suez Canal. He had appeared blameless—he'd executed several high-ranking military leaders to ensure his involvement in the attack was never discovered. Shortly after, he had disappeared into hiding, slowly receding into the back of her mind as the years had passed.

She'd had limited direct contact with him. He had slapped her once, but had mostly ignored her in favor of two of the other girls. In those days, she was more idealistic and far too weak to make him pay for his actions. She had closed that chapter of her life, but now that he was in front of her, there was no doubt in her mind.

He had to pay for what he'd done.

He had taken what she loved most. This man had worked closely with her lover Afshar, grooming him, putting him on special assignment, before finally having him killed. She remembered Afshar's face, their last tender moment together. His promise to put things right, to make sure this man would pay for his crimes at Suez. As soon as it was done, he'd planned to resign his military commission so they could have a life together. The timeline was uncertain, but the plan concrete.

Followed by the news he was dead, the life they might have had together lost.

Farah stepped to the side, steadying herself against the wall. Now that he was here, right in front of her, all she wanted to do was drive a knife into his heart. She bit her lip. She had to be smart about this. There were two men with him, and dying before she could take him out wouldn't serve Afshar's memory. With a deep breath, she moved back in front of the curtain, tapping the camera on her bra strap several times. She had to bring this to her handler. Farah would need help to bring this man to justice.

When she finally backed away, she sped to the dressing room, pleading for the universe to come to her aid. Whatever happened, she would find a way to bring him down. General Majed would pay for Afshar's murder.

\* \* \* \* \* \*

Farah waited in the alley instead of heading home, the minutes stretching interminably as she waited for General Majed to emerge. She had positioned her car around the corner from the club's main exit and held a lit cigarette in her hand as she kept to the shadows. She didn't actually feel like smoking. The delicious poison always relaxed her and right now she wanted to be on edge, to have every faculty at her disposal. The universe had sent her a boon, running into the general at the club, and she had no intention of squandering it.

Her patience was finally rewarded about half an hour later when General Majed and the two younger men emerged from the club. One of them was a regular, although she'd never learned his name. Her focus had always been on Reza, per her handler's instructions, and she had never deviated.

That was about to change. Farah stamped out the cigarette as the valet brought out a silver Lexus SUV. In a hurry, she tried to get a picture of the license plate, but the lighting was too dim. General Majed's companions got into the driver's seat—the one she hadn't seen at the club before. While the other two were getting in, she jumped into her car and followed as closely as she dared.

# Chapter 1

*New York, USA – Two months later, July, 2024*

"Baldwin, we have to stop meeting like this. It's beginning to feel like *Groundhog Day*—that's another movie from before your time." Petra smirked, staring down the young man on the other side of the table. The cool aluminum surface had become familiar, as had Rob, her interrogator, although she still chose to call him Baldwin in the hope of keeping him off balance. "Think we can finish any earlier this time? I have a gym class to get to."

As usual, he ignored her attempt at banter, instead focusing on attaching the polygraph sensors to her left ring and index fingers. "Have you watched any of the movies I told you about? I'm telling you, you look exactly like a young Alec Baldwin. You've got to check out his older stuff. Start with *The Hunt for Red October*. It's right up your alley," Petra continued. Badgering him with questions helped to maintain the image of nonchalance she had kept up since he'd conducted her first polygraph—she couldn't afford to show any sign of how important this was to her. So far, the investigation into Kasem had stalled, and she intended to keep it that way. This polygraph was no different from the last time, or the time before that. *Or the time before that.*

"Seriously, Baldwin, how many times do we have to go through this? This is the fourth time in less than a month, and you always ask me the same questions."

He raised his eyebrows. "I'm afraid that's above my pay grade. I'm just following orders."

"Fine." She kept her breathing shallow. The machine was designed to detect deviations in her physiological readings, but by keeping all the readings murky, none of her answers would look out of sync with her baseline. *You'd think this would be a piece of cake by now,* she thought, but the process was still nerve-racking. Each session made her skin crawl, but she shoved the emotions aside.

*Even if the investigation doesn't resolve, Kasem still has another shot.* Petra recalled the idea Rachel had run by her two weeks earlier. The recollection steadied her, and she met Baldwin's gaze. "Let's get this over with."

As usual, he opened with a series of basic yes-or-no questions. She confirmed her name, citizenship, place and date of birth, then he moved on to her history with the Agency, a multi-government independent intel organization commonly mistaken for the CIA where she had worked since graduating from university. As she answered questions about her status as a former field operative and research lead, Petra maintained the shallow breathing. Before Baldwin moved on to questions about the Ahriman, he returned to a few basic questions. She could tell he was shifting the order of his questions slightly to see if it would disrupt any of her readings. *Not going to fall for it.*

"Are you the daughter of Dr. Danielle Thomas?"

"Yes."

"Is the man Sir Edward took into custody in Burundi Kasem Ismaili?"

"Yes."

"Did you first meet him in Paris as part of an operation?" Baldwin kept up a poker face as he watched the screen on his side of the table.

"Yes."

"Is he the international assassin known as the Ahriman?"

The most important part of fooling the polygraph was to focus on a slightly different question when asked something that required her to lie. At the same time, Petra pushed her right thumbnail into the tip of her middle finger. The technique helped keep her grounded, automatically drawing part of her attention to the discomfort in her finger.

*Is he still the Ahriman?* "No."

\*\*\*\*\*\*

Forty minutes later, Petra channeled her pent-up emotions into a kickboxing bag. *Jab, cross, left front kick, right roundhouse.* She followed the instructor's sequence, reciting it in her head. The bag morphed into an image of the polygraph machine, then into Sir Edward, the slimy Agency higher-up who had arrested Kasem. Finally, it transformed into Kasem himself as she pictured herself railing at him.

*How could you?* she wanted to scream. He'd turned himself in without even telling her beforehand. Since then, she had devoted all of her energy to securing his release, but what would she do if that happened? When that happened… he would be lucky if she treated him as kindly as the punching bag.

The hour went by quickly, and when the instructor blew his whistle to end class, Petra couldn't resist delivering an extra three roundhouse kicks into the bag. Her anger had been seething and none of the more productive channels she'd pursued to manage it had made a dent. Every morning, she spent at least an hour at the gym pouring every ounce of adrenaline into maxing out weighted pullups or high-intensity intervals that left her lying on the floor, barely able to breathe. In the afternoons, she usually went to either a judo or kickboxing class, and she often did an hour of yoga back at the apartment in the evening. Some days she added an evening run, heading off on either the Reservoir loop through Central Park or the trail that ran along the Hudson River. Before bed she attempted a guided meditation, and she could only get through the fifteen minutes by imagining a punching bag in front of her. Each of these solutions offered a modicum of temporary relief from her built-up rage, but none of it addressed the deeper turmoil. Why was it she and Kasem always seemed to be left holding the bag? They had both made countless sacrifices to help the Agency and the CIA. Despite the mistakes they'd made along the way, she had no doubt they deserved a real life. A shot at a life without an operation at hand every other day, a chance to build their relationship on their own terms. It was true Kasem had done terrible things as the Ahriman, but he'd also done so much in the name of the greater good, at huge personal risk.

*And personal cost.* She thought of him alone in an Agency holding cell.

Petra evaluated her reflection in the locker room. Her café-au-lait skin was a tad darker than normal from all the time she'd been spending outside over the past couple of mouths. She shook out her long black hair and tied it into a fresh ponytail, then walked back to the apartment she had rented in Hell's Kitchen. She cut west on 30th Street to 9th Avenue, bypassing the crowds that swallowed up both Penn Station and Times Square, before heading north toward 46th Street. Her building was an old hotel that had been converted into apartments. The elevator was out of order, so she trudged up the stairs to the sixth floor, fiddling with her key to get the door open. The apartment featured the longest hallway in existence, before branching off in front of the kitchen. To her left was the tiny living room, which barely accommodated a six-foot couch and the television, with the dining room closed off with French glass doors just beyond it. Carlos had turned the empty dining room into a temporary bedroom, but he wasn't back yet. Stopping at the kitchen sink, she splashed water on her face and neck—anything to cool off from the thick humidity. She filled a glass of water and retreated to her bedroom on the opposite side of the apartment, where she blasted the window air conditioning unit and peered out the small window. The street below was bustling with the normal crowd of people for midafternoon on a Thursday. She sipped at the water and wondered how much trauma each of the individuals below kept hidden as they went about their day-to-day activities. Would she and Kasem ever again be able to walk freely together? How had they ended up here, at this point of no return?

When she'd first arrived in New York after his arrest, she had been optimistic. She was the Agency's best witness, and she was confident in her ability to hold up against their questioning. As the only field operative who'd had extensive contact with the

Ahriman, she had been nigh certain the Agency would release him following her testimony. His record also spoke for itself given the risks he had taken, plus the fact both Carlos and her former boss, Chris, had also agreed to speak for him. The past three weeks, however, had beaten that optimism to a pulp. Despite all their best efforts, the Agency showed no sign of releasing Kasem, instead justifying his continued custody on the basis that no one could prove he *wasn't* the Ahriman.

*Innocent until proven guilty, my ass.*

A ripple of fear passed over her, and she breathed through it, focusing back on her anger. When she reflected upon the anger, she knew she could only get past it by acknowledging the fear. But for now, she wasn't ready for that. If she let it in, the fear might paralyze her, as it would mean accepting the possibility she and Kasem might never have a life together. That thought was unacceptable, impossible, and the only way to ignore it was to sit in the anger. Her rage, while less than ideal, made her feel more powerful, more in control of the situation. By any means necessary, she would find a way to that life, even if it meant breaking Kasem out of an Agency black site.

The sound of the apartment door opening interrupted her thoughts, and she ventured back toward the kitchen.

"Hey, how are you doing?" Carlos asked as he made his way down the infinite hallway. "I picked up falafel from the place that you like." He pushed a white paper bag across the kitchen table toward her.

"Thanks, old man." She retrieved one from the bag and took a bite, savoring it. "Still not as good as back home, but it's about as close as New York can get." She finished off the hot, crispy treat and her stomach did a flip, making her realize this was the first thing she'd eaten all day.

"I'll find you one here that's as good as Kuwait. You mark my words, kiddo." He grinned and helped himself. "Eat up. You're looking thinner."

"Good luck." She grabbed another one from the bag and ignored his comment about her weight. At five foot seven and around 140 pounds, she was of medium build with a lean and muscular frame, although the recent exercise kick probably had her down a couple of pounds from normal. "How did your polygraph go?" she asked, changing the subject.

"Same as always. I told them I've worked with Kasem a few times, that he impersonated the Ahriman for us on an op, but that I never thought that's who he was. How about yours?"

"No change there either. They asked if he's the Ahriman, I said no." She bit her lip. "How many more times do you think we're going to have to do this? I can't live like this, constantly in limbo."

"We'll get him out, one way or another."

"I hope you're right." Petra sighed. She appreciated her old friend's reassurance, but in that moment, the future felt dismal.

"What about our friend from Langley? Have you heard from her?"

"Not yet. We talked last week, and Rachel said she was still trying to get some approvals before she could move forward. Anyway, I was hoping we wouldn't need to go down that route. I'm so done with all this crap—the fake promises, banking on one last op, one more mission. Whenever it's supposed to be the last time, it never is."

"I know the feeling. And I'm sorry for dragging you out to Madagascar."

Petra shook her head. "You know that op might actually have saved our relationship, so I should thank you," she said with a chuckle. "Besides, I shouldn't make this all about me. I'm sorry for bringing you back into all of this. I wish you hadn't gotten sucked in."

"We have to be there for the people we care about—that's the only thing worth fighting for. You're family, kiddo. You can't ever get rid of me."

"Thank you. I want you to know how much this means to me—Kasem, too, if he knew about it. Tell Diane that too. I know she can't be happy you're spending so much time here with me instead of back home, especially when you only just got back from Burundi."

"You are kind of cramping my triumphant return." Carlos cracked a grin. "Don't worry, this way, every weekend I get a special welcome... if you know what I'm saying."

"I don't need to hear anymore. Better not kiss and tell, but good for you, old man." Petra smiled. "I want you to know I'm really glad you're here. I think I would have gone insane these last few weeks if I were by myself." Her voice cracked, and she grabbed another falafel, not wanting to tear up.

On the days Carlos was back home with his wife, she felt Kasem's absence even more acutely, as if the empty apartment were a lead weight she was carrying on her shoulders. Despite her closeness with Carlos, the first few days in New York sharing the apartment had been tough. He'd been her friend and mentor for almost ten years, since she first started at the Agency, but when he had found out about Kasem's past as the Ahriman, he had felt betrayed. His reaction, while understandable, had left her feeling the same way; he hadn't waited to hear her side of the story before assuming the worst of Kasem. Over the course of the month they had all spent together during their most recent operation in Burundi, he had realized Kasem's past was far more complicated. Kasem had explained the entire story, and Carlos had apologized to both of them. Despite that, it had taken Petra a while to trust him again. She'd resented him for not giving her the benefit of the doubt. With everything he had done to help try and obtain Kasem's release, most of that resentment had dissipated, but slivers of it still resurfaced once in a while.

"Nah, you're stronger than you think, kiddo." Carlos hesitated, then asked, "Have you been to see them yet?"

"Do you mean my parents? Or his?"

"Either."

"No. I wanted to tell my parents that we were engaged, but now I don't even know if he'll ever get out. As for his parents—I can't go to his house and still pretend that he's dead. It's like losing him all over."

"I get it, but you know you have to, right? You should see them because he can't."

"I know." Petra took a deep breath, recalling her last visit with Kasem's parents. After his capture in Iran seven years earlier, Kasem had been declared dead, and because of his past as the Ahriman, he'd had to remain in hiding even when he returned to the US. He had never told them he was still alive, not wanting to put them through any more grief, as he would have had to disappear again, making them relive the trauma of his loss. When Petra had visited them, they had recognized her immediately from an old picture he had sent them and welcomed her into their home. The experience had been both wonderful and heartbreaking, one she wasn't looking forward to reliving, especially with the uncertainty around his future.

Before Carlos could press her any further, Petra's phone buzzed. She glanced at it and shuddered as she read the notification.

"What is it?" he asked.

"Rachel. She got the clearance she needed. It's a go."

# Chapter 2

*New York, USA*

Kasem stared at Rachel, dumbfounded and speechless. He remained silent for several moments, expecting to wake up from a dream. The situation was so obviously a product of wishful thinking that he was tempted to pinch himself.

"I know it's a surprise, and it's a big ask, but we need your help," Rachel continued. "We have new intel on his location. The first lead we've had since the drone strike in 2021, which he obviously survived. He's been eluding arrest since the British tried to take him out a few years ago, and we finally have a chance to get justice for what happened at the Suez Canal."

*Is this some kind of trap?* Kasem couldn't see how, but he still wondered if her offer was part of an elaborate scheme to lure him into revealing how much he knew about General Majed. Knowledge only the Ahriman could have. Knowledge that would effectively be proof to imprison him for life.

He remained silent. *I'm not falling for this.* Although the Agency's suspicions were correct—in another life, he had indeed been the international assassin the Ahriman—he'd split from that past over three years earlier. As part of that split, he had more than paid his dues, helping the Agency to stop a terrorist plot in Washington, DC, take down an illicit arms dealer, and stop a war criminal from executing a coup d'état in the East African republic of Burundi.

Instead of acknowledging any of that, the Agency had locked him up in one of their New York facilities. *So much for gratitude,* he couldn't help but think. Not that he would have expected anything else. The Agency was an intelligence organization—just a group of spies, and that's all they could ever be. If there was one thing that was true about spies, it was that they were experts at providing only part of the picture; the part that would make you do what they wanted.

Kasem finally broke the silence. "I'm afraid you're going to have to give me more than that. What new intel? If you know where he is, why not just send in a team?"

"It's not that simple. He's surfaced again. We have a confirmed sighting in Tehran, and a possible location, but we need more precise information before we can authorize a team. Besides, sending a commando team into Tehran might not be the best option anyway. It could attract a lot of unwanted attention."

"Reading between the lines—you know enough to force someone like me, a.k.a. expendable, at risk, but not enough to put your reputation on the line by sending in an entire team." *As a former Iranian operative, I'm obviously more expendable than any of her agents,* he was tempted to add.

Instead of taking the bait, she just shrugged. "Until recently, all we had on General Majed was that he'd disappeared. We had a few unconfirmed sightings—one in the Maldives, one in Bangkok—but nothing we could trace. This intel confirms he's back in Tehran, and we have a likely neighborhood and complex where he's probably hiding. It's not a home run, but I don't think it's a bad start. It's enough for this op to have become a major Company priority. We've got him in our sights now. We're not about to let him go."

"If you have the building, why do you need me?"

"Come on, Kasem. This is Tehran. You know better than I do that most major complexes house a few hundred people. Besides, I don't have to tell you how easy it would be to move him if he gets spooked before we have enough intel to move on the location. Plus, we need to confirm the intel. The source isn't exactly foolproof. Like I said, this is a priority op—General Majed is almost as high value as Bin Laden was back in the day. We need someone like you to make it work. Someone who knows the city and can hit the ground running with the intel we've got. Someone who can make it work without a lot of ground support. This is our chance to nail that bastard to the wall, make him pay for his crimes. I won't mince words—this is your chance to get out with a clean slate. If you don't do this, you're letting him win, letting him get away with Suez and everything else he's done." She leaned forward and her voice dropped to a whisper. "You'd be letting him walk despite all of that… including everything he did to you. Somehow, I don't think you want that on your conscience."

Kasem found himself speechless. *Is she right?* General Majed was scum, but why was it his responsibility to put his life on the line? If he declined, was he being selfish? Not that he had much choice—this op was probably the only way out of his holding cell. The bigger question was whether he could trust the CIA's offer. But even if there was only a minimal chance that Rachel was sincere, could he afford to let that pass him by? His choice to turn himself in had seemed noble and necessary, but now that he faced a lifetime in a holding cell—or more likely, a black site—he had to admit the future looked a lot bleaker.

Rachel drummed her fingers against the table, ousting him from his train of thought. "Look, I know it's a big ask. Sleep on it. I'll need an answer tomorrow. Before I go, I want to make one thing really clear—this op really does wipe the slate clean. No more interrogation rooms or holding cells, no more investigation, no more Ahriman. You get a clean break. No ties to the Agency, the CIA, or any other intel group. You'll be free to live whatever life you want, with *whomever* you want."

"I'll think about it."

# Chapter 3

*New York, USA*

Kasem rose early the next morning and crawled out of bed, careful not to wake Petra, who was still fast asleep. He made his way to the floor-to-ceiling window in the living room of his suite and looked out at the view. The corner below was empty by New York standards, with only a few pedestrians and cars spread across the intersection. He sipped a cup of egregious hotel coffee and watched the world go by for a few minutes—a sight he'd been deprived of over the last few weeks in custody.

In the back of his mind, the events of the previous day played on loop. First, Rachel's offer, then being moved from his holding cell into the hotel. He had an ankle monitor on to ensure he didn't run, along with a fixed radius around the hotel. Petra had arrived shortly after he had.

The left side of his face still smarted from the slap she had dealt him as soon as he opened the door. The rest of the night had been a blur—heated discussion about Rachel's offer, a tussle in the sheets, then another fiery debate. They had passed out in the middle of it, although they both knew what the decision had to be.

They had no choice, much as he wished it was otherwise. He didn't trust the CIA to live up to their end of the bargain, but they had no viable alternatives—not if they wanted to have a real life together.

He waited a half hour before he woke her gently with a kiss. She sat up in bed and he squeezed her hand, looking deep into her big hazel eyes. "Are you ready?"

"No, but nothing's going to change."
"I think it's time."

Petra nodded and reached for her phone. She opened a message thread to Rachel and typed out a single word.

*Yes.*

# Chapter 4

*Stormont Palace—Perth, Scotland*

Tim Collins surveyed the simulation zones he had set up through his binoculars, just uphill from the estate they would use as a training facility for Petra and Kasem before the operation in Tehran. Now that construction of the simulations was complete, he wanted to take a few minutes before their arrival to look everything over and make sure he didn't need to make any final adjustments. He breathed deeply and looked out from his vantage point, the highest spot on the estate. The grounds were immense, centered on an old Georgian hunting lodge, with three surrounding cottages and three hundred acres of land that included nearby woods, a meadow, and a series of small hills. The estate had long been used as a training facility by MI5 and MI6, with temporary warehouse structures that could easily be broken down and reassembled to simulate a wide variety of scenarios. More recently, the grounds had been used to set up and train two joint CIA and MI6 ops. Once Rachel had received clearance for the Tehran op, she had also gotten the go-ahead to use the facility for the necessary prep work. The last five days of briefings and preparations had been a whirlwind.

It had all begun a week earlier when he received Kasem's note.

> *I'll explain everything later, but we have a big favor to ask.*
>
> *Petra and I were assigned to a special op. I know it's a huge ask, but we could really use your help over the next few weeks. We need someone we trust in our corner. If you think you could make it work, call the number below and they'll give you more info. Either way, thank you. Separately, a wedding invite will be coming your way soon.*

Tim's first reaction was to break into a grin. He should never have doubted that Kasem would find his way out of Agency custody, and he was finally going to tie the knot. They had worked together in Burundi to prevent a military coup led by the former head of the Secret Police, but everything had turned bleak when Kasem turned himself in rather than allowing President Markov to be blackmailed into becoming an Agency asset. A second later, the note's meaning sunk in, and Tim sensed a shadow over the occasion, a foreboding deep in his gut. *What did they agree to?* Without knowing anything about the new op, he was certain it would at the very least be dangerous. If Sir Hoity Toity from the Agency board had agreed to set Kasem free, it was probably much worse. Tim had moved heaven and earth to rearrange his schedule to help prep them for the op.

All of that had been before Rachel had even briefed him. Now that he knew the details, the apprehension in his bones had worsened significantly. So far, Petra and Kasem had only received the bare-bones version on the intel—Rachel had wanted to wait until they arrived at the estate that afternoon—and Tim was appalled. How could the CIA use only two operatives on this kind of op? The mission was to capture General Majed, yet all the Company had was a brief sighting. True, they had a likely location, but so far it was unvetted, which meant they had yet to confirm the general was even staying there.

Tim thought back to his days as a cop and how much further he would have tracked down these leads before even considering this kind of undercover operation. *Even when you don't know what you'll find, you have to know where to look.* He grimaced at the mantra he'd always used as a Metropolitan Police captain in Washington, DC, when it came to undercover work. Prior to the op, headquarters had to know one or the other what the operatives would face and where. In this case, they had neither—no idea what protections General Majed had in place, and only an inkling of where he was hiding. When he'd raised his objections to Rachel, she had countered by explaining how intelligence operations were different. Part of the agent's responsibility was to cultivate sources to get them that information.

*Patronizing shits.* He had always thought that about the Company, and while Rachel was nice enough, her response had only cemented that opinion. If the CIA wanted Petra and Kasem to set up a network that would eventually lead them to General Majed, they had to provide both money and time. They had a moderate budget—nowhere close to enough—and as soon as they were on the ground, the pair would be on borrowed time. As former operatives who had worked in Iran, they would eventually come back onto the radar of the Revolutionary Guard, and they would have to locate and capture General Majed before that happened.

If there was anything Tim was willing to bet on, it was that the clock would run out.

He had minimal confidence in the building complex the Company had identified. The intel had come from an MI6 asset with limited training, and at this point was already almost three months stale. General Majed could easily have switched safe houses. The wheels of British and American bureaucracy might as well have processed the information at a snail's pace, and MI6 had refused to use their asset for follow-up confirmation. Even if they were lucky and the general was indeed still there, the Company had been unable to procure up-to-date blueprints or details on security arrangements. Had they had both, Tim would have advocated sending in a specially trained commando team. As it was, Petra and Kasem were expected to do the job of intelligence operatives to find and identify the apartment, then move in on the location with no backup whatsoever. In the last week, he had often wondered if intel organizations regularly sent their people into the lion's den without appropriate safety measures. He made a mental note to ask his buddy Carlos, a former field agent, if operations always stank this bad. Tim ran a security company outside of DC which provided onsite training for diplomats and aid workers that was required for travel to fragile and conflict zone locations. A decade earlier, as part of a cover legend, Carlos posed as a USAID consultant to be deployed in Afghanistan and had attended one of the training programs. Because of Tim's experience providing training to Afghan police officers, Carlos had been able to partially read him in prior to the op, and their friendship was born. They'd stayed in touch over the years, and when the op in Burundi had turned pear-shaped, Carlos had asked Tim and his team to come to their aid. Without hesitation, Tim had agreed—such was the strength of their bond—and Tim had now extended that relationship to include Petra and Kasem.

*Are they trying to bring them home in body bags?* Tim couldn't shake that question. He looked back out at the simulation zones. All he could do was prepare them as well as possible. Given the limited intel, he was reasonably satisfied with the four simulations he had put together.

The safe house they had identified was a standalone gated villa in Qeytarieh, one of the richest neighborhoods in Tehran. Tim had based his construction on blueprints the CIA had provided on other villas in the neighborhood, but it was a shot in the dark. In case General Majed had relocated, Tim had also constructed scenarios of an apartment and a wild card remote mountain house—the type of place Tim expected the general to be moved to if he were to catch wind of the operation.

Tim focused his binoculars on the scenario he'd had built on the adjacent hillside to where he was standing. Using two stacked double-wide trailers with a nearby single-wide, the site simulated a mountain house and guard station. Rachel had almost overruled him building this simulation, but he'd pushed back, and she had finally allowed it. Based on his reading of the general, he wouldn't stray too far from the city, but the mountains outside of Tehran contained a wide range of homes that could offer much better refuge than a place in the city. Even though Tim couldn't hope to generate an accurate representation of such a safe house, he had studied available maps and development plans to get as close as possible to the real thing. Most importantly, the various simulations would help to ensure Petra and Kasem could react and adjust appropriately to the different settings and situations they might find themselves in when moving in on General Majed's location. *I'll be damned if they don't know how to adapt,* he attempted to reassure himself.

The other scenarios had been easier to develop. Tim shifted his stance to look at the meadow six acres east. There, he had supervised another layout of trailers to mimic a series of villas side by side in a residential neighborhood. Unlike in the mountains, cover and concealment would be more challenging, especially in locating surveillance vantage points. Tim's plan was to use this site to ensure that, despite the poor visibility, they could access the central trailer without causing a commotion that could attract local authorities.

The third simulation site was only half an acre beyond the second and used stacked units to simulate an apartment building. That one was the most likely scenario, as the majority of residents in the building complex lived in the high- and low-rise buildings. Tim sighed. He would have preferred to stack more units to train for a higher building, but Rachel hadn't authorized the extra budget. However, given the resources he'd had access to, he felt reasonably satisfied.

He turned and looked west toward the edge of the woods to scan the last simulation site, which he had purposely left more impromptu—a single structure with a series of surrounding obstacles. The site was laid out so that he could easily and regularly modify the scenario while they were prepping for the op over the coming weeks. He particularly intended to use the site for nighttime training with minimal lighting and poor imaging, as he suspected that whenever the time came to move in on General Majed they would have minimal intel. Thankfully, he had seen both Petra and Kasem perform well in Burundi. So, he could hone and improve their skills from a well-developed base, but he still maintained the task was nigh impossible without a full commando team.

*All I have to do is teach them to be a SEAL team.*
*No problem.*

Tim stretched. He couldn't let himself go down that rabbit hole. The simulation zones were ready, and he would use them to drill Petra and Kasem on every possibility he could think of.

*Whatever happens, they'll be prepared.* He clung to that optimism. A gust of wind hit him, the frigid, damp air seeping into every crevice of his clothing, chilling him to the bone. He shivered, then swallowed the bitter taste in his mouth. The cold was a constant reminder of what he was sending the pair into, yet he had no control of the operation itself. They had agreed to it, and his apprehension was nothing compared to what they would have to contend with. He turned away from the ominous clouds over the horizon and walked back down the trail toward the hunting lodge to meet them.

# Chapter 5

*Edinburgh, Scotland*

Petra's emotions were a convoluted mess when their flight touched down in Edinburgh. She glanced over at Kasem's tanned olive brown skin and moderately sharp features as he awoke from a long nap. He turned toward her and she pretended not to notice, instead turning her attention to the window.

They deplaned from the business class cabin within a few minutes and were soon in a black Mercedes speeding their way into the countryside. The past week had been a whirlwind, beginning with Rachel's offer and their acceptance. She and Kasem had spent almost every moment since then together, relishing the ability to touch each other for the first time since his arrest. Despite all the time together, a wall remained between them, steadfast and unmoving. Petra found herself angry, happy, miserable, excited, and terrified, all at the same time, with the dominant emotion shifting at random. Whenever she was alone, and sometimes when she wasn't, she relived their first night at his hotel. The resounding crack as her right palm hit his left cheek. Her shock and surprise that she had actually slapped him, and the subsequent intimacy. And finally, the conversation that had followed.

Kasem had apologized multiple times for turning himself in without telling her and promised never to do anything like that again—take a decision that profoundly affected both of their lives entirely out of her hands. On the surface, she'd accepted it. Intellectually she even believed him, but emotionally she was lost. Could she ever trust him again? They had rebuilt their relationship against the worst odds. She had overcome his past as the Ahriman. He had let go of his anger that her life as a spy was the reason General Majed had captured and tortured him in the first place. When she had agreed to marry him, they'd decided to take on the world together, but at the first major test, he had reneged on that vow. She wanted to forgive him, to forget it had all happened, but the upcoming operation was a constant reminder of what he'd done.

"You promised we'd be partners, but you didn't even have the balls to tell me about this yourself. You let me hear it from Carlos." She had said those words to him that night at the hotel, and they echoed over again in her mind, destroying every instant of comfort. All she could do was bury the emotions and focus outwardly on planning for the op. Their last few days in New York, she had poured over every piece of intel Rachel could provide on General Majed. NSA transcripts of any conversation that mentioned or alluded to him. Last known reports on his location, all of which contradicted the recent sighting by the MI6 asset in Tehran. Profiles on his former associates.

Kasem had sat with her in her apartment scouring the documents. They'd taken up residence on the living room floor with printouts littering every surface of the couch and coffee table. Their conversations were limited to the intel and the op, interspersed by stolen moments in her bedroom, shower, and other parts of the apartment. Their attraction was heightened, as if every contact could be their last. They avoided emotions—guilt, fear, rage, all of which had threatened to destroy their relationship multiple times over. Most of all, they avoided the decision they had come to prior to accepting the op.

Neither of them trusted the CIA to make good on the bargain. After this operation, they were both clear their life beholden to blackmail had to be over. Which left them with only one option. One they had agreed upon, but one that was nigh impossible.

They would go through with the op, move heaven and earth to bring General Majed to justice. It was the right thing to do, and Kasem certainly had a score to settle. After that, they were done. No more ops, no more contact with the Agency, the CIA, or any other intelligence organization on the face of the earth.

There was only one way to guarantee that. A way that didn't involve placing their trust in such an organization, which would renege on their agreement as soon as it served their needs.

At the end of the op, the CIA had to believe they were dead. They had to cut ties with everyone from their lives, start fresh. It would be hard enough to execute the op, especially with how thin their intel was, but faking their deaths afterward would be a tall order.

Petra leaned her head against the window and watched the greenery outside as they entered the estate where the rest of their mission preparation would take place. Rolling hills, the woods, all of it was straight out of a postcard, but all she could think of was their plan. Would they be able to locate and neutralize General Majed *and* disappear successfully afterward? How many months did she have left as Petra Shirazi? And when the time came, would she be able to go through with it?

# Chapter 6

*Stormont Palace—Perth, Scotland*

The next morning began with a wider team meeting. First, Rachel debriefed them on how Farah Nassiri, an MI6 asset, had been working a separate target at an underground strip club and recognized General Majed from her time working in the military brothel.

"I know all of you have read the brief, but I wanted to revisit it since the entire op hinges on this sighting. We'll have real-time access as more intel from Six comes in, but since he hasn't been seen in the last two months, this is the best we have to go on." Rachel fielded a few questions from the group about the asset and her experience before closing the subject.

"Before we move on, Rachel, I wanted to ask about the underlying environment at Langley. There's something that's been bugging me. General Majed's been MIA for a long time. Why is he such a top priority now?" Tim asked.

"Isn't it obvious? He killed hundreds of people at Suez and set off the dominoes that led to a massive global recession. Not to mention all the other attacks that followed."

"True, but weren't those Al-Qaeda?"

Rachel shrugged. "You're right. His involvement in the other attacks was never confirmed. Regardless, the administration wants to treat him as one of the Company's highest value targets and—"

"Come on, tell him the whole story," Petra interjected. "Tim, the real answer is that he tried to have the president killed. General Majed would be a priority target no matter what because he orchestrated the attack on the Suez Canal, but the reason the

CIA's given Rachel this much latitude to go after him is because Reynolds wants him dead."

"That makes more sense." Instead of dragging out the discussion, Tim provided an overview of the scenarios he had constructed, on which they would begin practicing that afternoon.

Kasem leaned forward and looked at the projected simulations, amazed at what Tim had put together in such a short time. Kasem was even more impressed than when they had conducted a joint raid on the president's house in Burundi to stop a military coup executed by Chinese intelligence. They had made the right call asking Tim to come aboard. More importantly, Kasem was glad to have someone on the team they could trust completely, someone with no ties to the CIA or the Agency.

Nathan, their tech lead, whom most of them had worked with on a previous op in Madagascar, gave them an overview of the continued surveillance he had put in place. They had identified the two other men in the picture Farah had taken. The one fanning out bills was Mahdi Gul, a local businessman and real estate investor. He operated several mixed-use and residential buildings in Tehran, but the CIA suspected he also used these investments as illegal tax shelters and avenues for money laundering. The man seated behind Gul was his cousin Safar Kamali, a resident of Qatar who returned to Iran to visit family once or twice a year.

"Based on that intel, we're focusing further effort on Gul. We've traced the property Nassiri tailed them to back to one of his real estate funds. If General Majed is indeed hiding out there, then it's likely he or someone in his inner circle is paying rent to Gul for the property," Nathan concluded. "We could use that to get blueprints and security information on—"

"Whatever we can get on Gul's black-market dealings will also give us leverage, which we can use to obtain General Majed's location and any other information we need on the property," Rachel interrupted. "That's the most likely way I see this op going—a quick in and out setup. The two of you arrive and, within a few days, pick up Gul. That gives you the information you need to raid the property. Capture the general and we exfil all three of you. The whole thing shouldn't take more than two weeks from when you get there, tops."

*An op in Iran built on wishful thinking.*

Kasem raised his eyebrows and scanned the room. He could see traces of his skepticism on both Tim's and Carlos's faces. On the other hand, Petra was staring straight ahead with a look of grim determination, not making eye contact with anyone. Seeing her like that, he could feel the pressure cooker on the brink of bursting. He'd avoided broaching the subject, not ready for the storm that would ensue, but he could only postpone it for so long. Sooner or later they would have to talk, and the longer he waited, the more chance he gave her obviously growing resentment to fester. *Maybe after the meeting.*

He waited for someone else to bring forth his concerns about Rachel's plan, but the room remained silent. Instead, Carlos shifted the discussion to another operational point.

"How and where do you expect them to pick up Gul? We would need detailed information on his movements to grab him off the street, and that would be hard to do without any witnesses. Tehran isn't exactly a pedestrian-free village."

"Of course. I'm glad you brought that up. Gul is a regular at the club where Nassiri works, and the owner, Hashem Ahsani, is a long-time CIA asset. You should be able to come up with a strategy that lets you grab him straight from there."

"Could you tell us a bit more about Ahsani?" Petra asked. "The profile you gave me doesn't have much information."

"Not really. He's well connected, been a successful local businessman for the last couple of decades. We pay him well and he provides us with info. You can tell him you're making a snatch from the club and that he'll be compensated for it. Nothing else—no other operational details. You can't trust him or any of his people. When you're there, you'll be in enemy territory. That's why we need this to be a seamless in-out operation."

*What could go wrong?* Kasem couldn't help but think. The phrase 'seamless operation in Iran' struck him as an oxymoron, but he saw little point in raising his objections. When they got to Tehran, he and Petra would be largely on their own. No CIA, no backup other than whatever they could leverage from a few local assets, just the two of them and their wits, perhaps slightly bolstered by whatever prep they got under their belts with Tim's scenarios.

The meeting adjourned, and he watched Petra head straight for the CrossFit-style gym in the basement. He considered following her, but instead made his way outside. A short walk around the grounds would do him good. Taking in the greenery that surrounded him, Kasem plodded out of the main house. The sight of nature always had a calming effect, and even helped to soothe his aching muscles—likely a placebo, but the result was what he cared about. Although it was early summer, the air was brisk, but it felt exhilarating, awakening, especially after being cooped up in the basement for the last hour and a half. He crossed the wide stone patio and stepped out into the gardens, moving past the manicured bushes into the surrounding woods. Within a few minutes, the massive Georgian hunting lodge had faded into the distance, framed by the rolling hills behind it. The grounds were vast, composed of the main house, at least three smaller cottages, and the surrounding countryside, including its own loch. The estate bordered national forest land, so the surroundings stretched out even further, including the zone Tim had allocated for training drills. Kasem headed in the opposite direction, taking the trail uphill toward the loch. When he reached the water, he sat down on a large boulder and leaned back against a tree trunk to take it all in.

Staring out at the picturesque landscape, he imagined what it would be like to return to Tehran. The hustle and bustle, the view of the Alborz mountains, the food, and the warmth in everyday interactions. The constant dread of the Secret Police. Dissident protests and the subsequent crackdowns. Clashes between followers of the clerics and most people who just wanted to live their lives. People who wanted civil rights and secularism and to break free of the Islamist perception that had hung over Iran and every Iranian since the 1979 revolution.

In many ways, General Majed was even worse than the clerics. He didn't care about Islamic values, but he used them as needed to further his agenda. What he cared about was power, and to some extent, revenge. Revenge against Western powers for orchestrating the coup in 1953, revenge for their continued influence all over the country. Power at any and all costs, no matter what. That was what had led him to turn Kasem, then a political prisoner, into the international assassin and terrorist the Ahriman. What had led him to plan and orchestrate an attack on the Suez Canal that had killed hundreds.

"I don't like the circumstances," Kasem had explained to Petra that night in his hotel room, "but I think being part of something that brings General Majed to justice is worth doing. Some of that's selfish—he ruined my life, turned me into someone else, something horrible. I'd like to say I'm a bigger person than revenge, but when I remember what he did to me—what he did to us—I want to run him through at least a hundred times."

She'd been against capitulating to yet another operational request, at least not without continuing to explore other options, but he had finally convinced her. Despite the circumstances, he wanted to pursue this op. He had dreamed of it for years, since the day the Ahriman was born.

*Three hundred and sixty-seven.* It was so easy to imagine driving a knife into General Majed's gut that many times.

*One for each of my kills.*

Kasem shuddered at the magnitude, and how simple it was to picture the dark moment. He had made awful choices as the Ahriman, done terrible things. He had done them, no one else, and he was responsible for those choices. But all of it traced back to General Majed, and none of it would have happened without him. The general had envisioned the Ahriman, orchestrated each of the events that had manipulated Kasem onto that path.

"I made a mistake that day at Suez. I was so caught up in trying to escape that I never realized I was planting bombs, not bugs. I can't deny that I want revenge, but I also want justice. He should pay for what he's done, for all the people who died that day." Those were the words that had finally persuaded Petra. The importance of justice for the people murdered in the attack on the Suez Canal in June 2019, and for everyone who had died in the aftermath. Al-Qaeda had capitalized on Suez with a series of their own attacks at the Paris metro, Grand Central Station in New York, and multiple others.

Petra had teared up as she recounted her experience—the lynch mobs that had formed to attack anyone with brown skin, the Arab street gangs that had formed in retaliation. The gang wars that had gone on for almost a year afterward. "That's when I knew Al-Qaeda had won," she had said. "People were too scared to go about their daily lives. It was like the attacks drove a stake into each person's soul, multiplied by a billion for every person who felt threatened and unsafe. You're right—they deserve justice, and we can give it to them."

Kasem sighed and started back toward the lodge. Ruminating on his decisions would serve no purpose. He needed to focus on the operation and the path forward.

*Always forward, never back,* he said to himself, a motto at his high school.

Still, his mind wandered. He moved away from his past as the Ahriman and landed on where things stood with Petra. That night she had committed herself to the mission, but he wasn't sure where she stood on their relationship. Several times he had wanted to broach the subject, but he was too frightened to ask her outright. They had been to hell and back, but she still might not forgive him for his betrayal in Burundi. For taking such a big decision entirely out of her hands.

He hated himself for that decision, but when he looked back on it, he saw no viable alternative path. Not one that didn't compromise his values. He couldn't have stood by and let Sir Edward blackmail the Burundais president into a life of Agency service in exchange for the lives of his wife and children. What would Petra say if he told her that? If he took the plunge and said those words?

He entered the lodge and headed downstairs to channel his emotions into a two-hundred-pound barbell. Regardless, he was committed to his plan. They would go through with Rachel's op to capture General Majed, but when they found him, Kasem would take matters into his own hands. He would kill the general, and as part of the exfil process, fake their deaths. General Majed and the Ahriman would die on the same day, never to be heard from again.

*Always forward, never back.*

# Chapter 7

*Tehran, Iran*

Sami Khaled Majed, General Majed's nephew, stared at the report, unable to believe his eyes. He read it three times over before setting it down on his desk with a frown. His source within the CIA had never failed him before, and the report was abundantly clear, he just couldn't believe what it said. It belonged to an alternate reality, or at least a dream state.

He read the last paragraph over again:

> Based on this, I would wager the Company has confirmed intel that General Majed is alive and living in Tehran. There is a team dedicated to identifying his exact location, although I do not know how much, if any, headway they have made. The deputy director has, however, made this a chief priority due to the assassination attempt in Kuwait in 2021. I infer that they will send an operative in to neutralize the general as soon as they have more information on his precise location. I will keep you apprised as I learn more.

Sami folded up the report and drummed his fingers against a knot in the walnut wood surface of his desk. *They know he's alive, which means they'll be coming.* His gaze wandered to the window. *If they aren't already here.* The only questions were who they would send and how much they already knew. He smiled. Regardless, whomever the CIA sent had no idea he knew they were coming. He opened up his computer and accessed the anonymous profile he had set up on a local messaging app that mimicked the American Snapchat service. Whenever possible, he avoided using the platform. He hated how it deleted messages within moments of viewing them, meaning he had to screenshot his messages immediately so that he had enough time to decode them. Despite that, the app had its uses. The messages disappearing meant they were more secure for this type of communication.

He typed out a coded reply, grateful that he didn't need to include much detail. His source had enough training to know how and when best to follow up on his intel. All he needed was information on where to make his next delivery. Sami hit send, and his smile widened. Whatever happened next, whomever the Americans sent, he would be ready.

# Chapter 8

*Stormont Palace—Perth, Scotland*

Petra peered through her night-vision goggles and adjusted the focus to sharpen the image of the simulation structure on the edge of the woods.

"I'm not sure how realistic this is." Kasem grunted as he belly crawled through the tall grass and stopped next to her. "I don't know how many of these meadows there are in a big city."

"You know that's not the point. This is about us being able to react to whatever we find in there—and out here. Besides, we'll find other cover to use."

"Right," he said skeptically. "Remind me again why we're doing this? I mean, other than how much I love being wet—"

"Ahem, lovebirds, just reminding you that you have your coms on for this simulation," Carlos's voice said in Petra's ear. "Maybe get a room for the rest of that talk?"

Petra chuckled. "Don't tell me you get scandalized that easily, old man. We are engaged."

"We're soaked and covered in leaves," Kasem added. "Could be one of two scenarios, and I prefer the other one."

"Old man, huh? I think my wife would tell you I've got plenty of juice left in me—at least when I'm not out here worrying about you two kids. Now get back to work, so I don't miss her phone call in an hour."

"Yeah, yeah, yeah. We'll get you back in time for your phone date. Better get it when you can, Mary Poppins." Petra grinned. She had given Carlos that nickname on a previous op years ago because he always seemed to have every tool possible hidden in his jacket—anything from a lockpick kit to a fire starter. *Too bad we can't use one of his fire starters today.*

"I see two hostiles inside," she said, referring to the heat signatures in her night-vision goggles. She looked past the standalone structure toward the stacked site about two hundred meters past it. The standalone was meant to simulate a guardhouse on the grounds of a Tehran villa, while the stacked site represented the villa itself. Their task was to pass the threat in the standalone—either by neutralizing the guards or bypassing it without getting caught—and then move on to the stacked site. Since they didn't yet have confirmed intel on where General Majed was hiding, Tim had been testing them with all kinds of scenarios over the past three weeks to get them ready for their upcoming departure. Here, they had been given no information on the number of guards or security officers posted in either structure—prep for how little information they were likely to have if they had to move on General Majed at short notice.

"How do you want to play this, babe?" Petra whispered to Kasem.

"If we take them out, we risk sounding the alarm, but if we don't, that could bite us in the ass too," he said with a sigh, voicing her thoughts. He turned toward the stacked site. "I don't see any indication of major alarms on the building, but we have to get up to the second floor. The best way up is probably the emergency stairwell on the far side."

Petra followed his observation, focusing on the stairwell on the outside of the structure. "There's no line of sight to the stairwell from the guard post. I say we keep quiet, move past, and get over there as quickly as possible."

"Agreed. I'll set the distraction. You go for the villa."

"Other way around."

"But you're faster than me."

"Exactly, cowboy." She leaned over and gave him a peck on the cheek. "I'll catch up." Without waiting for him to disagree, Petra started moving toward the guard post. She ignored the temptation to break into an all-out sprint since she had to stay bent over to use the tall grass for cover. Moving as quickly as possible, she closed the fifty meters or so to the structure within a few seconds. "I'm in position," she said as she dropped to the ground once more.

"Ready when you are," Kasem replied.

"Standby." Petra placed her pack on the ground and unzipped it, then felt around inside for the cone shape of the fountain firecracker she had stashed inside, along with a cylindrical smoke bomb and a bag of party poppers. It was the next best thing to a fire starter—spectacle, noise, and a bunch of smoke. On special occasions, people in Tehran were known to set off firecrackers. While such celebrations were supposed to be limited to secluded areas, many still set off fireworks in residential areas, especially groups of teenagers. If there was anything that would draw out a couple of guards, it would be a group of hooligans setting off a bunch of illegal fireworks.

She laid down a small fire-resistant tarp—not part of the scenario, but she had no intention of starting a real fire that could spread across the estate meadow—then dumped the poppers out on top of it, with the smoke bomb next to those and the fountain in the center. "Good thing this grass is so damp," she grumbled, hooking a small ignition cable to the fuse at the base of the fountain cone. She was half tempted to ask Carlos if the tarp could really contain the fire, but stuck to the scenario. "Setting the distraction now," she said into her com. "Here goes nothing." Petra pulled the cable out to the edge of the tarp, activated the smoke bomb, then lit the end of the cable. After less than a second to make sure the cable had lit, she took off in a dead sprint toward the stacked structure.

# Chapter 9

*Stormont Palace—Perth, Scotland*

Kasem beat her to the simulated villa by about a minute, having started in that direction as soon as Petra set up the firecrackers. "I've reached the building, moving upstairs now." He took cover under the staircase for a moment while he readied his tranq gun and then made his way toward the second floor. Steadying his breathing with each step, Kasem couldn't help but think how strange it was to keep simulating this type of operation where he and Petra were out on their own. Both of them were well-trained, but breaching a structure like this without a team was far outside their area of competency. Tim's training had been invaluable, and their reactions and reaction time had certainly improved, but they would never be as effective as a SEAL or SWAT team.

*Even a SEAL team would have at least three people.* Kasem grimaced as he reached the second floor and crouched under the target window into the villa.

"At the base of the stairs," he heard Petra say through the com.

"I'm at the window." Raising his head to the ledge, he examined the access point. The window had a sensor lock in the corner, but other than that had a simple sliding mechanism. It led into what looked like a living room, with an open kitchen to his left. On the right was a hallway that split into two doorways, with a single doorway past the far end of the kitchen. "Two heat signatures off the kitchen, another three in two rooms on the other side. No movement."

"Coming to join you." Petra appeared behind him a few moments later, and Kasem thought quickly about how to proceed.

"I'll take the master off the kitchen," he said as he double-checked his tranq gun. "You take the other three."

"Roger that."

"We should be able to open the window without setting off the alarm. Be ready to move." He deactivated his night vision on a timer so that it would reengage in thirty seconds and turned on the headlamp on top to get a clearer view of the alarm. He squeezed his eyes shut for a second and opened them slowly to allow them to adjust. Two sensors jutted out of the window frame, one on the base and the other on the slide. The sensors were calibrated to measure the space in between, so that the alarm would engage if the slide was moved upward. Using a slim magnetic device from his pack, Kasem slipped it slowly into the space between the two. When nothing happened, he exhaled and placed the device on top of the frame sensor to keep it engaged. Using a tiny piece of electric tape, he attached the device to the frame sensor, then nodded at Petra as his night vision restarted. "Ready to breach," he radioed to Carlos.

"No movement on aerial, you're a go."

"Wait," Petra said softly and gave him a kiss. "For luck."

Kasem pushed the window slider up, praying that he'd been right about the sensor alarm.

# Chapter 10

**London, United Kingdom**

Kasem broke into a smile as he sipped on a flat white coffee at the Muffin Man Tea Shop just off Kensington High Street. Despite the stressful circumstances, he was very much looking forward to seeing his old friend Gaston. He'd arranged for the side trip away from Stormont Palace at the first viable opportunity.

By the time Kasem finished his coffee, his order of scones, two slices of Queen Mother's Cake, a looseleaf packet of first flush Darjeeling tea, and a Devon cream tea portion of clotted cream and raspberry jam was packed and ready. Years before the Ahriman, when he'd first moved from New York to London for a job in investment banking, he'd discovered the shop on a whim. It had quickly become his favorite guilty pleasure, although he rarely indulged to this extent. He picked up the paper bag and made his way toward a building on the east side of Holland Park, where he had booked a flat to stay during his trip. The bustle of the high street, the passing black cabs and double-decker buses, the hordes of people on the sidewalk—all of it reminded him of anonymity, of a simpler time. A time when he was just Kasem Ismaili, not an operative, not a wanted man, and certainly not a man who was officially reported dead.

Because of the number of CCTVs in the city, Rachel's team had processed an extra cover identity for this trip, one that gave him the freedom to walk around without fear of repercussions. He could be just another Londoner walking on the High Street dodging tourists. Rachel had wanted him to use an MI6 safe house, but he'd convinced her it wasn't necessary. With all the tourists and businesspeople who came in and out of London on a regular basis, booking an Airbnb would hardly attract any attention. It also provided a private place for him and Gaston to meet without involving higher-ups at either the CIA or MI6. Kasem hadn't bothered to mask his distrust of the intelligence agencies. Besides, if they relied only on information provided from those agencies, they would never get anywhere. General Majed would die of old age by the time they got anywhere close to his hideout.

Shaking off that train of thought, Kasem made his way to the third floor, using the code his host had provided for the apartment door. Once inside, he opened the kitchen window—it was a rare, beautiful afternoon in London, even for early August—and put the kettle on the stove. Sunlight streamed into the west-facing window. For a moment, he let himself believe he was just meeting an old friend rather than a source of potential intel.

While the water heated, he set out his purchases on the kitchen table, then glanced at his phone. Gaston had just sent him a text message: *Running a few minutes late, picking up some food.*

Kasem couldn't help but roll his eyes. *Old Frenchie doesn't trust me to get something good.*

Twenty minutes later, the two of them were seated at the kitchen table together. "This is quite the feast," Kasem said as Gaston set out a large quiche, three different hard cheeses, and two types of soppressata. "I'm glad I didn't eat breakfast."

"You Americans. A good meal in the afternoon has nothing to do with whether you had your petit-déjeuner. Food is a huge part of life. You have to enjoy it. Doesn't matter if it's the morning, middle of the day, middle of the night. I hope you have some decent food at your wedding—that's the most important part. Have you set a date?"

"Not yet."

"I hope you are taking time to smell the flowers."

"Of course." Kasem chuckled. *Some things don't change.* When he and Gaston had met during his last operation in Burundi, Gaston had several times goaded Kasem about how he couldn't seem to enjoy the simpler parts of life. "I got some scones and cake—it's supposed to be one of the best places around here."

"British high tea—it's a nice custom, but isn't chaussons aux pommes tastier than these plain scones? Now that cake, you could be right about that."

"Fair enough. Try the tea. It's really quite good."

"Of course, of course. I may be French, but I do admit the roast beefs know something special about tea. It's all from the colonies, of course, but it is good."

Kasem grinned at Gaston's colloquial reference to the British as 'roast beef.' Every time he saw Gaston, he couldn't believe the personification of a French caricature could exist in real life. He had met enough French people over the years to know most of them did not fit the stereotypes of American cartoons. *But one of them does, and I met him in Burundi.* "Sometime, I'll make you an Iranian meal. How about that? We're very particular about our kebabs."

"I look forward to it, my friend. I haven't had good kebabs since I left Tehran."

They munched on the food, sampling different things and telling non-consequential stories from their childhood. When he finished the last slice of quiche, Gaston set down his fork and looked at Kasem intently. "Tell me, Kasem, we've talked about everything except the present. When I last saw you, you told me the mission was everything, and I saw you carted off in handcuffs. Then, last week, you messaged me as if everything was fine, just on to the next op. Are we going to talk about what happened?"

"It's a long story, for another time."

"Are you sure? Sometimes the weight is heavier when you keep it to yourself."

Kasem hesitated, then recounted a summary of Rachel's offer and how he and Petra had decided to take it. He didn't mention his identity as the Ahriman or the name of the target, but even sharing a small portion of the story did indeed make him feel lighter.

"It's a difficult op, although one I'm sure you can follow through on. How is your stress these days?" Gaston asked quietly when he was finished.

"About as high as the last time I saw you."

"That bad? I'm sorry." After a protracted silence, Gaston added, "The deal sounds tricky, but worthwhile. Are you sure the Company will hold up their end?"

"We're, er, taking measures to make sure they do."

"What you should do, my friend, is disappear. Make it seem like you're both dead. If they're not looking for you, they can't find you." Gaston held his gaze. "If there's anything I can do to help, I will."

"Thank you."

"Anyway, I'll leave that to you. Going back to your message, the information you asked for—it's dangerous. Tehran is not an easy posting, even for someone who isn't marked."

"I know." Kasem wondered how much Gaston knew about his past or why he had been arrested, but decided not to ask. "Were you able to find anything?"

"Yes." Gaston placed a USB thumb drive on the table. "There are three files on there. One on Ahsani, the businessman you asked me to dig into. We don't have much, but he has quite an extensive network. We suspected he worked for someone else, so never thought of recruiting him. The second file may be even more useful; a woman named Tanya Mir. She'd turn on her own grandmother if you paid her enough, but be careful if you decide to contact her. Quite a piece of work—smart, beautiful, ambitious, but you and I have more morality in our pinkies than she does in her whole being. We are spies, so that's saying a lot. I'd advise you not to use her unless you absolutely have to. Trusting her is like… what's that English saying? Playing with the flames?"

"Playing with fire."

"Of course, play with fire and you might get burned," Gaston added.

"What does she do?"

"When I ran her, she worked with a supplier for the military brothels. Now she runs the outfit herself. Like I said, ambitious. You can only trust her when she knows another payday is coming, and that it's bigger than any others she could get."

"We'll keep that in mind."

"I mean it, my friend. *Prudence est mère de sûreté.*"

Kasem chuckled. "All I got from that is the word prudence. Petra's the one who speaks French, you know that. I don't have a clue."

"I knew she was the more civilized one. It means that even when things are going well, we must be cautious, act prudently. Especially in this line of work."

"Of course," Kasem agreed. "She did mention you knew a lot of old French sayings."

"I pride myself on it. Where do you think I get my wisdom from? Most of it is all mine, but I have to get my inspiration somewhere."

"Thank you. I need all the inspiration I can get." Kasem picked up another scone, spread the corner with butter, took a bite and then asked, "What about the third file?"

"I misspoke—the drive has only two. The last one is here, and it's not really a file, just contact info." Gaston slid a slim folio across the table. "As far as I know, the DGSE no longer has any deep cover operatives in Tehran. But if you run into any issues, this man will help you. All you have to say is that Gaston sent you. Davit is an old friend, and his association with me and the West is very much under the radar. He hates the direction the ayatollahs have taken the country, and as an Armenian, he's also dealt with a lot of discrimination. Don't go to him unless you have no other choice. Memorize the info and burn it before you go back—this one is not for the CIA, just for you. You and your chérie."

"I'll do that. Thank you." Kasem wanted to say more, to convey his gratitude for the risk Gaston had taken to hand over so much information. Without their personal connection, an intel request passed to French foreign intelligence at the DGSE—Direction Générale de la Sécurité Extérieure—would have taken a few weeks, required countless clearances within Rachel's team and on the French side, and would probably still only have yielded a redacted version of what Gaston had handed over. Even the most streamlined process would never have provided the emergency contact Gaston had just given him.

"You would do the same for me. I have no doubt." Gaston grabbed another large forkful of cake. "This bakery is really quite good, you'll have to tell me the name."

They spent the next half hour polishing off the remaining food, chuckling as Gaston shared stories from his recent travels. When the last crumbs had disappeared, Gaston stood up. "Tell your chérie I send her my love. My friend, my hope is that next time I see you, we don't have to talk about spy stuff. No operations, no intel, just food, drink, maybe some dancing. A celebration of your wedding and the future."

"I hope so too."

# Chapter 11

*Tehran, Iran*

Sami Majed sipped a cup of English Breakfast tea as he went through his morning ritual, which included skimming several local newspapers along with the daily intel briefing provided through the Iranian Security Service. He always read at least one or two of the reformist papers, such as the *Shargh* and *Eternad* in Farsi and the *Tehran Times* in English. While he steered clear of politics, he prided himself on remaining informed of the various perspectives circulating the country, especially keeping abreast of the local dissident pulse. He kept most of his opinions to himself, but he secretly had quite progressive views on women's rights and civil liberties. The few women whom he'd interacted with through his work in intelligence—assets operating around the world, many of whom were of Persian descent—had all been extremely competent, and he had noted they were allowed far more freedom than religious doctrine would dictate.

Since being recruited into the Ministry of Intelligence, also known as VAJA, straight out of the University of Tehran, Sami had grown increasingly disillusioned with the country's politics. Over various posts abroad, he'd been sheltered from the worst of this, but his transfer to the Revolutionary Guard had shattered his rose-colored glasses. Being stationed in Tehran made it impossible to ignore his country's plight. There was no disguising the truth; the clerics had debilitated his country and subjugated the people, and the Guard always played right into their hands.

On foreign policy, however, Sami was extremely nationalistic. He saw no reason Iran should be subject to the whims of American or British policy. Whenever he thought about how the West had interfered with, and in many ways destroyed, Iran's former secular political trajectory, he was overcome with a deep-seated rage. He and his old friend Abbas had often privately discussed what the country could or would have been like if the CIA's plan to depose the former Prime Minister Mohammad Mossadegh in 1953 had failed.

*Perhaps we could even have been together.*

Sami pushed that thought aside. He preferred not to acknowledge it, even to himself. They were the closest of friends, the most trusting of companions. On several occasions, Sami had asked himself if his feelings went further than that, if he sought something more from their friendship. Questions he had never had the courage to voice aloud, and which had faded into the background five years earlier after Abbas's wedding. They were still in touch and caught up from time to time, but it was a far cry from the evenings they had spent together several times a week before that. Partly as a coping mechanism, Sami had immersed himself in postings outside of Iran, while Abbas had done the same in his family life.

Sami let out a long sigh and set the *Shargh* newspaper aside—he still preferred paper copies—to open the daily intel briefing on his computer. When he reached the end of the document, he sat back. He wished he could be back on assignment outside of Tehran. With Abbas otherwise occupied, his time in the city was primarily spent attending to his uncle, a task he would have preferred to avoid. Given his source's most recent report, taking another posting was out of the question. If the CIA had a lead on General Majed, it was up to him to stop them from locating him.

Sami reopened the series of three reports that he'd received. The first had provided the initial direction of the CIA's operation, but since then, the source had only made limited headway. Sami reread the key lines he had highlighted across the three reports with a feeling of deep frustration. There was little he could do until the source provided more information. He was tempted to round up a group of American expats to stir the pot, to see if the CIA made any mistakes when pushed into a corner.

"Deputy Director continues to consider the investigation a top priority…"

"… conjecture that agent(s) have been or are likely to be deployed, but the operation remains largely off book."

"Budget allocations indicate the operation has likely started, but I cannot yet ascertain if operatives are on the ground in Tehran."

Sami scowled. The lack of actionable intel was enough to make him want to ram his fist through the wall.

*I could be working an entire network of assets. Instead, I'm on babysitting duty.*

His first assignment had been in Shanghai, where he had lived on and off until his posting in Kuwait in 2021. As a field agent, he'd been incredibly successful, identifying and recruiting two high-level Chinese government assets, both of whom had yielded priority intelligence. The two assets had remained active since he'd handed them off to another agent, but he missed the process. Upon his initial return to Tehran, his uncle had requested his help on what he'd called a personal assignment. Sami had worked alongside General Majed and Lieutenant Afshar, often butting heads with both of them, but ultimately it had been engaging and rewarding. That assignment had turned out to be training and grooming the man who would become the Ahriman. They had turned a privileged geek into one of the world's deadliest assassins and kept their names out of it. *No evidence to bite us in the ass.*

Those were the good old days. He and his uncle had also orchestrated the Suez Canal bombing, nursing the idea from infancy, setting it up step by step, moving each of the pieces on the chessboard. Although Sami had initially been skeptical of recruiting the "boy"—as they had referred to the Ahriman during his training—he eventually had to acknowledge the general's brilliance. The boy had turned out to be a godsend, a means for them to orchestrate massive attacks, to tip the balance of power in their favor without the risk of negative consequences. The Ahriman had been his greatest success, until the operation in Kuwait when he had disappeared. Despite the desire to take another international posting, Sami had remained in Tehran afterward, managing his uncle and trying to keep busy. Few people knew of their role in the attack at Suez, but those who did would never forget it. As a spy, Sami was used to operating with less visibility, remaining in the background while he watched events move forward according to his prescription. He had always relished the sense of power that came with operating from the shadows—he could wield influence and control while most people barely knew of his existence, let alone his impact.

Sami shut down his computer and was about to make himself another cup of tea when a text message notification appeared on his phone. *Your appointment at the Maham Shooting Range is confirmed for Tuesday at 11:00.* He broke into a small smile. The only reason his source would ask for an in-person meet would be if he had news, which meant Sami could soon take action. Perhaps he had the names or profiles of the operatives the CIA were sending? Or something equally juicy? Regardless, the Company would be caught with their pants down when Sami got hold of their agents. Their days were numbered.

# Chapter 12

### Stormont Palace—Perth, Scotland

Petra's stomach did somersaults as she zipped up her suitcase and did a last check around the room to make sure they hadn't forgotten anything. *This is crazy. We're crazy,* she thought, memories of how she had fled Tehran years earlier slamming into her like a tidal wave. She breathed through it, summoning other recollections, some of her best memories—walking along the beach on Kish Island with Kasem, cooking dinner together for the first time at her apartment, beating Jamal and his girlfriend at a knockoff game of Pictionary. *Tehran was never all good or all bad. Ups and downs, like anything in life,* she reminded herself as the burst of panic passed.

On her way out, she paused at the door and looked back at the bedroom that had been their home for just under four weeks. *Should have been a honeymoon suite,* she thought with a sad smile. She turned out the light and headed toward the living room, suitcase and laptop bag in hand.

"How do you feel, kiddo?" Carlos greeted her when she walked in.

"I don't know, a bit all over the place, I guess." She shrugged.

"Lover boy's gone for a walk with Tim, but the car's here whenever you guys are ready. No rush since your flight isn't till tomorrow morning. How about a drink, for old times' sake? We've still got some of that Côte du Rhone you like."

"Sure."

Carlos handed her a glass of the red wine and poured himself two fingers of whiskey. "To you kids," he said, raising his glass. "To a long and happy marriage."

"I think you already made that toast." Petra's voice caught as she tapped her glass against his.

"Can never make it too many times, kiddo."

"Do you think we're doing the right thing?" she asked quietly. "Think we'll live to see the other side of it?"

"I hope so. I will say one thing—you've done all you can to be ready for it. You did well at the simulations, and even though whatever you face out there will be completely different, you'll be better prepared. React to it better. I have faith in you both." He took another sip. "Now you have to go out there and prove me right. Prove you can do what they're asking you to do, no matter how impossible it seems. I promise you I wouldn't bet on anyone else. If anyone can do it, it's you. Besides, even if things don't go well officially, I know you two will make it through." He sighed. "I know as your mentor on the op I shouldn't say this, but if you two decide to disappear afterward, I'll help you. And if that's the way it goes, Diane and I will miss you both."

"I'll hold you to that, old man," she replied, unable to say more at the prospect of never seeing her old friend again. They both knew the best option for her and Kasem would be to run as soon as the op was over. Petra savored the moment with her old friend, taking in the wine's earthiness. She'd always found it to be grounding, a reminder of the freedom she felt every time she was out on a hike.

They sat together in silence, the minutes stretching past until Carlos asked, "Did you see Rachel before she left? I know you spoke last night, but she said she knows you're going to do great out there. She was sorry she couldn't stay to see you off."

Petra chuckled. "You'd think we're off to the Olympics with all this talk of achievement. But yeah, I saw her this morning. Besides, it's better this way—without the boss around. Like you said, we've got some time, might as well enjoy it while we can." She took another long, slow sip, picturing the green canopy of the trees outside. Whatever happened next, she intended to relish these brief moments.

As if he could read her mind, Carlos raised his glass once more. "Taking a page out of Gaston's book, I'm going to lay out a good old proverb. Love like you will live forever, but live like you will die tomorrow."

******

After loading her suitcase into the car Rachel had arranged for them, Petra left Kasem in the car and returned to their room. She'd already double-checked, but a redundant sweep gave her something to focus on rather than the impending sense of doom. Carlos had disappeared, so she was alone, a sensation she knew would accompany her throughout the op, even with Kasem alongside her.

She took five deep breaths and switched off the light. On her way back through the hallway, she ran into Tim.

"Petra, hi, I'm glad I caught you."

"Me too. I'm sure Kasem already said this, but we wanted to thank you for all your help. I know how big of an ask it was for you to come here so last minute."

"I appreciate that, but I'm glad you asked. Good luck out there. The conditions aren't ideal, but you both kick ass. You've got this."

"Thank you." She gave him a hug and released him. "We don't know each other that well, but I'm pretty informal."

"Me too." He hesitated, then added, "There is something I wanted to tell you—a piece of advice."

"Of course."

"You already know how I feel about such a small team if you have to move on General Majed's apartment. We ran the simulations, and they're not ideal, but you guys can handle it."

"We think so too." Petra waited for him to say more. She could tell he was working up the courage.

"I know we did some alternate scenarios, like the mountain house. That's the one that concerns me."

"I don't think we have to worry about that. I'm glad we ran different scenarios, but General Majed wouldn't move out to the middle of nowhere. He loves being in the thick of it."

"I'm sure you're right, but if something like that happens, you're going to have to improvise," Tim said.

"What do you mean?"

"The two of you on your own infiltrating an apartment in the city is bad enough. The mountain house, that's another ball game. No matter what simulations we ran, I don't see how that ends well. Not without a commando team. So, if they move him to a place like that, I want you to do one of two things. Get some backup, no matter what you have to do to get it. If that's not possible, you call it off. Abort. The end. Capisce?"

Petra nodded. "Okay. I still think whatever happens will go down in the city, but I got it."

"I hope you're right."

# Chapter 13

*Tehran, Iran*

By the time they arrived in Tehran, Petra's anxiety had transformed into a sense of hyperawareness, one she knew was fake despite how it felt. At each corner of the airport, she caught strange details in the carpeting, flickers in the lighting, and random movements made by guards and employees. The feeling was disconcerting, but she welcomed it, a far cry from the more debilitating somersaults her stomach had been doing when they first boarded the flight. Time crept by as they made it through immigration and customs without running into any issues.

When they reached the international arrivals zone, Kasem spotted a driver holding a sign that read: Kareem and Asma Jafari, Partners for Development. They maneuvered their way through the crowd, narrowly avoiding bumping their luggage cart with someone else's on three separate occasions. Approaching cautiously, they went through the protocol Rachel had set up. Kasem spoke first, in purposely broken Farsi, then asked about traffic and if the driver had had time to pick up tea with honey for his wife. When the driver shook his head and motioned toward a coffee stand nearby, Petra's shoulders relaxed.

They followed him toward the coffee stand and were on their way to the parking lot a few minutes later. Once they had exited the airport grounds, Petra breathed a sigh of relief; every moment in Tehran would be dangerous, but the airport was a flash point she was glad to have behind them.

"I've started the air conditioning. It should cool down within a few minutes," the driver said.

Kasem leaned over the back seat vent as the whir sound of the air became more pronounced. "Thanks."

The driver glanced back toward them. "We can speak freely in here. We have the car checked for listening devices every day, plus extra jamming in the air conditioning to make sure no one can use a directed mic. I assume you've already installed the security software on your phones and computers?"

"Yes." Petra nodded. "But we were told you would run an additional diagnostic on the phones before we use them with local SIM cards."

"I'll check them when we get to your apartment. Leave them off for now."

"Of course," she agreed. Detecting his accent and the way he spoke about headquarters, Petra guessed he was probably a junior case officer with MI6. "Do you always work as a driver for your cover?"

"Driver, handyman, various odd jobs for expats around the city. It's not too bad. Lets me move around the city a lot easier than most people who are posted here. My dad's Persian, so I look the part well enough. I'm Jamal. Forgot to introduce myself earlier."

"Nice to meet you." Petra's throat went dry, recalling the name of Kasem's closest friend in Tehran. She had helped his Jamal escape Iran, but after that, they'd had to cut off contact to help him remain under the radar. Kasem had checked on him from a distance a few times over the years, and he was doing well, but Petra was sure the reminder would feel like a knife in the gut. She turned toward him, trying to catch his gaze, but he seemed fixated on the fuzzy gray covering of the passenger seat.

"Good to meet you, Jamal," Kasem said after a few seconds of silence.

"I'll be one of your primary conduits to the Canadian embassy when you need it, but your contract allows you to visit the World Bank offices whenever you want. You can link into their servers and use that for casual communication, but if you need something more secure, the embassy is the better option. Officially, I'm a private driver, but both embassies have vetted me and my car for occasional use. You can call and set up a visit to Isfahan or another tourist site and use the opportunity to hand over intel and I'll run it up the chain. Be careful in your apartment. It's been swept for listening devices, and we'll have a housekeeper keep that up three times a week. Use your own tech to check anytime you get home. Your biggest danger is obviously your phones, so don't let them out of your site and run regular diagnostics and sweeps. Use secondary or burner phones when you communicate with assets, all the normal precautions. When in doubt, use the Moscow Rules—someone is always watching, always listening. Never let your guard down."

"Got it," Petra answered. She was grateful Jamal obviously didn't know they were seasoned field operatives, but he still seemed too young to be lecturing them on protocol. She turned her attention to the window, watching the traffic as the images in front of her mixed with her memories. Half listening as Jamal continued to explain obvious bits of procedure, she took it all in. She had been so focused on how Kasem would react to their return to Iran that she hadn't given much thought to how it would affect her.

Tehran had been her only deep cover Agency posting, and when she thought back, it was like looking at someone else's life. She'd been hungry and highly effective, especially for an operative so young, but blind to the danger. Faces swam in front of her—old assets, friends. Dinner parties, restaurants, cafes, laughter. The fear that had always been at the back of her mind, now more front and center. She remembered visits to dead drop sites in and around the city. The constant vigilance to keep a lookout for the Secret Police. Travel to incredible historic sights, places she would never otherwise have seen. The few moments other than her time with Kasem when she had allowed herself to be fully immersed in the wonderful yet wounded country where she'd been deployed.

And love. This was where their story had really begun.

Petra blinked several times, realizing her eyes had welled with tears. She kept her gaze fixed on the city going by, brushing the tears away before they became noticeable. Although they were at the beginning of the morning rush hour, they were making unusually good time. Rather than pushing the pain aside, she leaned into the memories, letting them envelope her, but at the same time trying to disengage. She had learned in therapy that resisting the most painful memories gave them more power. She could either pretend they didn't exist, meanwhile letting the memories and thoughts control her actions, or she could acknowledge them and be a spectator as they went through her mind. At the end of the day, they were only thoughts. Whatever power they had was what she gave them. Remembering that lesson brought her a modicum of comfort, and the rest of the drive passed more quickly.

When they got off the highway, they drove past the Ararat Sport and Culture Center. A large crane hung over the street corner with a body dangling from it. She swallowed bile and squeezed her eyes shut. It wasn't the first public hanging she had seen in Iran, and it wouldn't be the last.

A few minutes later, they drove past Mellat Park and a more pleasant wave of nostalgia hit her. She and Kasem had walked around there many times, although they'd always been careful to limit any public displays of affection. Ahead of her, the mountain peaks were etched in the distance—imposing and beautiful figureheads overlooking the city. They passed the colorful archway leading into the Safavieh Shopping Center, where she had set up one of her many drop sites to exchange intel. They turned right onto Aramesh Street and stopped in front of their new home.

Jamal transformed back into the perfect driver, attending to their every need. The elevator was out of order, so he helped them carry their suitcases up the two flights of stairs to their apartment. Before he left, he did another sweep of the apartment, and Kasem handed him a tip.

After Kasem shut the front door, Petra took his hand and led him toward the floor-length windows in their living room. It wasn't much of a view. They weren't high enough to see over the nearby buildings, but they could feel the hustle and bustle of the city below.

"How are you?" she asked.

"It's not as nice as my view was." Kasem's voice sounded hollow. When they first got together, his place had a similar view to this one—nothing to write home about. Which meant he was referring to his place after being captured by General Majed, where he had lived as the Ahriman. Kasem would have been able to look out at the city every day, all the while knowing he couldn't experience any of it.

"But maybe I should be asking you. You were getting a little emotional in the car."

"I didn't realize how much it would bring up," she said.

"We'll get through it together."

"I'm okay."

"You know, you're not a very good liar." His eyes twinkled, and she burst into a nervous laugh. Lying was central to their job description, just not with each other.

"Neither are you." She kissed him on the cheek.

They looked out at the view in silence until Kasem spoke. "How long do you think we can be here... before they find us?"

"I don't know. A couple of months, at most."

"Agreed." He walked across the living room to the open kitchen, where there was a calendar hanging on the wall. Petra joined him, looking at the scenic view of the mountains on the picture above the boxes that marked the days of August. Kasem flipped down two pages to October and marked the 7$^{th}$. "That's our deadline. Two months from now, we leave here no matter what. Hopefully that will be with General Majed in a box, but either way, before this day we have to be dead. The day we die, the day we start over."

"All right."

"I'll approach Gaston's contact, but we won't mention that to Rachel or the Company team. His name's Davit Simonyan. Gaston said he would help us. We can use him to secure our escape route. You focus on Farah, I'll take Ahsani."

"Fine."

Kasem hesitated. "I want to talk to you. I know what I did in Burundi was awful. I should have spoken to you about it before—"

"You should have done more than that. We should have made that decision together."

"Do you really think you could have made that choice?"

"I don't know."

"I know it was awful, and I wish things had gone differently, but do you see why I had to do it? I couldn't sit back and let Sir Edward blackmail Markov into becoming an Agency pawn. He was going to force Markov to turn the power contract his way. I had to stop him."

When she didn't reply, Kasem continued. "I shouldn't have let you find out the way you did, or decided unilaterally. You're right about that. But do you see why I had to make that choice?"

*No.*

*Screw the greater good.*

Much as she didn't want to acknowledge it, she did understand. She'd been choosing the greater good over her personal life for years—how could she fault him for doing the same?

"I understand." She sighed. "But you better not do anything like that again. *Never.* We're in this together, no more unilateral decisions. Promise me."

"I promise."

"I really hope that's true. We won't survive it if you do anything like that again."

"When we're out there, we lie, scheme, cheat, whatever it takes." He gestured toward the window. "But in here, I want everything to be real. At home, we need to feel safe, need to *be* safe. No secrets, no lies, not even white lies. That's how we find a life on the other side."

# Chapter 14

*Tehran, Iran*

Kasem grabbed a seat at a table in the back corner of the run-down coffee shop as he waited for Ahsani's signal. The coffee shop was one of many of Ahsani's fronts—a means to turn his black-market income, especially payments received from the CIA, into legal 'white' money. As he looked at the operation, Kasem couldn't help but be impressed. The café had only a limited menu, but everything on offer was supposed to be of high quality, a marked contrast to the drab interior and ambiance, which helped justify the low price point. They churned massive volume, making it much easier to disguise the steady trickle of illegal earnings mixed into its revenue.

Since most of the details were classified, Kasem knew very little as to how the CIA had recruited Ahsani, but he could tell the setup was remarkably effective. He even looked forward to visiting Ahsani's other establishments now that he'd seen this one. In addition to his firm commitment to the op, he'd been in the spy game long enough to know the days were long and tough. Little pieces to enjoy amidst all the subterfuge helped keep the anxiety at bay. Otherwise, most of it was just waiting—endless hours of patience interspersed with moments of more fear than most people experience in a lifetime. On the rare occasions when he reflected on it, he wondered why his anxiety and paranoia hadn't sent him to the emergency room a hundred times over. Yet somehow, they kept being dragged back into the game. Neither he nor Petra wanted to admit it, but they enjoyed the adrenaline, regardless of the fact they wanted out.

*We're basically addicts. Instead of cocaine, it's the secret world.*

Kasem took a small sip from his Turkish coffee and broke into a smile as the caffeinated spice hit his taste buds. He'd expected the coffee to be good, but it far surpassed his expectations. He looked around with additional appreciation, recalling how much he and his old friend Jamal would have enjoyed discovering a place like this. They had frequented more upscale establishments, minor indulgences to make them feel wealthier than they were. Savoring every sip, he finished off the draught. Outside the Middle East, finding a decent cup of Turkish coffee was almost impossible. He remembered searching for one in Paris, the culinary capital of the world, yet still coming up short. Kasem signaled the waitress to order a second. He might as well enjoy a few more minutes before the meeting began.

The waitress returned with a fresh coffee and a plate with three traditional small cookies. "With our compliments," she said in Farsi.

"Merci," Kasem replied, returning her smile. He broke off a large piece from one cookie and waited until she returned to the counter. The sweet walnut flavor filled his mouth, evoking a similar dessert his mom used to make. At the very least, Ahsani had good taste in signals. He wolfed the rest of the plate down and left cash on the table to cover his bill, along with a tip.

He ventured down the back hallway toward the bathroom. When he found it, he knocked on the door immediately after it, a scratched-up dark wooden door with a sign that said "Storage" in faded Farsi letters. The door opened and Kasem found himself face-to-chest with one of Ahsani's bodyguards.

Kasem looked up slowly, then almost took a step back to get a full view. He recognized the face from Ahsani's file, but the description had neglected to mention the man was a giant. At just over six feet, Kasem was tall, especially by Iranian standards, but the man in front of him had to be at least six inches taller.

*Did Ahsani hire Colossus to be his bodyguard?*

The similarity was uncanny. The bodyguard looked like a tanned version of the metal-armed superhero from the *X-Men* comics he'd read as a child. Kasem wondered if he was trapped in a weird dream.

"Inside," Colossus said in Farsi. Before the door had clicked shut, Colossus patted him down, not bothering with any preamble. Kasem noted with discomfort that the girth of the man's bicep was wider than Kasem's head.

After confirming he wasn't carrying any weapons, Colossus led him up a stairwell that looked like an indoor fire escape. They went up two flights, turned down a long hallway, and finally stopped at a drab waiting room. The room had a desk in the back with a bookshelf wedged behind it, and two armchairs in front that were far past their prime. The red upholstery had faded to a dirty pink and several spots were so worn through the internal cushioning was visible.

Kasem shifted his weight between his feet, wondering how long Ahsani would keep him waiting. He recognized the tactic—keep your target off balance by making them wait—and unfortunately, it was working. Colossus remained standing, so he did as well, not wanting to lower his vantage point even further. The room was freezing, adding to the discomfort; the wall-mounted air conditioner was working overtime.

*Ahsani is an ally,* he reminded himself. *This is just posturing, probably part of his cover.* Still, the lack of trust surprised him—at least based on this first impression—especially after Rachel's assertions of how long he had been working for the CIA. *She did say we shouldn't trust him.*

Almost on cue, the door on the opposite side of the room opened and Ahsani appeared. He and Colossus spoke quietly. Kasem strained his ears but couldn't make out a word over the loud hum of the air conditioner. After a few seconds, Kasem decided to take back control of the situation and moved toward them without waiting for an invitation.

Ahsani frowned, but then the expression disappeared, replaced by a beaming smile—the perfect host. "Please come in." He motioned to the room behind him.

Kasem stepped into a large conference room in pristine condition, the complete opposite of the waiting room. He walked past the head of the bright cherry wood table and took one of the leather seats on the opposite side. Interlocking his fingers behind his head, he leaned back in the chair, doing his best to portray an image of outward confidence. Why had he convinced Petra he should do this meeting on his own? Meeting with Ahsani, ally or not, was basically like meeting with the head of the mafia, even if Kasem was Ahsani's second cousin, according to his cover. Kasem resisted the impulse to shift in his seat. What had the CIA told Ahsani in advance? Was Kasem expendable relative to their long-time asset?

He silenced the stream of thoughts, unsure where they had come from. He hadn't felt this unsure of himself on an op since his initial training. Being back in Tehran had shaken him to the core.

The catastrophic outcome of his last time here.

Losing control and the need to get it back.

To make sure nothing like that ever happened again.

*Pull yourself together. You may not be the Ahriman anymore, but you're a trained operative.* The thought calmed him, redirected his focus. He had a job to do.

"Don't you think it's time to start this meeting?"

Ahsani, who was still at the doorway, turned toward him with an amused expression. "Indeed." He took the chair across from Kasem and Colossus sat down next to him. "This is Ramshad. Most people are scared of him. I like to call him my second in command. If you ever can't reach me, he's the one to talk to."

"My inner seven-year-old is doing a tap dance. He looks exactly like Colossus, one of my childhood heroes, a character from the *X-Men*."

"The metal guy in *Deadpool*?" Ahsani's eyes twinkled. "It's an apt comparison."

"Absolutely."

"Ramshad is privy to all of my activities, almost like a brother."

Kasem raised his eyebrows, wondering if he had correctly understood. Did that mean Ramshad knew of Ahsani's work for the CIA?

"I chose him as my bodyguard when I started working for the Company," Ahsani continued. "But now he knows as much as I do, although it's an egregious violation of protocol. They say little about my methods because I don't tell them much. More importantly, the intel I provide speaks for itself."

"I'm sure it does."

"We don't know anything about you, though, or what you and your wife are doing here. I'm not sure how much you know about me."

"Not much," Kasem said with a nod. Ahsani had deliberately shared something against CIA protocol in the hope Kasem would reciprocate. He chose his words carefully. "What did they tell you?"

Ramshad was the one who answered in perfect English. "You were sent here to locate and neutralize a high-value target. Your cover is that you're my distant cousin, and while you do freelance work with the World Bank and the Australian and Canadian embassies, you want to make a few side investments in our underground network, which would give you more freedom to move around the city. I believe you know about our network—three underground bars, one club, and several legitimate operations, like the coffee shop downstairs. We're well-connected with the police, even the Revolutionary Guard and the Secret Police, along with some important public figures."

"Yes, they told us that."

"Then how about you return the favor? Tell us who your target is." Ramshad crossed his arms.

Kasem drummed his fingers against his pant leg, taken aback. The more information he and Petra shared, the more that could jeopardize their safety, although Ahsani already knew they existed. Nothing he said now would compromise them more than that, and he needed them to trust him and Petra.

Before he could respond, Ahsani interjected. "Why don't we start with something lighter? Officially, we're cousins, so you and your wife should come over, have dinner with us tomorrow night. My wife will make something special. Afterward, we can visit one of my bars. I believe you'll find the clientele quite interesting. Ramshad will give you a rundown on the attendees. I've set up a special whiskey tasting just for you."

# Chapter 15

*Tehran, Iran*

Sami Majed headed into the Maham Shooting Range, where he had learned to fire a gun in his early teens. His father had first brought him there at thirteen. Officially, only adults were permitted to use the shooting range, but the staff didn't strictly enforce the rule. Sami had seen other families there on occasion, teaching other teenage boys how to shoot. As soon as he was old enough, he had secured an annual membership at the facility, and the range quickly became his sanctuary in between his early postings outside the country.

He went straight to his locker and retrieved two of the guns in his collection—a Colt AR-15 semi-automatic rifle and a Glock 18 pistol, both off the local black market—along with some ammunition. Although he often carried his service weapon, at the range, he preferred to switch them up to maintain and hone his skills across different weapons. His source Behraz approached him, posing as a porter. Sami deposited the two weapons in his hands before they walked over to the nearest available roofed firing point. The range was deserted since it was late morning on a Tuesday, so it was only a short walk. After handing over a a tip, Sami gestured toward the weapons. While he didn't need help loading his firearms, it would give them more time to talk.

"How long are you here for?" Sami asked.

The porter wiped the barrel with an old rag, keeping his gaze focused on the gun as he answered. "Delegation's here for another two days. I'll head back to Istanbul at the end of the week."

"This isn't the usual protocol."

"I know it's not standard, but I felt we needed to meet. I didn't want to leave this at a drop."

Sami nodded. He had figured as much when he got the message about the appointment at the shooting range. "What did you want to tell me?"

Behraz picked up the old rag, and Sami pocketed the thumb drive that had been concealed underneath it. "It's a recording I think you'll like. Not that much information yet—you'll be able to tell the team lead is holding back—but now that I have a clear in, I'll get more."

"How did you get this?" Sami asked.

"I don't ask you to tell me your secrets."

"Fine. Give me the gist."

"The deputy director confirmed they're sending in at least one agent, possibly two. They may have already arrived and the whole thing's going down off book. There was something strange. I can't verify, but it sounds as if neither candidate has any history with the Company."

"Do you know what determines which one—or both?"

"Not yet."

Sami frowned, processing the other piece of information Behraz had shared. Why would the CIA use fresh operatives for an op in Iran? "That last part—when you say they have no history with the Company—does that mean they're new? Completely green?"

"I very much doubt the Company would send in rookies, not here. Plus, the recording also implies they've both got local experience. My guess is they're seconded from another agency. It would still be a first, but less of a stretch than newbies."

"Makes sense. Anything else?"

"Word is their training happened out in Scotland. The first—whichever they chose—probably just got here, maybe in the last week at most." He gave Sami's shoulder a condescending pat. "I'm sure you can figure out who they are. There aren't that many viable covers."

"Unless they're Persian."

"I'll let you know when I hear more."

"All right." Sami adjusted his glasses, then picked up the rifle, pretending to weigh it slowly in his hands.

"The other piece—not in the recording—is that they're using some kind of connection to an underground club or restaurant."

Sami frowned. There weren't that many successful clubs, but they each had plenty of bartenders, dancers, and customers. It was a good lead, but he couldn't possibly put surveillance on every single underground establishment. "The asset works there?"

"Potentially. They could also be a regular."

"I need more info on how you're getting this intel, otherwise I can't trust that it's legit."

"You know we don't talk about my methods. My primary informant is the same as always—a team lead out of Istanbul. We've been spending more time together," Behraz said, handing Sami a pair of earplugs and noise-cancelling headphones. He shrugged. "Phones are great as recording devices, but the secret is that alcohol and hedonism make for loose lips."

*Alcohol, hedonism, and sex.*

Sami set the rifle down on the table and picked up the Glock pistol, which Behraz had already cleaned and loaded. He lined up a shot at a target on the retaining wall ten meters in front of him. For a moment, the op no longer existed. All that was left was his weapon and the target. He squeezed the trigger and fired off six shots, then set the gun on the table. "But everything you've got, you're sure it's credible?"

"As long as I buy the drinks, he always delivers—in multiple ways."

"Fair enough." Sami knew Behraz's methods involved copious amounts of alcohol, followed by seduction. The results spoke for themselves, and Sami had no interest in the details. *So long as he never tries it on me.* "Anything else?"

"The woman who's running the op from Istanbul is relatively young, I think. A guy in the meeting calls her *mademoiselle*. I'll keep feeding that resentment; there's a goldmine ready to tap."

"Get me her name and I'll make sure you get a fat bonus. Same thing goes for any information on the cover legends their agents are using."

Behraz smirked. "Will do."

Sami picked up the rifle again, and they walked over to the neighboring station, which had long-range targets set up at a distance of fifty and one hundred meters. After another round of shots, he reviewed the paper targets. Most of the shots were well placed, split between the head and heart, but there were a few that were off. He was far better with a pistol than a rifle.

"Too bad we can't make bets on who's better at this," Behraz said as they made their way back to the short-range station.

*I know better than to make bets with you.* "Too bad, indeed," Sami replied, glad Behraz's cover as a porter prohibited such an arrangement. "Any idea when you'll be back?"

"Two months or so. We'll have another mission to Dubai or Qatar, so I can justify popping home for a few days."

"Just let me know when."

"Next time, let's meet at a bar."

"Sure," Sami agreed. Part of him hoped they would—an underground bar in Tehran offered better cover than the shooting range. They would look like another gay couple taking advantage of the anonymity. But another part of him wouldn't dare go to a bar with Behraz. He was far too good at seduction to risk meeting him at a place that would give him the upper hand, especially since Sami had to admit he found him attractive, a fact they were both uncomfortably aware of. "As long as there are some pretty girls to look at," he added in a feeble effort to clarify there was no chance of anything other than a conversation.

"There are always pretty girls."

Behraz ejected the magazines from both weapons, made sure both were empty, and placed them in a carry bag along with Sami's headphones. Together, they walked back to the lockers. Once he reached his car, Sami sat down in the driver's seat and scratched his chin. His gut said that even if the recording implied the CIA was going to choose between the two agents, both would be deployed in the end. *They wouldn't go through the trouble of training two if they were only going to use one.* What confused him was the fact they weren't Company operatives. Given the training venue in Scotland, his best guess was the CIA must have seconded agents from MI6. That said, the situation still didn't sit right. On the outside he could have imagined the Company using *one* seconded agent, but two?

*Unless the agents or covers are connected.* He drummed his fingers against the steering wheel. Of all possibilities, that was the only one that held water. Which meant the operatives he was looking for had to be using a joint cover.

*A couple. A couple who've worked in Iran before.*

Sami nodded to himself and set off back toward his apartment to listen to the recording. Behraz could hit on him a thousand times for the intel he paid back. He was by far the most productive asset Sami had ever recruited. While stopped at a traffic light, he sent two quick texts to his junior team members.

1. Need a detailed dive into any foreign couples arriving in the last two weeks. Flag any European embassy connections.

2. Go over underground clubs and restaurants. Identify any with known Western or dissident ties. Look for any fresh faces connected to the owners.

# Chapter 16

*Tehran, Iran*

Petra rubbed her eyes as she made her way to the Bab Homayoun bathhouse near the Tehran Bazaar. The last couple of nights had been exhausting. She and Kasem had attended Ahsani's whiskey tasting, followed by a middle-of-the-night excursion. After monitoring the street where General Majed's apartment was believed to be located, they had placed cameras at key points along the street. It was too risky to breach the wall before they confirmed his location, but the street-side view would hopefully provide more clarity in the coming days. "It's worth a try, anyway," she had justified to Kasem, although she wasn't holding her breath. There was a reason General Majed had remained in hiding this long—she suspected he was mostly confined to his safe house.

Stepping inside the bathhouse drew her out of the exhaustion. She felt transported to a different time. Most of Iran's traditional bathhouses had been converted into teahouses, restaurants, or museums, and while she had visited a few hotel spas that tried to replicate the experience, she had never sought the traditional bath experience. Farah's MI6 handler had proposed three different meeting places, and Petra had decided a traditional Persian hammam offered the most anonymity, while giving them enough privacy to speak freely so long as they chose a time when it wouldn't be crowded. That had been easy enough—Farah worked in the evenings and at night, and Petra was free to move about the city during the day. Petra had chosen late morning on a Wednesday so both the bazaar and the bathhouse would be on the quieter side.

Now that she was there, she wished she had made the effort to visit during her earlier stint in Tehran. The entrance split off into separate men's and a women's sections, and the lobby to the women's section looked straight out of a tourist catalogue. A series of pointed archways connecting to traditional Islamic columns made up the ceiling. The shaft was composed of a smooth off-white stone, with the column capital done up in an elaborate saffron pattern. Delicate cream and white tiles in a floral mosaic adorned the walls. Seating areas with wood lattice benches surrounding circular fountains in blue and auburn tile completed the visual. She stopped at the reception desk and bought a day pass, then ventured through the seating area into the more private part of the bath.

As Petra made her way to the changing room, she was struck by the contrast between the serene and quiet bath and the bustling bazaar just one floor above. She could hear water dripping down the corners of the walls, mingled with the relaxing meditation music playing through the speakers. She passed the second sitting area with dimmer lighting, where Farah had said she would meet her.

The changing room itself was mostly empty, with only three lockers occupied. Petra donned her swimsuit, the green bathrobe she had brought with her, and a pair of flip-flops, then checked her hair in the mirror, pulling it into a bun on top of her head and wrapping it in a towel that matched her bathrobe. She hated that style, but the approach protocol she had set with Farah was to look for the woman in a green bathrobe and hair towel. Once she was ready, she poured two cups of tea from the station in the center and grabbed a seat in a round booth in the far corner of the sitting area.

"Asma? It's so good to see you," someone said to her about fifteen minutes later. "Did you run into a lot of traffic getting here?"

Petra looked up and recognized Farah from her picture. Following the greeting that she had laid out, she replied in English. "No, actually I took the metro. What about you? It's wonderful to see you after so long. Come, sit, let's catch up. I grabbed you a hibiscus tea. I hope that's all right."

"Of course. Did you add honey? That's my favorite—hibiscus tea with honey."

"I think they already added sugar. I hope it's not too sweet."

"I'm sure it's fine. Did you go to the steam room yet?"

"Yes, but it was a bit too hot for me. I had to take a break," Petra answered, reaching the end of the pre-determined greeting.

Farah sat down and pulled the sheer curtain across the entrance to the booth. "I'm glad you're here." She took a long sip from her teacup. "I was starting to think they weren't going to do anything about him."

Petra detected the edge in Farah's tone. *A personal stake.* The interaction confirmed the suspicion she'd had since reading Farah's file. "Bureaucracy is slower than ideal, unfortunately. Now that I'm here, could you take me through it from the beginning? Right from the start, even before you spotted him."

"Of course." Farah described the encounter—how she'd been tasked with attracting the attention of a young party boy who frequented the club in order to clone his phone. "That part was easy enough. We went to a private area for a lap dance. There were other girls there, then it was just me, and I used the device my handler gave me on his mobile. I was on my way back to the dressing room when I walked past another curtained booth. That's when I saw him."

"How did you recognize him?"

"I used to see him years ago when I was with some men in the military."

"Were you ever with him?"

"Not like that. There were two other girls he favored. He had his pick, you know, since he was the general. Twice he lined up all of us, like an inspection. He yelled at us, then slapped the girl on the end. I didn't know her well, but she didn't deserve that. She looked at him the wrong way, I guess. He just left her on the floor. Then he walked down the line, looking at us again one by one, then went back to the beginning. She was just getting up, and he pulled out a baton." Farah shuddered, and a tear ran down her cheek. "He didn't beat her, just yelled and waved it around. When she was finally up and back in line, he threw the baton at the wall and dragged her out. I've never been so scared. But I felt so guilty. None of us did anything to help her, just let him treat her that way. All I could think was that I was glad it wasn't me."

"You couldn't have done anything to help her."

"I don't know. Doesn't that make us just as bad, letting him do that to us?"

"You were just trying to survive."

Farah was silent for several moments. "Men like him, they shouldn't be allowed to breathe air. By the time I got out, I knew I had to do something. Anything to make sure my country wasn't run by people like him."

"I'm so sorry." Petra knew how empty the words must be, but she said them anyway. There was nothing she could say or do to lessen Farah's pain.

"It could have been so much worse. I know that, even if it doesn't take away the memories. I would have left the brothel sooner except for Afshar."

*Afshar?* Petra almost sat up straighter, but stopped the reaction in time. Officially, Lieutenant Afshar had executed Kasem a few months after his capture in Tehran on the charge of being a spy. *"Lieutenant Afshar is dead,"* she remembered him shouting when she had mentioned his name. Kasem had described him as captor, traitor, and trainer. "Afshar? Who is he?" she asked, maintaining a neutral expression.

"His name was Dariush Afshar. He was a lieutenant who worked for General Majed. We met in the brothel. He saw me once by chance. He had this smile, like there was nothing bad in the world. At first, he was shy, stopped in just to see me, never asked to be alone. When he finally did, it was like a courtship. He'd visit me and bring me gifts. Sometimes we'd just cuddle and look out the window, talk."

"Did he tell you what he was working on?"

"Not much. The odd bit here and there. As we got closer, he shared more—not about what he was working on, but the people he was working with. I'll never forget the things he said about General Majed."

"What do you mean?"

"At first, it was nothing. Afshar told me the general was a pompous ass, then later, that he might be brilliant. I didn't tell him about that day in the lineup. I knew it would upset him, and there was nothing he could do. Anyway, he told me he was working with General Majed to train a recruit; the two of them and someone else. I don't know who. Sometimes he treated Afshar like his protégé, other times like his servant. Afshar was never sure if he could or should trust him. That was the beginning."

"And then?"

"Then he told me about Suez. That was after the attack, after it had all happened. He said we'd never prove it, but the whole thing was General Majed's plan, that he set it all up. A few weeks later, Afshar was dead." Farah wiped her eyes with the back of her hand. The tears were falling freely now. "That bastard killed him. I'm sure of it. He wanted to make sure no one could tie him back to the attack, so he took care of everyone who knew about it."

Petra reached out to touch her hand. "I'm so sorry," she whispered again. "We will end this."

"You have to. That's why I followed him that night. I'd never seen him at the club before, and I couldn't let him get away."

"You did the right thing. Tell me more about what you saw when you tailed him."

Farah described how she had followed General Majed's car, had watched him go inside the house in Qeytarieh. "I wanted to do more, but I didn't make it to the gate inside."

"Did any of them notice you?"

"I don't think so."

"Thank you, Farah. We won't let him get away with everything he's done."

"Tell me how I can help. Please, I'll do anything. My handler said they're not pursuing this, but I have to see this through. He has to pay for what he's done."

"The first step is we have to figure out if he's actually staying in that house, and if not, where." Petra paused. "The report said one of the other two guys in the pictures is a regular. Do you know how often he comes into the club?"

"He comes in almost every week, usually more than once. I've seen him there most Saturdays, sometimes during the week too."

Petra gulped down the last bit of her tea. "So, he'll be there this weekend?"

"He should be."

"Do you dance at the club every night?"

"Only Wednesdays and Saturdays. I work at the bar on Fridays."

"Are there any couples who come in to watch the show, or is it just men?"

"It's always packed. Definitely more men on show nights, but there's plenty of women too, especially on Saturdays. Wednesdays are whiskey tasting, quieter. The show is more like a dance than a striptease. But on Saturdays, sometimes the women even join us on stage. The men always love that. We make a lot more in tips if we can make that happen."

"All right, I'll be there tonight." Petra weighed their options. They would have to tread carefully, and grabbing Gul that evening would be next to impossible. Even with a few days to plan, Saturday would still be a stretch. Difficult, but possibly a viable option if they could identify the extraction point. "Could you draw me a floor plan for the club? Where the bathrooms are, the exits, the bar, dance floor—all of that." She hesitated, then explained. "I'll need to get him out of the bar alone, ask him what he knows about the general, then get him back in as if nothing happened."

"Sure."

"Pay attention to the details. How many tables there are, how many dressing rooms. Where the exits are, the windows.

How long is the hallway. Things like that. I'll walk around myself and build a detailed schematic, but I don't have as much access as you do."

"I'll have it for you tonight."

\*\*\*\*\*\*

That night at the bar, Petra recovered the plan Farah had sketched from an empty box of pads in the trashcan under the bathroom sink. Although they weren't expecting anyone to be searching the trash, she had instructed Farah to use that concealment method as an extra precaution. The men involved in an Islamic police force like the Revolutionary Guard found such things repulsive and were unlikely to open such a box. She had also neglected to mention Kasem in any of her discussions with Farah. A key part of maintaining operational security was to make sure no single asset, regardless of how close they were as an ally, knew all the details of an operation. With Ahsani and Ramshad, they'd been unable to disguise the fact they were both working on the operation, but Petra planned to limit contact with them as much as possible. The less they knew, the better.

Retreating into a stall, Petra examined the map. Eight curtained-off tables where guests could sequester themselves for an extra fee flanked the bar and dance floor. The restrooms were located down a hallway behind a bar. Further down the same hallway were the dancers' dressing room and two storerooms. The staff entrance was in between the dressing room and the first storeroom and opened out onto an alley. There was an additional hallway on the other side of the bar that led back to the kitchen.

Petra considered her options and decided exiting into the alley would be their only play to grab Gul. Farah had marked the three tables Mahdi Gul frequented. One was by far the more convenient option closest to the hallway. She examined the latch on the bathroom window, then folded the map up and stuffed it into her bra. After a couple of minutes to reapply makeup, she let her headscarf fall onto her shoulders—most of the women inside the bar had done the same—and ventured back out into the hallway.

She turned right and took a quick round past the dressing and storerooms before finally returning to her seat at the bar. When she sat down, she moved her hair across her right shoulder, a signal to Kasem that she had completed her review. The next part of the evening was up to him.

# Chapter 17

*Tehran, Iran*

Kasem clinked his glass with Ramshad and took a sip of the Balvenie single malt whiskey.

"Be careful with that one—it goes down smooth, but it'll catch up with you later. Tell me, how have your first couple of days here been?"

"Fine, just settling in."

"I imagine you and your wife have been here before?"

"Yes, of course." Kasem nodded. He saw no reason to keep that to himself. According to their cover, he and Petra had visited a few times, with one extended stay five years earlier. Besides, Ramshad wasn't an idiot. He would know the CIA wouldn't have sent them in on this type of operation with no prior in-country experience.

"What do you think of the bar? We didn't get to talk much the other night when you were here."

Kasem looked around once more, appreciating the simple walnut wood décor of the bar top and the glass shelves behind it stacked to the ceiling with all sorts of liquor. "This place is amazing. It's like an old speakeasy straight out of New York. I'm glad we got here a little early. It's nice to see it without many people."

"We actually modeled it after an American speakeasy. Not just one; we visited several before we came up with the design of this one."

"Do you remember which ones?" Kasem asked, fondly remembering a few of his favorites.

"A few. The Lower East Side Toy Company. I think that was the biggest one we went to. Then there was the Gibson in DC and Franklin Bar in Philly."

"I'm impressed. You may have been to more speakeasies than I have."

"What can I say? Research is important."

"Absolutely." Kasem chuckled, tipping his glass back to polish off his drink.

Ramshad waved for the bartender to top off their drinks, then looked over at Kasem once more. "Going back to business—there's a group of regulars who come to most of these whiskey tastings. The last one was special, scheduled just for you, but we do them more informally once a week. Sometimes the wives come, but it's mostly men coming in for an escape. Some of them smoke cigars too. It's pretty informal. The bartender introduces the whiskey, gives a few tasting notes to the group, then everyone socializes. Later in the evening, the girls perform."

"Sounds good."

"Your wife fits right in." Ramshad motioned toward Petra, who was at the bar. "Also, here's the item you requested." He slid his hand across the table, and Kasem retrieved the offering and placed it into his pocket.

"Thank you. And you're right, she's much more social than I am." Kasem savored another sip, thinking ahead that he would also evaluate the attendees as potential sources of information. "Tell me about your favorite speakeasy, out of all the ones you visited," he prompted Ramshad. In the back of his mind, he wondered about Ramshad himself.

*Colossus always had a heart of gold.* Instead of dwelling on it, he focused on his task for that night. Gaston's contact, Davit Simonyan, would shortly be in attendance.

# Chapter 18

*Tehran, Iran*

Kasem rose early the next day and shook Petra awake. "Let's get a real coffee, and we can scope out the café at the same time."

"Sure." She yawned and crawled out of bed, "Every time I deal with jetlag, it gets worse and worse." She stretched her arms overhead, leaning her torso from side to side, then bent over and touched the floor.

"Much as I like the view, you should get dressed," he grinned, eyeing her curves and long legs. "It never gets old."

Petra chuckled as she disappeared out into the hallway. When she returned from the bathroom ten minutes later, she looked fresh with her black hair combed out. She pulled on a pair of jeans and a t-shirt, then nodded toward the bedroom door, "Are you ready? Get your shoes on." She slid on a pair of black flats next to her, suitcase, "Let's go."

On the way out, Kasem grabbed the keys to one of the SUVs parked in their driveway. Petra held her hand out, "I'm driving."

Kasem tossed them to her with a shrug, heading for the passenger side. When he opened the door, he saw the steering wheel on the right side and jumped in, "Too bad you went to the wrong side—it's a British style car."

"Fine," she grumbled as she handed back the keys.

The ten-minute drive to the café passed in silence as Kasem mulled over the intel he'd read, still contemplating what Kevin was involved with. They parked just down the street and ventured in on foot, each ordering a coffee and croissant—Café Gourmand was famous for its baked goods. Kasem carried their tray upstairs to the rooftop, where they sat at a table in the corner, far from the stairwell and relatively isolated. It was early in the morning, so both the café interior and rooftop were almost empty, but he suspected that that wouldn't last for long.

After draining his coffee, Kasem looked around, considering how they could grab Kevin at this location. "Did Veronica mention where he usually likes to sit? We'll have to run surveillance for at least a week."

"I don't think so—since we're setting up a meet, I'm sure we could do it however we want."

"The meet could be here on the rooftop—early to mid-afternoon when the sun's too hot for most people to come upstairs. Maybe that one?" he motioned toward the table directly opposite the stairwell.

Petra frowned, "The problem isn't how or where to meet him, it's how to get him out afterward. If we knock him out, everyone will notice, and if we try to subdue and lead him out at gunpoint, we risk a fight." She rubbed her chin, "What about a window from the bathrooms?"

"That won't work either, it's a crowded street."

"Right." She drummed her fingers against the table, "What if we have Veronica's contact do the meet?" She considered further, and a smile spread across her face, "I've got it—it's simple, we drug him."

"But how do we get out of here then?"

"In an ambulance—no one will think anything of it."

"Her contact would have to be really connected to make that work. We'd need a local ambulance, uniforms, the whole shebang. Do you think Veronica can pull that off?"

"She's Agency, isn't she? She'd better be able to pull it off." Petra wolfed down the last bite of her croissant, "I think we better go tell her."

"You go ahead, I want to walk around a little, then I'll take one of those taxis on the street back. There's a gym nearby as well, so I'll check that out too."

"You sure? Let me know if you want me to pick you up. V said team meeting at noon, so don't get lost, okay?"

"Sure."

Once Petra headed off into the stairwell, Kasem moved to the edge of the patio and finished munching on his pastry. The rooftop offered a good view of the surrounding area—most buildings in Buja were only two stories, so he had a decent vantage point. He oriented himself, tracing the road they'd use to get there and identifying the street that would lead him into downtown so that he could get a better feel for the city. *And perhaps the contacts Kevin was meeting with.* He hadn't told Petra, but he had his eye on *Arena* in particular, the restaurant and bar which was frequented by one of Kevin's contacts. Veronica's file hadn't provided much detail, only that Kevin had been seen there, meeting with the Deputy Head of the *Agence d'Electricite,* which regulated new power developments. Under normal circumstances, it would be too early to visit—the restaurant only opened in the late afternoon, but Kasem had noticed that there was a gym on the same property. He could kill three birds with one stone, knock out his workout, get a feel for the city, and start setting up a contact or two to help with his to-do list.

# Chapter 19

*Istanbul, Turkey*

Rachel Fleming walked out of the regional department meeting reeling as if she'd had the wind knocked out of her. She had expected to deal with bureaucratic red tape, unnecessary security clearances, and countless check-ins with her boss, but nothing close to the animosity she had just experienced from her colleague Devon Marsh. She couldn't think of anything she could've done to offend him. *Did I wrong him in another life?* They had completed training around the same time. He'd been sent to Istanbul, while she had stayed at Langley, albeit covering assignments across several regions. As far as she could remember, they'd had minimal contact in the last eight years, and judging from their previous interactions, she'd expected a cordial greeting.

She tamped down on the fury building within her. Was she overreacting? Devon had been derisive and misogynistic, but no one else in the room seemed to have noticed anything strange. James, the department leader, was a huge fan of his. *Why?* She saw no reason for it other than the fact they were occasional drinking buddies.

Rachel reached the conference room where she had set up her temporary office, shut the door, kicked off her shoes, and massaged her soles gently. Her pumps pinched at several different points, but despite the dress code that advised limited heels, most of the women at Istanbul station wore at least a low heel, so she stomached the pain. Rachel rolled her chair closer to the floor-to-ceiling windows, then released the lock at the base of her Herman Miller chair so she could lean all the way back, soaking up the natural light.

A million thoughts streamed through her head, and she struggled to get a handle on all of it. The most unfortunate piece was that despite running their operation entirely off book, the rumor mill had caught on to far more than she had predicted.

*The whole department knows we're going after General Majed.*

She gritted her teeth. There was only one way that information could have circulated so rampantly—James must have told the other team leaders who worked under him.

*If you were going to tell them anyway, why are we bothering with an off-book op?* She wanted to confront him, but it was too late to do anything about it. There was nothing to do but pray none of it would compromise the success of the op. Or Petra and Kasem's safety, although she didn't want to think about that. She already had nightmares that ended with their deaths because she couldn't get them out in time. A particularly vivid one included her waiting for them at a border checkpoint. They approached on foot, but before they could make it across, General Majed turned into a zombie and attacked them.

On top of her fears, she couldn't help feel like everyone was laughing at her behind her back. Except for Devon, her fellow team leaders appeared overly sympathetic, to the point of being condescending. They were expecting her to fail. That was the gist of their behavior. She had received what should have been a highly prestigious assignment, but no one expected her to pull it off. Based on poorly vetted intel, the Company had allowed her to send two seconded operatives into one of the most dangerous destinations on the planet. The only explanation was the CIA couldn't care less if they never returned.

And Rachel had fallen for it, hook, line and sinker. She shuddered. For the sake of her pride, she hoped the op would succeed, but at this point, all she cared about was getting Petra and Kasem out safe. To hell with the rest of it. However, she couldn't count on their objectivity—not with the bargain she'd struck to get Kasem out of Agency custody. If they didn't deliver General Majed, Kasem would end up in an Agency black site.

*Whatever happens to them will be my fault.*

Rachel breathed through her emotions and forced herself to shift focus to her computer. She and her local team had been scouring all information available on Mahdi Gul's assets to find definitive proof of his illegal activities for Petra and Kasem to use in their upcoming confrontation. So far, they had come up empty, and time was running out. To help speed things along, she had hoisted even more of the task onto Nathan. Originally, the plan was only to have him help during the training phase, but she had leaned on him even more since the op had officially begun. He had worked with her, Petra, and Kasem during an operation in Madagascar a couple of years earlier, one which had revealed he wasn't at all suited for field work. Since moving back to an office job at Langley after that operation, he'd been much happier, but she had somehow cajoled him into helping with this op. He was a genius with everything computer-related, and she would trust him with her life. With the way the other team leaders had treated her at the department meeting, she clung fervently to that. Something was wrong, even if she couldn't put her finger on it. The only thing she could do now was try to keep the circle as small as possible.

After spending the next half hour on her emails, Rachel checked the clock on her phone, which read 5:30 p.m. Right on cue, a text message popped up on screen, and she broke into a smile. Nathan's flight had landed, and he would meet her at her apartment off Taksim Square. She grabbed her computer and notepad off the conference room table, scanned the room to make sure she hadn't left anything out that could compromise her or the op, then headed out. Deep in her gut, she had a feeling that Nathan had found something. She tried to temper her anticipation, but it bubbled up incessantly on the tram ride home.

"What did you find?" she asked within less than a minute of Nathan's arrival.

"Straight to business, hmm? Don't ask me how I'm doing, how the flight was, or anything? No thank you for taking my time to help you *again*. Just the same as back in Scotland—all business and favors, nothing else."

"I'm sorry. It's good to see you. You don't understand how great this is—to be around someone I don't have to posture with." Rachel sighed and shook her head. "Anyway, the point is I can trust you, and I really appreciate all your help. How's that for a better greeting?"

He gave her a pout and sat down on the couch, then broke into a grin. "It'll do for now. So long as we get some time to explore the city later. I'm burning vacation time here, so I better get some actual vacationing in, not just decoding spreadsheets on my days off."

"Of course."

"Good. Let's get the shop talk over with and then we can get to vacationing."

"Sounds great," Rachel agreed, slightly taken aback by his decisiveness. When they had worked together in Madagascar, Nathan had been anything but commanding, always unsure of himself. "Nice to see you like this. Looks like the change in jobs has done you some good," she said as she watched him set up his computer.

"What can I say? There's nothing like getting out of field ops."

"You could be right. I might be too old for this too."

Nathan turned the computer screen toward her, ignoring the comment. "I went through all the spreadsheets you sent over. The numbers tell an interesting story. Each of the three spreadsheets represents a different fund, with investments coming in from a bunch of different sources. The money is pooled into separate funds and then reinvested. But we need way more to get this guy. There's nothing here that's definitive. It just looks shady."

"So, we've got nothing unless we can get hold of his records. Reminds me of Nguyen's ledger," she said, referring to the target of their operation in Madagascar.

"Yes and no. The inbound part is a lot like Nguyen's ledger—a mess to decode and decipher. Nguyen was trying to hide his illicit arms investments by buying agriculture equipment and inputs, then funnel the returns back to his investors. I'm not sure where this guy is putting his returns, but the sketchy bit is on the inbound. He's using black money to make investments under the table, most of which are legit real estate assets. What that real estate is used for is another thing. I'm sure some of it is illegal bars or whatever, but we don't have anything to pin on him yet."

"Hmm," Rachel glanced at the ceiling, considering the implications. "So, Gul takes black market money and funnels it into a bunch of different investments, stuff that's probably legit."

"Exactly. If he's hanging out with your target, he could be doing that for him too."

"Right. Which means General Majed is channeling funds through Gul's investments."

Nathan raised his eyebrows. "Why not just pick him up now? I bet he would talk."

"We can't risk it. It has to be catch and release, otherwise we risk the Guard catching wind of it. And if the Secret Police realize Gul's been kidnapped, that could compromise Petra and Kasem. So, whatever we have on Gul has to be good enough to make him cooperate."

"Has your Company team looked at this yet? We might be able to find something in NSA intercepts, but it'll take forever for me to go through on my own."

Rachel hesitated. "There's something off about the team, maybe the department. I don't know what it is yet, but I don't want to risk it."

"So that's why you want me to do all this." Nathan looked at her for a few seconds of protracted silence. "Here's what I propose. Let's go out, get some food. I'm starving. We can talk about this over a meal and some drinks."

Rachel was once again surprised by the decisiveness with which he spoke. "All right." Despite the temptation to keep pushing, she stopped herself. It wouldn't do the op any good if she alienated one of the few people she could trust. "How do you feel about Turkish food?"

\*\*\*\*\*\*

Rachel led them to a round booth in the back corner of the Taksim Bahcivan restaurant. "This is my favorite place here," she said as they sat down. "Crazy enough, it's also one of the cheapest. I like to come here when I'm starving and load up on kebabs."

"Challenge accepted." Nathan chuckled.

Ten minutes later, they had before them a spread of adana, iskander, and shish kebabs, along with a Turkish-style lahmacun pizza, spinach borek cigar-shaped pastries, a chopped cucumber and tomato salad with pomegranate seeds and feta cheese, and several rounds of pide flatbread, along with a couple of beers. By the time the food arrived, Rachel realized that she, like Nathan, was also famished, and they both dug in with minimal conversation.

Once she had finished her first serving of kebabs and accoutrement, Rachel looked over with a smile. "I may not deliver on a real vacation, but I can make sure you eat well."

"You should know better than to bring up a heavy subject on an empty stomach."

"It's not empty now." She nodded toward his plate, already bare of the three kebabs he'd started with.

He mopped up the juices with some flatbread and popped a morsel in his mouth. "Fine, we had an agreement. I'm temporarily satiated, so let's talk."

"There's not much to say. I really need you to stick around. I don't think I can trust my assigned team, or at least, the broader circle within the Company. Like I said, it's too risky. I already sent Petra and Kasem into the lion's den. I can't risk anything that might compromise them."

"How are they holding up? It's too bad we didn't really have time to catch up in Scotland."

"It is."

"Are they solid now? The two of them, I mean."

"I think so." Rachel shrugged. "They've had their issues like any couple, I'm sure."

"I just remember things were messy back when we were all in Mada, but that was a while ago. Anyway, I'm glad they're doing well."

Rachel took a large gulp of her beer, taking the time to choose her words carefully. "I'm sure Petra would have liked more time to hang out with you. The two of you were pretty close."

"We had some good times—*Bake Off*, self-defense classes."

"That's not what I meant."

"I know. I had a crush on her, obviously not reciprocated, but she was also my friend. Kasem too, I guess, although we didn't get to know each other very well."

"He's a good guy, but you're right, difficult to get to know."

"Sure." Nathan helped himself to another plateful of food. "What did you mean when you said something's off about the department?"

"It's just a feeling, but something I can't shake. I've been in this business long enough to know not to ignore it."

"When did it start?"

"I'm not sure. We never talked about how I ended up on this op, right?"

"No."

"We're going to need more of these." Rachel finished her beer and waved at the server to bring over another round. "I was pretty excited when I got assigned the op back in May. General Majed, he's a huge target, top priority, all of that stuff. He was always on the radar, ever since we discovered his involvement in the Suez attack."

"Right. I remember that from the briefing packet you sent me."

"Exactly. So, huge, priority target, and we got this new intel he's alive, hiding out in Tehran. Before that, we thought he'd died of a stroke, but then we had this new lead and there was all this energy behind it. We were going to find him, bring him to justice."

The server delivered the next round of drinks and Nathan passed her a beer. After wetting her throat, Rachel continued. "The whole thing was pretty prestigious, especially since I don't really get along well with my supervisor. So I was pretty honored to be given the assignment. A couple of weeks in, though, I realized it was a setup. The Company had intel to confirm General Majed was still alive, but we couldn't confirm his location. All we knew was that he was in Tehran. I tried to get clearance to use the girl who spotted him for a honey trap, but she'd only seen him the one time and the Brits told us to steer clear."

"I guess they burned their hands pretty well when they tried to catch him a few years ago, right?"

"For sure."

"That op was such a screw up, even the tech trainees joked about it. Anytime someone messed up, they called it the Big Botch, just like the op."

Rachel nodded. "It was a big-time screw up. I don't remember the exact numbers, but it cost them several million, blew at least three covers, and got both the team leader and department head reassigned."

"General Majed's pretty good at pretending to be dead, isn't he? First, the Brits thought he was dead after their op, then somehow, he makes us think he died of a stroke last year."

"He must have a great PR team. Anyway, when they wouldn't authorize any of the local case officers to investigate further, I realized it was a setup. That's when I was talking to Petra and came up with the idea to use her and Kasem."

Nathan frowned. "On a side note, how did you get them to agree? I thought they were done with this... really done. They said as much when we left Mada."

*Oops.* Rachel had almost forgotten she hadn't read Nathan in on Kasem's past as the Ahriman. "That's a long story for another day. We figured out an arrangement. They were perfect for it. Both had a lot of experience in Iran."

"An arrangement? Right."

"Exactly."

"If the Company wouldn't let their case officers investigate, why did they authorize the op?"

"I didn't give them much choice." Rachel ignored his skepticism. "Assigning the op to me was basically a way for my supervisor to give me a giant middle finger. I went over his head to get clearance. It's our one shot at General Majed, so I pushed it through. After I got here, things went wonky. The op is supposed to be off book, but all the other team leads know the target and that I'm running it. I'm required to stand up at the department meetings every week, and it's like I'm on trial. Everyone wants to know everything, like they've forgotten the need-to-know principal. So far, I've been able to keep the circle small, but I'm not sure how long that will last. In the department meetings, one of my colleagues now refers to me as 'mademoiselle' while he rips at me about running an op on a priority target without Company agents. He shouldn't even have known we're using a seconded team. He kept grilling me, as if they were already dead and I should hand the entire op over to him. I'm still in shock. How could he know all that?"

"Your supervisor?"

"It has to be."

"All right. So your supervisor isn't sticking to protocol, but if this weren't off book, it would be fine for another team lead to know the basics, right?"

"I guess…"

He reached across the table to grasp her hand. "I get it. You're worried about them. It's not ideal. That guy's an ass, but I'm sure he'll keep that stuff to himself. We're not talking about a mole, just a breach of protocol."

"It's like there was this rage, this vindictiveness against me. Like he wanted to take me down because I got assigned the prestigious op instead—"

"I thought you said the op was a setup."

"It was, until we figured out a way forward. Now we might actually have a shot at finding General Majed. I'm telling you, Nate, he's got it in for me."

He slid across the booth and put his arm around her. "Even if he does, he can't do anything. A guy like that, it's just posturing. He wants to make himself feel better, look bigger. That's all this is about."

"I hope you're right."

"Let's enjoy the rest of this meal, then I'll hit the ground running on those NSA transcripts. In the meantime, they should approach Ahsani to see if he can get any more dirt on Gul. We don't have time to waste. Besides, I want to make sure I get to see *some* of this beautiful city."

Rachel gave him a small smile. She hadn't realized how much emotion she had been holding back. Nathan raised his beer and motioned toward hers. "When I'm right, I'm right. Cheers."

"Can't argue with that." Her smile widened, and she clinked her bottle against his. "Thank you."

# Chapter 20

*Tehran, Iran*

"There's something I have to tell you."

Petra set her glass on the coffee table. "I opened the bottle of wine Ramshad snuck us from the bar. Sorry, it was too tempting—I helped myself."

"All good."

"Before we get to that, I talked to Rachel. They haven't found enough to put pressure on Gul. She thinks we should ask Ahsani for dirt on him."

"Fine. I have a check in with Ramshad tomorrow anyway." Kasem doled out a second glass for himself and sat down on the floor across from her. He tapped his fingers against the wood surface, and Petra noticed the nervous energy enveloping him.

"What is it, Kasem?"

"I should have told you this before. I know I said we wouldn't have any secrets between us. Not anymore."

"You're telling me now."

"I don't know if you picked up on it, but I was pretty uncomfortable about using Simonyan as one of our assets."

"I figured it was because he was our best option for an escape route."

"That's part of it... but there's more."

Petra took a long sip to shut off the alarm bells going off in her head. Since meeting Farah the day before, she too had been grappling with her own secret. Should she tell Kasem about Farah's connection to Lieutenant Afshar? She remembered it like it was yesterday, her first conversation with Kasem when their paths had crossed in Kuwait three years earlier.

*"...we got word that you were killed by a Lieutenant Afshar."*

*"Lieutenant Afshar is dead!"* Kasem had yelled.

*"Was he your captor?"*

*"Captor, traitor, trainer—it's all the same. He's dead now. Why does it matter?"*

She suppressed a shudder and gripped the stem of the glass more tightly. "What is it?"

"Simonyan was a close friend of Commander Derderian."

"I know. It was in his file."

"Derderian was investigating General Majed's involvement in the attack at Suez."

"Are you sure?" Petra thought back to the brief mention of the commander in Gaston's file. According to French intelligence, Derderian and several other family members had been killed in a gas leak explosion. She swallowed a sinking feeling in her gut and banished all thought of telling him about Farah's relationship with Lieutenant Afshar.

"When General Majed got wind of his investigation, he had a team pick him up on New Year's Eve. Along with half his family—women, children. I was there that night, part of that team. We drove them out to an old horse stable that was converted into a warehouse. The whole place was wired with explosives. Then he had us separate the children, load them up into a van. I'll never forget what it looked like—this navy blue cargo van, and we just threw them in there like pieces of luggage. After that…"

Petra circled the coffee table and sat down next to him. He leaned into her chest, and she wrapped her arms around him.

"After that, he ordered me to set off the charges. He said that they'd found you, that they would kill you if I didn't comply. I remember holding it in my hands, this tiny piece of metal and plastic. I couldn't move, couldn't do anything, but then he reminded me of the consequences. So, I did it. I pushed the button—something so small. And then he made me watch the warehouse burn down."

# Chapter 21

*Tehran, Iran*

"How did it go the other night?"

"Not bad," Kasem replied as he sat down at a back table in the coffee shop where he had first met with Ahsani and Ramshad earlier that week.

"That's it?" Ramshad raised his eyebrows. "The circle of trust should go both ways, shouldn't it? You're still holding back your target, yet you want us to keep helping you."

"You know how this business works—it's all need to know. If I tell you, it puts us both at risk."

"You have access to the club anytime, and we haven't pressed you for more information. Seems like we're the only ones putting anything on the line."

Kasem ignored the statement and slid his phone across the table, the photo of Gul open on screen. "Do you have any idea who he is?"

"I do. He's a regular."

"All we have is his name, but we need leverage."

"Is he your target? He's not particularly high profile."

"No, but he could help us get to him."

"I see."

"Our team said you've probably run across him in some black market circles. Any information you have could be very helpful. My wife and I are here on borrowed time."

Ramshad's expression softened. "I like you, Kasem. You and Asma both, and so does Ahsani. The man you ask about is a banker, handles money transfers, estate tax, things like that for people in the black market. We haven't done business with him directly, but he's certainly in our orbit. I'll look into it, see if we have anything else on him."

"Thank you."

"How did you get the picture?"

"Asma took it," Kasem answered. They had to protect Farah's identity. Ahsani might not like that one of his employees was also helping them, even if technically they were all on the same side.

"I thought as much." Ramshad replied, although he looked skeptical. "Gul is very good. You won't find any of his transactions out in the open. If you're tracking one of his money trails, you won't get very far, not without talking to him. Would you like us to pick him up next time he's at the club?" He snapped a picture of Kasem's screen with his phone. "Just in case."

"Let's see what we find first."

"Fair enough. Now, have you had brunch here yet? They have an amazing spread here."

"I should probably get go—"

"Nonsense," Ramshad interrupted. "Is there anything you don't eat?"

"Maybe another time."

"Come now. If I go home right now, my wife is expecting me to go with her to visit my in-laws. I told her I had work so she should go without me, but if I get home before she leaves, I'll have no choice. Besides, the food is excellent, and I'm hungry."

Kasem broke into a smile, recognizing that Ramshad was making a peace offering. They might not always be on the same page regarding the operation, but they could certainly be friends. "You make an excellent case, and I'm hungry too. The food is the best thing about being back here."

"Now we're talking." Ramshad leaned closer and spoke in a hushed tone. "Normally this place is dry, but I have a few connections."

"I'll follow you."

"I can't tell you how great this is. My mother-in-law is so sweet, but she wants to control everything. No matter what I do, I can't seem to do it well enough, and Amira likes to see her every weekend. I can usually get out of it once or twice a month, but I swear to God, I've gone the last three weeks. I can't take another comment about how I need to lose weight or take her out more often. Travel more and drive a fancier car. Live in a different house. Or magically make all the traffic disappear."

"I get the gist."

Ramshad waved for a waitress and ordered a spread of nans, cheese, jams, two types of traditional Persian omelets, and a plate of Halim porridge. "Do you like Kaleh pache?" he asked.

"It wasn't my favorite." Kasem shrugged. His mother had made the sheep's head soup on special occasions, but he'd never really enjoyed it. When he was a kid, he could usually get away without eating any, but as he had gotten older, he'd eaten it begrudgingly. She had made too much of an effort for him to refuse.

"The one they have here is amazing. Let's try it. If you don't like it, I'll have it. My wife never lets me eat it anymore. Too high in cholesterol."

"Sounds good."

"Next time you see her, this never happened, okay?"

"My lips are sealed, but there's a price."

"A price?"

"I get to call you Colossus. Your new nickname. Give a guy his childhood dream."

Ramshad burst into a guffaw. "I love it. You can call me that anytime, no blackmail required."

The food arrived a few minutes later, and the two of them spent the next hour feasting and drinking. Kasem even gingerly tasted the Kaleh pache, but after swallowing the first spoonful, shook his head. "Still not my cup of tea."

"No problem, my friend. More for me." Ramshad pulled the enormous bowl toward his side of the table.

"Don't forget about the rest of the food." Kasem gestured toward the other dishes. "You can't leave me to eat it all."

"Don't worry, we'll finish it."

Despite his doubts, Kasem found they were quite capable of devouring the spread. By the time Kasem made it home, he was stuffed to the brim and pleasantly tipsy, although he made sure to drink two cups of coffee before attempting to drive.

He plonked down on the couch and had almost forgotten about the picture on his phone burning a hole in his pocket. When Petra joined him a few minutes later, he recounted what Ramshad had shared about Gul. They sent the details off to Rachel, and instead of discussing the operation any further, he and Petra spent the rest of the day wandering around their neighborhood. Deep down, he had to admit he loved this city—despite all the harm that had come from his time there, despite all the restrictions. If only he could erase its connection to his former life as the Ahriman.

# Chapter 22

*Tehran, Iran*

"What do you think? Should we help them? They won't find anything on Gul—he's too careful. But we have the records they need for leverage." Ramshad looked across the table at his boss, referring to files Ahsani had acquired and kept on most of his black market contacts.

"Did you tell him we've worked with him?"

"I didn't say anything, just that I would look into it."

"Good. I'd rather the CIA not know about those dealings." Ahsani poured two drinks from the crystal flask at the end of the table and handed one to Ramshad. "Did he share anything else about the operation?"

"Just that Gul could help them locate their target."

"Any idea how they got that picture?"

"Looks like it was taken at one of our clubs. He or his wife could have taken it." Ramshad opened the picture on his phone. "It's not a great shot, just a screen grab before the auto delete."

Ahsani glanced at it and shook his head. "Neither of them could have gotten that close. Not unless she dressed up as one of our girls. She certainly has the rack for it."

Ramshad smirked, leaning over to look at the picture more closely. "She could have snuck in one night, but how would they know when he comes to the club?"

"He comes in with people all the time, but that means someone must be helping them. The same person who took the picture. The question is who. See what you can find out when you talk to him again."

"What should I tell him?"

"Give him some high-level info about what Gul does. Act supportive, but don't hand over anything that could implicate us. The CIA network has been helpful to me, but not enough to turn over that kind of evidence." He paused. "And reach out to Gul. Let's relocate the money he scrubbed."

"I'll take care of it."

# Chapter 23

*Tehran, Iran*

Davit Simonyan read through one report Kasem had given him for the fourth time, grappling with his new reality. He had been told his brother-in-law Commander Derderian and several others in his late wife's family had died because of a gas leak on New Year's Eve seven years earlier. After their deaths, he and his wife had adopted Derderian's daughter, Tala, and raised her as their own. She had sent him an email that morning, telling him how much she was enjoying university. Her apartment was walking distance to Covent Garden, and she and her friends had already been to several shows, taking advantage of last-minute discounts and standing tickets. He was sure she was also getting into all kinds of other trouble, what with the concentration of pubs within less than a block of her campus, but he could tell she was having fun. She deserved to rebel, to have a few secrets, as long as she was safe and enjoying herself. It had been a long time since she'd been truly happy. Life had been difficult since his wife's death.

Although he missed her terribly, he was grateful she was outside of Iran. She deserved to be free. The poor treatment of women was the main reason he had worked for French intelligence. He had applied for immigration, but instead been approached to serve as an intelligence asset. After adopting their daughter, he had taken a step back, unable to stomach the danger. Gaston had helped him to get out, acting against his superior's orders. Simonyan was grateful for that time, but what was his excuse now?

*Tala is safe.*

He walked over to his sideboard table and picked up a picture of the three of them together. Tala was safe and his wife

Maya was gone. Perhaps his days of standing on the sidelines were over.

*There was no gas leak.* Simonyan had always thought the investigation into the gas leak was weak, but had chosen not to look into it—that would have been far too painful for both his wife and daughter. Kasem's report provided a credible explanation—General Majed had been responsible. He had hunted Derderian down to silence his investigation. An investigation that had stumbled upon General Majed's plan for the Suez Canal attack. An attack he had executed without facing a single consequence.

He recalled the last time he had seen and spoken to Derderian. The two of them had laughed about a childhood exploit when they had snuck out as teenagers and taken his father's car to go to a friend's party. They'd both been so sure they would get away with it, until Derderian's dad had shown up at the party to take them home. Simonyan remembered the chilling silence on the ride home—the most stressful moment of their lives up to that point. *If only it had stayed that way.* He couldn't help but smile. They were fast friends throughout school and university, although when Simonyan had begun a relationship with his sister, tensions had run high for a while.

As an only child, Simonyan had always thought of Derderian as a brother. He missed the nights they used to hang out watching soccer and drinking whiskey, the times they'd played soccer, gone hiking and skiing together, and the times when they had sat around doing nothing. Reading the report on his death made Simonyan feel as if it was happening again. The wound had reopened. It was fresh and hemorrhaging blood.

Simonyan switched his screen to Kasem's other report, a direct account of how General Majed had planned and executed the Suez attacks.

*Could this be true?* He knew in his gut that it was. The account was too real to be fabricated. Which left the more important question: what should he do about it? Kasem had obviously left the ball in his court as to the next step, but there was no mistaking his intent. Kasem had provided that intel for a reason.

While Simonyan couldn't pinpoint exactly what or who he worked for, the underlying message was clear enough. Whomever Kasem worked for, they wanted him to spy for them.

A shiver ran up his spine. Intense paranoia and moments of utter terror had characterized the short time he had worked for the French DGSE. Could he really venture down that path again? If he chose not to, if he stood by, what did that make him? Especially now, when he had nothing to lose except his own life.

His time in the military had always been a fight. As one of the few Armenians rising up the ranks, he'd endured offhand comments and sideswipes about his ethnicity on a daily basis, even among the more tolerant officers. Sometimes the comments were overt, other times more subtle. They had asked him to explain his traditions. How he could be an Iranian, despite the fact his family had lived in Tehran for four generations.

*You'd have to be a traitor again.* The thought had been lurking in the back of his mind since he'd first read the reports, but he had staved it off. No matter what discrimination he had faced, growing up and in the military, he was Iranian to the core. But his loyalty wasn't to the oppressive regime that gave his orders. His loyalty belonged to the people. People who had been subjugated by the clerics. People who deserved better.

*You would be a patriot again.* He took a deep breath and clung to that thought. He had to believe it in every part of his being to take the next step. Had to hold on to it at all costs, even with the line he was about to cross once more.

*What should I do, Maya?* She had always been the voice of reason, his voice of clarity. He had so many questions. Who did Kasem work for? How had he procured the intel he'd shared? *Why me, and why now? What do they want from me?* If it involved General Majed, Simonyan wasn't at all sure he could be helpful. The general had been underground for some time. Simonyan had heard rumors of a stroke, and that he was being hunted by Western intelligence, but he'd never given them much credence.

Simonyan glanced at the clock and sighed. There was only one way to answer those questions, and if he took that step, there would be no going back. He took a deep breath and solidified his decision.

*She would want me to do this. For Tala, for us… and for Iran.* And if General Majed had indeed killed her brother?

*She would want him gone.*

# Chapter 24

*Tehran, Iran*

Ramshad stared at his computer screen, his thoughts replaying his earlier conversation with Kasem. He looked at the spreadsheet from Ahsani's file on Mahdi Gul and wondered why Ahsani didn't want to hand over the information.

Ahsani had used Gul to clean a number of larger transactions so they wouldn't bring attention from the local tax authorities. In turn, Gul also tapped Ahsani's legitimate investments to bring other clients' black market money out into the open. Gul would pool cash investments from several of his clients, package them into a Special Purpose Vehicle, and make an above-board investment. Ramshad wasn't entirely sure how the process worked, how Gul funneled the cash and absolved most of his clients' tax liability. What he did know was that as part of the coverup, Gul constructed spreadsheets that contained records of each client's investment. The spreadsheets served as insurance—a record of the transactions he scrubbed that implicated both Gul and his clients. As a form of leverage, the spreadsheets were essentially the Holy Grail, exactly what Kasem and his wife needed to get Gul to cooperate. Ramshad couldn't make head or tail of the records, but Ahsani had kept copies of all the documentation—insurance for his assets and blackmail material on many of his customers—to be used on an as-needed basis.

*If they could even decipher the records.* Ramshad wanted to justify Ahsani's decision. Still, if anyone could do it, he would bet on the CIA, or the Company, as Ahsani referred to them.

*They haven't always been on the right side.*

The Secret Police had killed his grandfather before he was born, and everyone in his family was skeptical of the West.

Rightfully so, in his opinion. Despite that, Ramshad had continued to work with Ahsani even after being read in on his involvement with the Company. Whatever wrongs they had committed, and there were many, especially in Iran and other parts of the Middle East, he had to believe in Western values. At the end of the day, those values stood above what the Iranian government had become—a tool for fundamentalists to remain in power. A system that silenced progressive voices, that subjugated women. One that placed religion above all other things. One that couldn't be further from a true interpretation of the Quran.

When Ahsani had first shared his connection with the Company, Ramshad had wondered if Ahsani was a traitor and if that made him a traitor too. While taking the metro home after that conversation, he had noticed a woman in a burka, covered from head to toe with only a slit for her eyes, talking to another woman in a loose headscarf and pants, both waiting for the same train. Tehran was full of such contrasts, opposites that gave the city life and vibrancy. Most Iranians had once celebrated and championed that contrast, at least according to the stories his grandmother had shared. In a time before the Shah, before the mullahs had destroyed it all. Pieces of that spirit remained despite all attempts to reduce it to ash. The work Ahsani did with the Company, distasteful as it might be, was to fan those flames. To restore that spirit and bring it out of the shadows.

*I could help them.*

Kasem and his wife, Asma, were risking their lives to locate their target. Ramshad couldn't help but root for them. He wanted them to survive the op. Whoever their target was, he had to hope they were worth capturing.

Ramshad gazed out the window toward the Alborz Mountains, which framed the north side of the city. He remembered the first time he'd ridden the gondola from the Velenjak valley up to the Tochal ski resort as a kid. He had taken in the city view with all the hope and optimism of childhood. Later, he and his family had breakfasted at the resort hotel, a similar spread to what he and Kasem had eaten earlier that day, although not quite as delicious. Ramshad smiled at the memory. He hadn't returned to the resort since his parents had passed five years earlier. Less than a year later, his sister Zana had left, too, for a job in Qatar.

*"I have to get out of here. It's not safe to be a progressive. I'm one step short of a dissident. If the Guard ever investigated us, they would find out our great-grandmother was Jewish. There would be no mercy imaginable for a Jewish dissident. Next stop, hanging."*

Asma reminded him of his sister, something in the cadence with which she spoke and how she carried herself. They had lost touch after her departure, but they spoke occasionally over the phone, always wary the authorities might be listening in to their conversations. Ramshad thought of their Jewish great-grandmother. He'd never met her and no one in his family was very religious. Their home was secular but had maintained an outward Islamic demeanor to limit attention from the Guard. His Jewish relatives had all left, either for Israel or the United States, but the family that remained in Iran kept those ties a secret. As a child, his parents hadn't even dared take them to visit the city of Isfahan, where that part of the family was from. If they'd officially been a Jewish family, that would have afforded them some official protections, but as a mixed family, they deemed it too risky. To this day, Ramshad had yet to visit Iran's third-largest city.

*For Zana. And the rest of us.* Taking a deep breath, he turned to his computer and saved the spreadsheets onto an encrypted USB thumb drive. With the drive in hand, he went straight to his car and drove south.

******

Ramshad stopped near Mellat Park, where he had asked Kasem to meet him. It was just past dusk, so while there were still quite a few people around, it would be hard for anyone to make out faces. It would be best to meet out in the open as if they had nothing to hide rather than showing up at Kasem's apartment. He also didn't want his car's GPS to show he had gone anywhere particularly unusual, and he visited the nearby Safavieh Shopping Center across the street often enough.

Ramshad sat down on a bench on one of the main paths next to a bed of pink roses and pulled out his phone. He pretended to read an article while he kept an eye out for Kasem or anything suspicious. Ten minutes later, Kasem joined him on the other side of the bench with a quick nod. "Why did you want to meet?"

"I have something for you," Ramshad said quietly. "The boss didn't want me to share it, but it's what you asked for. I'm not sure you'll be able to decipher it in time—I certainly couldn't—but if you can, it's yours."

"Why are you giving it to us?"

"I don't know who your target is, but I have to believe you're trying to make things better. To make things right for the people here. All this time we've been working with the Company, it has to mean something."

"It's a good target."

"I'll take your word for it." Ramshad wedged the thumb drive between two of the bench slats.

"Kheily mamnoon," Kasem said softly, using the most formal and earnest version of 'thank you' in Farsi.

"Like I said, I have to believe in something." Before he could second-guess what he'd done—the betrayal of a boss who had given him everything—Ramshad stood and walked away.

# Chapter 25

*Istanbul, Turkey*

"Rachel, I reviewed the files you sent through. Thanks for that. I have a few questions."

"Of course." After another grilling department meeting, she had finally acquiesced to hand over the files to her supervisor James. She took a seat in front of his desk and clasped her hands together. Anything to prevent them from tapping on the armrests. She had beaten the nervous tick years ago, but it had returned with all the stress of the last few weeks. The habit had ballooned since her arrival in Istanbul, but she'd first noticed it while reviewing files at the estate in Scotland.

"They're obviously qualified operatives, both with experience in Iran. However, I fail to understand why we needed to use them specifically. We don't have many Company field agents who've worked in Tehran, but we certainly have a few."

*Because you wanted them to be expendable.*

Rachel nodded as if she were clueless about the CIA's true motivation. Since she had purposely sanitized some of Kasem's and Petra's field history before handing the files over, she'd expected this question. *Smoke and mirrors. That's what we do here.* "The male agent is particularly suited for this since he's had direct experience with military assets in Tehran. The female operative worked with him during that op, and they eventually made it out."

"Doesn't that put them at even higher risk? They were both blown."

"In a way, but that doesn't substitute for their experience. We've never had anyone with as much access to higher-ups in the Iranian military as he did."

"I see. So, I'm guessing some of those details aren't in the files? One of them doesn't even have a photo."

"Standard protocol—just like we don't put their real names in the files, we don't include every detail that could be used to identify them."

"Fine. At least it's clear they're qualified, even if they are from another agency." He shrugged. "Plus that makes them less valuable, expendable even. Maybe it was a good idea." He turned toward his computer, then looked back at her with a frown. "Was there anything else?"

*You called me in.* "No, sir."

"Very well. I'll see you at the next department meeting."

Rachel walked out of his office with a sinking feeling in her stomach.

*It's fine,* she consoled herself. Maintaining redundancy on operative and asset details was standard Company protocol, even if it wasn't typical for off-book ops. *No big deal.* Now that he had reviewed the files, maybe the department meetings would be a little less gruesome. Devon, the colleague who seemed constantly out to get her, would have to be silent now that she had provided the information he'd been so skeptical about. She had bigger things to focus on now. Petra and Kasem would be kidnapping Gul from the underground club tomorrow. The information Kasem had received was perfect. It had provided the leverage they would need to get him to cooperate. Gul would provide General Majed's location, they would move in and neutralize him, then she would exfil Petra and Kasem. The op would be tied up with a bow, and they could all move on with their lives.

Still, she couldn't silence the feeling of dread in her stomach that something was about to go terribly wrong.

# Chapter 26

*Tehran, Iran*

He was hanging naked with his hands tied to a metal ring attached to the ceiling. The rope had left deep red open sores on his wrists. Every part of his body screamed with pain, so much that he could no longer place where it was coming from. The skin on his chest and abdomen had turned various shades of black and dark purple from the beating they had inflicted. His back was covered in gashes from the whip. The slightest muscle twitch sent convulsions throughout his body.

The cell was lit by a dim halogen bulb in the far corner that had yet to be extinguished. He had lost all perception of time—he could have been in the cell for a week, a month, or a year. He had been given food a few times, but there was no semblance of routine. Sometimes the guards would come in and ask questions. They would throw cigarette butts at his feet and jeer. A few times, they poured water in his face and forced morsels of rice down his throat.

No matter what, they would inflict more blows.

The whip was the worst. The last couple of times, his back had bled too much, so they had whipped his legs instead. He longed for daylight, for a bed, even just to be horizontal. He thought of his parents and his sister, but most of all, his thoughts hung on his girlfriend. The future he wanted to build together.

The cell door opened, and he recoiled at the extra light. When his eyes adjusted, Kasem tried to shrink away. Every time he saw the general his blood turned cold.

"Did you really think you could come back to Iran, and we wouldn't find you? That we wouldn't find your girlfriend?" General Majed spat at his face. "I created you. I made you. And then you come back to hunt me down?" He broke into a guffaw. "Get him down," he said to someone behind him. "It's time for you to prove your worth."

The room dissolved, and Kasem was standing in a stadium with a knife in his hand. Lieutenant Afshar was in front of him, and just beyond, he saw Petra. She stood on a stool with her head in a noose.

"Petra," he shouted and tried to run toward her. The surrounding ground turned to quicksand, and he struggled to pull his feet from the mud. With each attempt, he sunk further. "Let her go," he screamed. "Afshar, help her."

General Majed appeared again, this time floating atop the quicksand. "Only you can save her. But you must pay the price—kill the lieutenant, here and now, and I'll let her live."

Kasem's gaze darted between Petra and Afshar. "Help her," he pleaded again. Why wasn't she struggling? Why wasn't she fighting back? She stood there immobile, like a statue. He looked down at the dagger in his hand and tried to take another step toward her. He sank to his knees and floundered.

"You'll can only move toward Afshar. It's the only way you can save her."

"I'll help her, Kasem. Don't move," the lieutenant spoke for the first time.

General Majed snickered. "He can't even save himself, let alone anyone else."

Kasem shut his eyes and this time willed himself a foot closer to Afshar. He felt himself flying, free of the quicksand. He landed in front of the lieutenant and their eyes locked.

"You must do what you feel is right."

Kasem drove the dagger forward into Afshar's gut. The lieutenant collapsed in his arms and, a moment later, there was blood everywhere. All over Kasem's hands, his arms, the stadium floor. He dropped Afshar's body and ran toward Petra. The few seconds it took to reach her felt like an eternity. He pulled the noose off her head, but she remained motionless.

She was asleep, that had to be it. Asleep.

He lowered her to the ground, laid her down and groped for a pulse. Nothing. Her pulse was gone. Her body was cold.

"No!"

\*\*\*\*\*\*

"Kasem, are you okay? Wake up."

He bolted upright, his face covered in sweat. He looked around frantically, his whole body shaking. His breathing was shallow and rapid, but started to slow as he realized where he was. Their apartment in Tehran. Petra was in front of him, looking at him with an expression of deep concern.

"Just give me a minute. I'll be right back."

When he returned from the bathroom, Petra was on the couch, her expression unchanged. "Are you okay?"

He steadied himself against the armchair across from her and lowered himself to the floor. "I am. It was just a nightmare."

"I didn't know they were back."

"Just a few since we got here."

"A few? How could you not tell me this? Kasem, this isn't just a nightmare. You had PTSD and now it's back."

"I'm fine. It's not as bad as they were before."

"You're not fine, and it looked bad enough. What would have happened if I hadn't woken you up?"

"Babe, all we have to do is finish the op and get out of here. If they keep happening after that, I'll go back to therapy. I swear."

Petra hesitated. "We're moving on Gul tomorrow and probably on Majed a few days after. Are you sure you can handle this? I need you to be a hundred percent."

"I'll be on my game, I promise."

# Chapter 27

*Tehran, Iran*

When Petra arrived at the club her heart was racing, although she portrayed an outward calm. They were on the early side, so the club had only just started to fill up. Kasem took a stool at the bar, and she excused herself to freshen up.

She walked toward the bathrooms and, after making sure the hallway was empty, went past them and opened the door to the storeroom just past the dressing room. A moment later, Farah joined her.

"Did anyone notice you leave?" Petra asked.

"They were too busy handing out ecstasy to notice. Besides, they know I never partake—it makes me too woozy to dance."

"Did you place the cameras in the booth closest to the hallway?"

"You're all set."

Petra tapped the app on her phone to engage the cameras and checked the feed. She could see two angles of the round table and purple studded couch cushions that comprised the booth. "Looks good." She locked the screen and put the phone back in her purse, then retrieved a small vial. "After you get him into the booth, add a few drops to his drink. The laxative will make him rush out of there within a few minutes. Leave the rest to me."

"He probably won't be here until eleven, maybe even later."

"That's fine. You marked the booth reserved like most of the others, so it doesn't matter when he arrives. We'll be ready."

# Chapter 28

*Tehran, Iran*

Kasem ordered a finger of Auchentoshan 18 while he waited for Petra to return from the restrooms. He took a small sip. The first taste of whiskey was often too sharp for his liking, but by the second, he could enjoy the flavor with less of a burn. For show and his own pleasure, he savored it, alongside the hope it could help steady his nerves. Both he and Petra were on edge. He could sense it, but they were also experienced operatives who could put those emotions aside when the situation demanded it. Kasem's relief at having told her about the triggers that recruiting Simonyan had pulled was palpable. When she was ready, he could only hope she would reciprocate. For now, they had dealt with the worst of their trust issues, at least on the surface. She clearly still resented the decision he'd taken in Burundi, but they were working toward a new normal, one that left the past where it belonged.

As he sipped his whiskey, he listened to the various conversations in his vicinity. Behind him, four men were discussing having watched Manchester City play Arsenal during the last season of the English Premier League. "The stands were loud there, but nothing compared to here on a Saturday night," one said with a chuckle.

Kasem tuned them out and focused on a group of six men and women in their early twenties on the opposite side of the bar. There were three conversations in the group—gossip from a recent party, a discussion on the most recent round of political protests, which were becoming increasingly tense, and a heated debate on which stripper was the best looking.

With his third swallow of whiskey, he turned toward the stage. The emcee had just appeared and was attempting to get the crowd riled up ahead of the first act, a group number including all the club's dancers, when he felt a tap on the shoulder.

"I know you said you'd come by on Monday, but I thought I'd see if I ran into you here."

Kasem forced a smile and greeted Simonyan. "Davit, it's great to see you." In his peripheral vision, he saw Petra pause on her way toward them and then head to the opposite end of the bar as if she were searching for a better vantage point to watch the show. He gestured toward the empty stool next to him. "Have a seat. How do you like the show here?"

"Not bad. I've seen it a few times."

Kasem felt his earlier trepidation return. Of all times for Simonyan to show up, tonight was the worst possible. His arrival meant Petra would have to handle Gul on her own unless he could quell Simonyan's doubts quickly.

"What are you drinking?"

"Auchentoshan 18. It's excellent."

Simonyan ordered the same and settled on the stool next to Kasem, both facing the stage. "Cheers." He waited until the music for the first act picked up before he spoke again. "I read the books you gave me. Where did you get them?"

"They're firsthand accounts."

"I thought the Ahriman was the one responsible for Suez. At least that's what all our intel suggested. But the other details line up—the exact time of the attack, the type of devices used, the precise locations the bombs went off." Simonyan frowned. "None of that was public."

"They're not fake. I can promise you that."

"My friend's death. Because of his position, most of the details around that were classified. So, I have to ask again, who is your source?"

"We had someone inside. He's dead now, but he worked for General Majed," Kasem answered, using the story he and Petra had come up with when they'd decided how to bring Simonyan into the fold.

"Then why not stop the attack at Suez? I can understand why you wouldn't care about my brother-in-law, but—"

"We only got the intel after, once it was too late."

"Who do you work for?"

"I think you already know."

Simonyan pretended to cheer as the dancer on stage executed a pirouette around the pole. "What do you want from me?"

"Help us locate and capture General Majed. Get justice for your brother-in-law, for the people who died at Suez."

"And if you do?"

"If we thought he would face real justice in an Iranian court, I'd be the first one to turn him over." Kasem stopped there. He preferred that Simonyan fill in the blanks, come to his own conclusion rather than being explicit.

"Are you going to kill him?"

"I'm not sure I see another way."

"What can I do?"

"You could get us the intel we need on his safe house. Security details, blueprints. If he's there, his nephew Sami Khaled's fingerprints will be all over it. Then once it's done, we'll need help to get out."

"What's the address?"

Kasem recited it quickly. "Will you do it?"

"I'll think about it."

"Davit, over three hundred people died in the attacks at Suez, another eight when he killed your brother-in-law. Don't they deserve justice?" Kasem watched Simonyan's microexpressions before he played his last card. "Doesn't your daughter?"

# Chapter 29

*Tehran, Iran*

Petra waited in the first stall in the men's bathroom and watched the camera feed. Gul had arrived at the club almost an hour after the show began. Despite Simonyan's surprise appearance, the evening had gone as planned, at least so far. Farah had captured Gul's attention and led him to the first booth with one of the other girls. She'd spiked his drink less than five minutes ago, and he would need to exit momentarily.

*Three, two, one.* He stood with an uncomfortable expression on his face, then bolted out of the feed.

When the adjacent stall door slammed shut, she emerged and locked the main door after placing an 'Out of Order' sign on the side facing the hallway. She waited for him to emerge, and when he did, he had a dazed expression on his face.

"Are you all right? I think you're in the wrong restroom."

"I'm sorry." He stumbled toward the sink and she caught his arm.

"Perhaps we should call a doctor?" The protrusion from her ring pricked his skin and his expression glazed over. A moment later, he passed out. She braced herself as his weight descended on her and grunted as she dumped him into the cart she had wheeled in earlier from the storeroom. She dumped the basket of dirty hand towels over his unconscious form and sent a message to Kasem.

*Got the package. Meet me at the van.* On her way out, she yanked the sign off the door.

# Chapter 30

*Tehran, Iran*

Sami Majed checked his phone and tapped on the chat notification.
*Out for delivery, 14:00 today.*
Sami checked his watch. He had about ten minutes until it arrived. He checked his email quickly and went downstairs to the building lobby two minutes ahead of time. Right on schedule, a young man dressed in a local postal service uniform arrived. Sami signed for the package and returned to his apartment.
He ripped it open and tossed the obvious cover materials—a set of travel brochures that covered ten different scenic destinations in Turkey and the cost of associated tours. At the bottom of the box, he found what he was looking for—a set of branded knickknacks. One of them was a key chain. He ran his fingers over it, slid the lid off the USB thumb drive, and plugged it into his computer.
After a quick virus scan, he opened the first pdf on the drive. The file took a moment to load, but when it did, he almost lost his grip on the glass of water in his hand.
*It can't be.*
The woman's face was different than he remembered, and the photo was blurry. Her hair was longer, and she wasn't wearing a headscarf, but the resemblance was unmistakable.
*Lila Tabbas.* At least that had been her cover legend at the time. He would have to determine what name she was using now.
He skimmed the profile that followed her picture, although it provided little detail. Nothing on her cover, just the fact she had previously worked in Tehran in close contact with an asset within General Majed's inner circle. He could fill in the blanks, and knew she had indeed worked with such an asset. The

Ahriman, albeit before the general had shaped the boy into that character.

An idea formed in his head as he went through the document once more. Perhaps she could be of use to him. There was a chance, however small. But another question superseded that one by a long way.

Who had she come to Iran with?

A wave of anticipation hit him as he waited for the second file to load. *Was it possible?* As far as they knew, the Ahriman was dead. But if the girl had returned to Tehran, who was to say he hadn't as well?

The second file did nothing to assuage his suspicions. It contained a cover report from Behraz stating he had yet to confirm whether the second agent had been deployed but that the operative was male. The female agent would lead the operation. His contact had not seen the other file, if it indeed existed. In his conclusion, Behraz confirmed both operatives were seconded from a partner agency and had extensive experience in Iran, although he was still procuring specific details.

Sami reread the two documents twice, unable to move, unable to believe what he was seeing. His instincts had never failed him before, and he wasn't about to stop trusting them now. If the girl was back alongside a male agent, that could only mean one thing.

The Ahriman had returned to Iran.

# Chapter 31

*Tehran, Iran*

Petra's phone vibrated with an alert a few minutes after they parked in front of the storage unit Ramshad had set up for them. It was in an industrial area, so the place was quiet late on a Saturday night. She helped Kasem unload Gul and secure him to a chair before she bothered to check the message.

Five minutes earlier, Rachel had texted. *Call me back. Urgent.*

Before she could dial, the phone rang, and Petra picked up. "What is it?"

"Thank God you're okay. We have to abort. Now."

# Chapter 32

*Tehran, Iran*

Petra put her head in her hands, unable to process what she'd just heard. *This can't be happening.* "What do we do, Kasem?" she whispered. Under normal circumstances, she was good at adapting to changing situations. But everywhere she turned, the options were too bleak to contemplate. She leaned her head back against the wall and squeezed her eyes shut, her heartbeat ringing through her ears.

"It's going to be okay."

"How?"

"We find another way. Capture General Majed, then get out of here. We were always going to exfil on our own. Now we just have an added task."

"But she ordered us to abort."

"It's Rachel. I bet you could convince her we've still got a shot. If we leave now, you know what happens."

*You go back to an Agency cell. Or worse.*

"Why don't we just run? Let's go. Now, tonight. We could just disappear."

"That's not what I want."

"What do you mean?"

"Isn't it obvious? How can I leave now? When we have the man who destroyed our lives—my life—in our sights. I can't do that, and I'm not going to."

"So having a life together, that's second to revenge? Is that where we are?"

"It's so easy to say, isn't it? He murdered hundreds of people and turned me into a puppet. Today, I have the opportunity to even that score. How can you ask me to let that go?"

Petra was silent for a long moment before she asked, "Do you really think we still have a shot?" *What are you smoking?*

"Of course we do."

"If Sami Majed knows I'm here, he'll have doubled the security detail around that house. There's no way we can move on it without a full commando team."

"Then let's find an alternative."

"Like what?" she said with a sigh.

"Think about it. General Majed stayed sequestered in his safe house for weeks, maybe months, then he gets spotted one night at a strip show at Ahsani's club."

"What are you saying?"

"I'm saying that if we can't get to him inside the house, then we lure him out."

Petra sat up straighter as her brain finally began to function once again. A million scenarios ran through her head, and she took a deep breath to get a handle on it all. "Okay, you're right. If Gul could lure him out once, maybe he can do it again." She glanced to her right toward the room where they had stashed him.

"Exactly. Instead of going to him, we get him to come to us."

"We'll need something special, not just a regular night at the bar."

"We'll figure it out. Or at least, Ahsani will." Kasem picked her phone up from the table and handed it to her. "You've got this. Call Rachel and convince her, get her on board."

"All right. Whatever it takes. I'm not letting you go back to prison."

# Chapter 33

*Tehran, Iran*

Petra watched Kasem walk into the interrogation room through the video feed they had set up at the warehouse. It had taken her over twenty minutes on the phone to get Rachel to agree to their new plan, but it might as well have been three hours. Every muscle in her body felt sapped, and the sense of despair that had abated earlier was already returning.

"Who are you? What have I done?" Gul cried out.

Kasem pulled up a chair and sat down in front of him, a bottle of water in his hand. He took several long gulps and set the bottle down on the floor. "Mahdi, are you thirsty? Perhaps you'd like some water?"

"Yes, please."

"Why don't you give me something first? Tell me about who you work for."

"I work for my clients. I buy real estate and rent it out, clients pay for it."

"So everything about your business is entirely aboveboard. Is that right?"

"Of course."

"I'm afraid the information I have contradicts that." Kasem placed the first page of a printout of the spreadsheets Ramshad had provided on the table in front of Gul.

"What is this? Where did you get this?"

"Does it matter where I got it? I suppose you think we wouldn't be able to decode it, but you'd be wrong." He unfolded a second printout with the summary Nathan had put together and read the first few lines. "It seems the Montazavi family added another two million dollars to the fund you used to buy the Safavi construction site. I believe the mall there is about to open, isn't it? I'm sure the tax authorities would find that information very interesting. Then we have another million from Ahsani, five hundred thousand from the Farzanehs, just shy of a million from Faraz Shah, all for your purchase of the high-rise complex out in Qeytarieh." Kasem drummed his fingers on the table. "More than the authorities, you've gotten into bed with some shady people. I bet they wouldn't be happy to find out you weren't able to maintain their confidentiality." He pursed his lips. "I believe they get pretty angry about that kind of stuff."

"What are you going to do?"

"That depends on you, Mahdi. I don't *have* to do anything with this. I could just keep it to myself, hold on to it for safekeeping. But to do that, I need something from you."

"What did I ever do to you? Did I sleep with your wife? Threaten your children?" When Kasem didn't rise to the bait, Gul added, "Tell me what you want from me."

"It's quite simple. We need your help to get to one of your contacts." Kasem showed him the picture in which both Gul and General Majed were sitting, doe-eyed and mouths open, as they received lap dances at the club. The table in between them displayed two bottles of whiskey, one of which was knocked on its side. "The picture itself is pretty damning in the right hands. You're obviously drinking, and I suspect the empty baggy on the table contained another illegal substance. But like I said, we're not after you. I don't give a crap who you touch or sleep with or whatever the hell else. What I care about is General Majed. Help us capture him and it all goes away. The spreadsheets, the photos, everything."

"I can't help you. He'll kill me if I do. Please. I'll do anything else."

Kasem got to his feet, shoved the metal table aside, and with one stride, his face was less than an inch from Gul's aquiline features. "Do you think this is a joke? You can't help me because he'll kill you? What do you think is going to happen if I send this information to the Montazavis? Are they going to throw you a party?" To punctuate every few words, he slapped Gul hard. Left cheek, right cheek, until the older man had turned bright red and raw.

"Please. His nephew will kill me if I help you."

Kasem shoved his hand against Gul's neck, tilting the chair back to slam his head into the wall. He held on for five seconds before he let go and shoved the chair to the side. It toppled to the right, and Gul sobbed as his body rammed into the ground.

Outside the room, Petra shuddered and looked away from the screen. She hadn't seen Kasem interrogate someone before, and she hoped never to again. *It could be so much worse.* The reminder didn't seem to help.

Twenty minutes later, Kasem emerged and squeezed her hand. "I'm sorry it got that far."

"It's okay. You've seen me do worse," she said in reference to an interrogation in Madagascar that had gone awry two years earlier.

"I think we've got him now. He agreed to everything, and right now he's writing a list of Sami Majed's investments."

"Great. All we have to do is convince Ahsani to throw a big party."

# Chapter 34

*Tehran, Iran*

"I don't care how much money you throw at me. I refuse to cooperate unless you tell me who the target is," Ahsani repeated for the third time. "How do you think I've survived this long? I have the right contacts in the government and in the police, but I stay under the radar. Now you want me to turn my club into the site for a CIA operation, and you expect me to go along with it as if it's just a regular day? I can't do that, not unless you put something on the line. Not unless you tell me why."

Petra exchanged a glance with Kasem. So far, he had run the meeting since all their interactions with Ahsani had been through him, but he had also let Ahsani control the discussion. She didn't think that was the right way to handle an asset like Ahsani. *Maybe Ramshad or Simonyan, but not Ahsani.* She knew Ahsani's type well. She had dealt with many assets who would only respect authority if it came at him with aggression or caused fear. Kasem had too, and as the Ahriman, she was sure he had approached most of his contacts with all the control in his hands. So why was he playing it this way? Since she didn't have an answer, she remained silent and let the conversation continue a little further.

"Information on the target is not up for grabs. If you want to negotiate, let's talk about the price," Kasem said, this time with more of an edge to his tone.

"Look, I can throw you a party. I can throw you the biggest shindig on the planet. But I will not keep taking risks if you can't be bothered to read me in on such an important detail. The Company can kiss my ass if they think that's how I'll work. How do I know you won't bring the police down on top of me? At some point, you're going to have to trust me."

Petra readied herself to step in—she had the arguments for why not reading in Ahsani would actually protect him on the tip of her tongue—when Ramshad interrupted.

"I want to hit pause on this conversation. Everyone here wants the same thing. We believe you when you say it's a good target. If we didn't believe that, we wouldn't have worked with the Company for all these years. That said, Ahsani is right. Any time we host a special event, we risk bringing the authorities down on us. Security has to be set, bribes have to be paid. For your snatch and grab to work, all of that has to be doubled. So, please, just meet us halfway. We're not going to interfere, and we'll do everything we can to help. All we need is the name."

*Don't give it to him.*

Before Petra could intervene, Kasem replied, "General Majed."

# Chapter 35

*Tehran, Iran*

Simonyan grimaced as he handed over a file on Sami Majed, including everything he'd been able to dig up from his contacts in military intelligence. A big part of him still couldn't believe he was doing this, that he was diving back into the secret world once again. How could all the sweat and blood he had poured into his career have amounted to this?

*If I get caught, nothing else I've done will matter.* The sobering thought kept him from looking Kasem in the eye.

"Thank you," Kasem said. "This file could help us identify other hiding places in case he moves his uncle to a new location."

"I don't need gratitude. Just do what you promised and I'll hold up my end of the bargain. I'm working on getting the security details for that house like we talked about."

"Change of plans. We're going to have to lure the general out instead." He continued with an overview of the special event to be held at the club in less than a week.

"I see. What do you need from me?"

"Security coverage the night of the party. We'll need you to run interference so we can get him out."

"It's risky." Simonyan's earlier thought about what would happen if he got caught returned full force.

"We'll make sure it looks credible."

"Forgive me if I don't share your confidence."

"Isn't it worth the risk? To capture General Majed after everything he's done?"

"Fine. But I won't do anything that makes it obvious I'm working with you. My daughter's already lost too much."

"I wouldn't ask you to."

"Not intentionally, anyway." Simonyan shrugged. He was committed to the cause now, and he had to believe that Kasem wouldn't burn him at the first test. His old handler and Gaston wouldn't have provided his details to Kasem if that were true. Besides, he had chosen this op for a reason. *For my daughter.* Thinking of her in this context was even more painful. Kasem had been right—she deserved justice. And he wanted it too, for his brother-in-law and the rest of his wife's family. Yet he couldn't deny that a small part of him was glad Derderian had died that day. How could he not be? That event had brought him and his wife their daughter.

"I'll be in touch." Kasem held out his hand and Simonyan grasped it, finally meeting his gaze.

"I'll be there on Saturday," Simonyan added. Despite his misgivings, he was in this now, with both feet. "I appreciate your candor. I only met General Majed once, but I'll do what I can to help if it's needed."

"We'll be in touch."

A moment later, Kasem had disappeared from the other side of the alley. Simonyan pulled a pack of cigarettes out of his pocket and stared at it. He'd finally quit eight years earlier after repeated attempts and near-constant prodding from both his wife and his daughter, but he had picked up the pack right before he went to whiskey night to meet Kasem the week before. He pulled a cigarette out and raised it to his nose. As he sniffed it, he remembered all the times he had savored the poison, how it had leveled out even the most extreme of emotions.

"You never give yourself enough credit," he recalled his wife saying. "You think you need them, but you can go days without one. It's time to stop. If not for me, for our little girl. She can't lose anyone else."

*But we both lost you,* he wanted to reply. He stared at the cigarette for a few more seconds, then placed it back into the pack and pulled out his phone instead. As a precaution, he had turned it off when he'd set off to meet Kasem. He turned it on as he left the alley, heading in the opposite direction from

Kasem. Once it had booted up, he called his daughter over the Telegram app.

"Baba." Her face lit up his screen and she beamed at him.

"Jigar tala," he said. "It's good to see you."

"Is everything okay? You hardly ever call me that anymore."

"I was just thinking of you, that's all. I wasn't sure you'd have time for your dear old dad, but I tried anyway."

She gave him a skeptical look. "Are you sure?"

"Absolutely." Simonyan nodded, hoping to convince her, even though she was right. He wanted to kick himself for using that expression. He hadn't intended to alarm her, but he rarely used *jigar tala,* a play on her name and a Farsi expression for love that meant "golden liver." When they had first adopted Tala, she had doubted they really wanted her, that she hadn't upended their lives. It was such a tremendous burden for a child, and he and his wife had struggled with how to explain that even with the terrible circumstances that had brought her to their home, they were over the moon to have her as their daughter. The first time Simonyan had gotten through to her was when he'd used that expression, using the words "golden liver" to convey that she was essential to their lives. That she meant everything to them. He had hardly used it since, only in the most serious of conversations. "Where are you off to?" he asked to change the subject, taking in the shifting scenery behind her.

"I'm meeting some friends at The George, then we're going to get some lunch."

"The pub before lunch?"

"Baba, you don't have to worry. I can take care of myself."

"All right, I know." He gave her a wry smile. "Let's chat properly tomorrow? I want to hear all about your classes and that boy you were talking about."

Tala's cheeks flushed. "Dad, I just got here and there are people around," she hissed. "Okay, we'll talk tomorrow."

"Love you—"

She hung up before he had the words out, and he looked down the street with a sigh. It was late afternoon, and the pack of cigarettes was burning a hole in his pocket. He walked toward the Gholhak Metro Station a few blocks away, his resolve bolstered by seeing his daughter's face. He was grateful to have her, but now that he knew what had happened to her first father, he couldn't live with himself if he did nothing. Before he headed into the station, he stopped at a trash can and tossed the pack. No surprise, but his wife had been right. He didn't need them to discern true north.

# Chapter 36

*Tehran, Iran*

That evening, Kasem pretended to smoke a cigarette while he stood at the entrance to the alley that ran directly behind Ahsani's club in the Darband neighborhood. The sky had just turned to hues of pink and red as dusk set in, and he took a moment to look up while he waited for Gul to meet him. The gamble he and Petra had taken by blackmailing Gul and then releasing him had yet to pay off, but so far, it at least had not blown up in their faces. Since he hadn't turned on them yet, Kasem hoped he would deliver as promised.

Kasem watched the sunset for another couple of minutes as the sun ducked behind the nearby mountains, creating a halo effect. He held the unlit cigarette in one hand and brought it up to his lips. He'd decided not to light it—he wasn't a fan of the stuff—and he had a story about trying to quit ready in the unlikely event anyone besides Gul walked into the alley. The street in front of him was bustling. Happy hour—albeit with the alcohol kept hidden—had begun about an hour earlier, and with the warm weather, the patio tables on the street had filled up. Few people frequented the alley behind the club at this hour—it was too early for even the staff.

*Gul had better show up.* Kasem breathed deeply, glad he hadn't lit the cigarette. Petra had hated it when he'd smoked a cigar at a dinner party one night in Paris. He imagined the smell of cigarettes in his hair and clothing would be just as bad.

A few minutes later, he spotted Gul on the opposite side of the street. Without even glancing behind him, Gul made a beeline toward the alley, much to Kasem's chagrin.

"Were you followed?" Kasem handed Gul a fresh cigarette. He scanned the street behind, looking for anything that seemed out of place. When nothing caught his attention, he turned his focus to Gul, still maintaining diffuse awareness directed at the main street.

"I didn't see anyone," Gul said.

"Did you speak to General Majed?"

"Yes. I told him there's a special event at the club on Thursday. Invite only, and that I would pick him up that evening."

"And?"

"He's in."

"Did you have to press him?" Kasem frowned, hoping Gul hadn't inadvertently tipped him off.

"Not really. He's all for an excuse to get out of the house, especially one that involves strippers."

Kasem's heart did a momentary jig. He could hardly believe their plan might actually be working. Soon, he and Petra could leave this life in the rearview mirror.

*After I make him pay.*

The thought of revenge sobered his anticipation, a reminder of how much of a role he had played in his own dark transformation. Before he got too wrapped up in his thoughts, he turned his attention back to Gul.

"Has anyone asked where you were on Saturday?" Kasem asked regarding the night of the abduction.

"No, everyone at the club was too, er, occupied to notice anything amiss."

"Good." Kasem repeated Gul's role once he and the general arrived at the club, then nodded. "See you on Thursday."

"I'll be there. Afterward, you'll hand over the files?"

"When it's done. Just make sure you show."

"I know what someone holding a gun to my head feels like."

Kasem watched Gul walk away, and for a moment wondered if he should have some sympathy for the guy. He shrugged it off. Gul wasn't scum, but he was hardly a Good Samaritan; he had no scruples on whose money he laundered.

*All about the Benjamins.*

A few minutes later, Kasem exited the alley with a spring in his step. He was nervous about the upcoming op, but it was time. Time to confront General Majed for his crimes.

*Three hundred and sixty-seven of them.*

# Chapter 37

*Istanbul, Turkey*

"We have a serious problem." Rachel slid the file across the desk and took a seat.

James gave her a skeptical look. "Can't this wait till later? I'm in the middle of something."

"It can't." Conway, James's direct supervisor, appeared in the office doorway with a grave expression on his face. "You better listen to her, James. I'm just a fly on the wall for this conversation."

He opened the folio and flipped through the two pages inside. "What am I looking at?"

"It's a translation of a wanted bulletin that went out in Tehran," Rachel replied. "As you can see, they have a picture of one of our operatives."

"How did this happen? Did they have a run-in with the Revolutionary Guard?"

"No, nothing like that. The Guard hasn't located them, which means they don't have enough information on their cover legends to find them. At least not yet."

"What exactly are you saying?"

"Isn't it obvious? There's a leak. Right after I handed you those files, that photo showed up on every police bulletin within a hundred miles of the Alborz Mountains."

James stared at her with a blank expression, which turned into a frown over several seconds of silence. "That's not possible. You're deflecting, turning the attention away from your agents' screw ups."

"I wish that were true. If they had screwed up, we could probably get around it. Figure out how to fix it. Their only alternative now is to proceed with the op without my team's support."

"So, the leak could be from within your team?"

"It's possible, but unlikely. My team has had access to those photos for a while. That bulletin came out two days ago, less than a week after I gave you a copy of their files."

"I don't like what you're insinuating."

"There's no insinuation here. I'm making a statement of fact. On Tuesday, I handed over the information you asked for, and by the weekend, our operative's photo blasted out all over the country." Rachel let the silence linger before she added, "Did you show anyone the files?"

"I did, but—"

"How many people?" Conway interrupted.

"I gave them out to three of the department teams."

"Why would you do that?" Rachel exclaimed. "This was supposed to be off book. It's not a training exercise for you to hand out to every recruit in the building."

"That's enough, Rachel." Conway sat down next to her and looked at James. "She's right. We need a list of everyone you showed those files to, and everyone who had access to them this past week. Everything else is on hold until we find the source of this leak." He turned toward Rachel. "Your operatives—they're Agency, right? Seconded over to us?"

"Yes."

"Get over to their local station, just you and a skeleton team. Maybe even just a tech lead. I'll call Alex over there and tell him to expect you."

"All right."

"In the meantime, James and I will work on figuring out how this leak happened. A quiet investigation, so to speak. If we're lucky, we can flip it back in our favor. Feed the Guard some false info."

"Sure," Rachel agreed, keeping her skepticism to herself.

"It's a long shot, but worth a try," Conway said. "We'll also have to assess how many ops this leak could compromise, without showing our hand. Given what's happened, Rachel, do you think they can still make this work?"

"I don't know. They came up with a new plan, but it's a stretch. They're going to have to abduct General Majed from a crowded party venue."

"Should we abort?"

Rachel shrugged and answered with a question. "When are we going to get another shot at this? Majed's eluded us for years. We can't call it off, not when we're this close."

"That's fair. What about local support? Anyone they can rely on?"

"Our asset runs the club, and they're working with a British asset. But there's no other trained operatives. It's Tehran, not Paris. We can't exactly call in the cavalry."

Conway nodded. "I'll give my counterpart at Six a call. See if I can wrangle some backup. James, you better hope they can still pull this off. If they can't—well, it's safe to say that whatever happens to them, it's on you."

# Chapter 38

*Tehran, Iran*

Sami glanced at his watch for the third time, his frustration beginning to seep out of his pores. Gul was always late for their assigned monthly meeting, but even he'd never been over thirty minutes late. Sami briefly wondered if anything could have happened to him, but dismissed the possibility. If there was anything Gul had a knack for, it was self-preservation. A knack that Sami had used to his advantage multiple times over. Even before his uncle had gone into hiding, Gul had been funneling money away for them, providing a safe haven to keep it away from prying eyes and paying substantive returns in the process.

Sami waited another fifteen minutes, and when Gul still hadn't shown, he grimaced and headed home. On his way, he called a trainee he worked with at the Ministry of Intelligence.

"Fahad, I need to reassign you to something else."

"Of course, sir. What would you like me to do?"

"I'm sending you a profile on a businessman—Mahdi Gul. He has suspected ties to some black-market dealings, and we may want to bring him in for questioning. I need a report on what locations he frequents and anyone he meets with. Start with backtracking data from his phone."

"I'll get on it right away."

"Put a detail on him as well—ongoing surveillance."

He was about to leave, giving up on the meeting, when a taxi pulled up. Gul got out, looking flustered and disheveled.

"I'm very sorry," he said as he approached, slightly out of breath. "I was running late and there was a big accident."

Sami gave him a quick nod as Gul continued to provide excuses. "It's fine. Let's get on with the meeting."

Gul ran through his standard monthly updates on their returns, handed over a cash dividend, and left within fifteen minutes. Once he was gone, Sami reached for his phone to cancel the assignment he'd given to Fahad.

*Cancel report on Gul,* he typed into the phone.

Before hitting send, Sami hesitated; something about today's meeting didn't sit right. After vacillating for another moment, he deleted the message. Even if it turned out to be an unnecessary exercise, it couldn't hurt to see where Gul had been the last couple of days.

# Chapter 39

*Tehran, Iran*

Petra couldn't help but smile to herself as she passed the Tehran Bazaar and approached the Bab Homayoun bathhouse. Even with the unfortunate turn the op had taken, the bathhouse offered a modicum of comfort. *Self-care and spy craft, all in one.*

When Farah sat down across from her, they exchanged an informal greeting, with a kiss on each cheek. Petra gave her a brief update. They had discovered the security detail on the apartment where General Majed was hiding was too well equipped, so they would have to draw him out instead.

"I heard about the event. They said it was for a special guest, the owner's son or something. All the girls were called in. They want us to rehearse a new burlesque number this afternoon. They're even bringing in extra staff from his other restaurants."

"I'll be there too. It will be a lot more crowded, but the basic plan is the same as we did for Gul."

"I don't know if I can get him to the same booth. What if he recognizes me?"

"Gul will take care of that part. Just use the rest of the vial for General Majed's drink."

"I will."

"I'll see you then." Petra stood and was about to return to the locker room to get dressed when Farah grabbed her hand.

"You'll get him, right? We have to make sure of it."

Petra lowered herself back into her seat and grasped both of Farah's hands. "We will, I promise."

"It has to be fate, you know?"

"What do you mean?"

"General Majed disappeared years ago, but I'm the one who saw him at the club. I'm the one who recognized him. I have to do this for Afshar, for everything we could have had together."

"I know how important this is to you."

"You think you do, but you don't. Afshar and I were going to get out together. We couldn't get married here, but he had a plan to get to Turkey. All we wanted was a life together." Tears were streaming down Farah's face. "The general took that from us. He has to pay. You have to kill him, like what he did to Afshar. He can't get away with this."

"I won't let that happen."

"Promise me."

"I promise." Petra squeezed her hands again. "After it's done, we'll need to get you out of Iran. You're too close to all of it. It'll be too risky to stay."

"Did you know my brother was a dissident?"

"No."

"He took part in a bunch of student protests at Tehran University. He and his friends marched for women's rights, for civil rights, for the end of the ayatollah government. They were part of this commune of sorts. They had underground parties, organized rallies, stuff like that." She let out a long sigh. "I never had the courage to join him. I told him somebody had to earn some money to send back home. He resented me for it, and as he went further into the commune, he started taking drugs—ecstasy, ketamine, maybe crack. He lost his grip on reality. We drifted apart, and the next time I had news about him, my mother told me he was dead." She rubbed her eye. "That was a year after Afshar died. That's when I started to work for the British."

"I'm so sorry."

"Don't say you're sorry. Let's get these bastards."

"We'll get them, then we'll get you out."

"No, Asma, I'm not leaving. I need to be here to keep helping right the scale. If he were still alive, then I'd have something to run away to, but now there's nothing for me out there. My family's gone too, but I'm still here. I have to do what

I can to change things. For all the other girls like me, for everyone who has a chance at a real life."

Petra held her gaze in silence for a few seconds before she finally nodded. She had grappled with her feelings about the greater good and how intelligence organizations like the Agency and the CIA trampled on the values they claimed to uphold on a regular basis. None of that had changed, but in Farah's eyes, she saw the reason for those values written in block letters. She reiterated her promise and excused herself, but the encounter played over again as she left the bathhouse.

*We're doing the right thing.*

She had known it intellectually, but she could now feel the emotional truth behind that thought. Kasem was right. Whatever his reasons for going after General Majed, the mission was just. They could bring him to justice—for Farah, Afshar, and everyone who had died in the Suez attack and in the aftermath.

*And for Kasem.*

# Chapter 40

*Tehran, Iran*

Sami skimmed the report on Gul's GPS records from the previous two weeks. Nothing in particular stood out to him after the first review, so he decided to work backward. The most interesting detail was that the GPS was deactivated for a few hours both of the past Saturday nights. This fact didn't surprise Sami; he would expect Gul to turn off his phone whenever he was visiting an underground club or restaurant. Since he had first vetted Gul, he knew Gul visited such establishments on a regular basis. However, the length of time the phone was off for on the most recent Saturday evening gave him pause. *Seven hours instead of three the previous week.*

Sami reread the records from that day and considered the possibilities. It looked like Gul had gone to dinner at a restaurant in the Darband neighborhood, then the GPS had reactivated at his home. Perhaps he had gone to visit someone after the club? *But Gul doesn't have a mistress.* Sami recalled his earlier investigation of Gul. Although that investigation had been completed three years earlier, he knew from experience men who kept a mistress tended to always have at least one at any particular time. He sent a quick reply to the report requesting additional information on the restaurant and any traffic cam footage that was available.

While he waited for the reply, Sami turned his attention to the instant messaging app he used to communicate with his CIA source. It had been several days since the last update, and he was waiting for any information Behraz could provide on the cover legends the two operatives were using. Sami could still hardly believe the Ahriman had returned to Tehran. It was hard enough to process the fact the Ahriman could still be alive after everything he'd been through. But that he would dare to return was beyond comprehension.

*Frankenstein's monster has returned.* For the second time that day, Sami wondered if he should relocate his uncle to a new safe house. The unfortunate reality, however, was the general hated being moved and usually reacted poorly. On top of that, the best available option would be to move him to a house in the mountains. The remote location would provide additional cover, but his uncle had been adamant he wanted to remain in the city no matter what. *The increased security on the house will be enough,* Sami tried to convince himself. He also knew that he should visit himself, but their relationship had become increasingly strained as Sami had to take on more of a caretaker role. The three women who stayed in the house now took care of day-to-day needs, and Sami preferred not to disrupt the routine they had formed. That routine had taken months for everyone to get accustomed to, and he refused to let 'the boy' take that from them.

Sami thought of the boy. His name had been Kasem Ismaili, although Sami could scarcely remember ever using his name. He had always said *the boy* with every ounce of derision he could muster. Yet that boy had turned into a monster in his own right. Sami was under no illusions of what would happen if that monster was finally able to confront the general. There was only one reason the Ahriman would have returned to Iran after all this time. He was out for blood.

General Majed's blood.

His train of thought was interrupted by a message on his phone that contained details on the restaurant Gul had visited. The message also linked to a video snippet. Sami clicked on it and watched the eleven-minute clip to the end before replaying it.

At 10:37 p.m., Gul had emerged from the restaurant with two other men. Sami didn't recognize them, but they were well dressed and he assumed they were business contacts.

At 10:43 p.m., the oldest of the men got into a black car. The remaining two walked to the end of the block.

At 10:47 p.m., the two men disappeared into another restaurant on the far side of the street.

Sami frowned as he recognized the place. It was called Fire and Ice, one of the restaurants owned by prominent local businessman Hassan Ahsani. Sami had never directly encountered Ahsani, but he knew of his reputation. More importantly, he'd heard of the reputation associated with Ahsani's businesses—they were considered some of the most hopping bars and clubs in the city.

*Their cover is connected to the black market.*
*An underground club or bar.*
*One of Ahsani's clubs.*

# Chapter 41

*Tehran, Iran*

Kasem walked into the underground café where Ramshad had asked to conduct their last meeting on high alert. Instead of choosing one of Ahsani's bars, Ramshad had picked a new place, and something about their text exchange had felt different. Perhaps it was only because Ramshad had provided the information on Gul behind Ahsani's back, but Kasem was determined not to be complacent. They were too close to the end to let anything slide.

On top of that, Ahsani's loyalty was at best questionable. His first and foremost loyalty was to money, and as such to his business. *He would sell us out in a heartbeat if it made him enough money.* Rachel had staunchly disagreed when he'd mentioned that point on their most recent call that morning. Even Petra believed Ahsani was more nuanced than that, but Kasem was sure he was right. All he had were his instincts, and they had kept him alive thus far. He intended to trust them.

The front room of the café looked like any small fast-food place. It reminded him of the Burger King he had sometimes convinced his parents to visit as a kid. The only difference was this place sold kebabs, naan, and French fries instead of burgers, along with the fact it was almost always empty. Instead of going up to the counter, he walked over to an old jukebox on the left side of the room and picked out a Celine Dion song called "Think Twice." As soon as he selected it, he heard a click in the wall behind it. The jukebox was on gliders, so he was able to easily slide it to the right and open the low doorway concealed behind it. He stepped through to a small landing and walked about twenty feet to the end, where a well-dressed young woman stood at a podium.

"Did you make a reservation?" she asked in Farsi.

"Yes." Kasem gave her the name of the song he'd chosen. She checked a clipboard in front of her, then nodded. She pressed a button on the wall behind her and the door slid back in place, no doubt along with the jukebox.

"Please go ahead." She motioned toward the stairwell that continued downward.

Kasem gave her a cash tip and ventured down the stairs, emerging into a dimly lit room with a series of small booths along the left and right walls, with a small bar at the center. He walked over to the bar and ordered a Laphroaig 10. Something about the smoky taste just seemed right in the dark atmosphere of the underground bar. Glass in hand, he settled down at a booth in an alcove offset from the main line of tables.

Ramshad arrived a few minutes later. He grabbed a drink at the bar, then looked around and spotted Kasem.

"I was surprised you chose to meet here," Kasem said as Ramshad sat across from him.

"Just mixing it up."

"What are you drinking?"

"Woodford Reserve. There aren't many places that stock bourbon, so I enjoy it when I can."

"Maybe I'll follow you on the next one."

"Right."

Kasem frowned as he picked up on Ramshad's discomfort. "Are you okay?"

"No, I'm not." He drained the contents of his glass and returned to the bar for a refill without elaborating further. When he finally returned, he set the glass on the table with a resounding thud. "I met with one of our contacts at the police earlier today. We always let the people in our corner know ahead of time when there's going to be a special event. It's easier to make sure everything goes smoothly that way."

"And?"

"I saw a very specific bulletin at the station afterward. I couldn't believe what I was reading." Ramshad slid his phone across the table.

With a sinking feeling in his stomach, Kasem leaned forward to look at the picture. He scanned the bulletin with Petra's photograph and met Ramshad's gaze. "We probably should have told you about that beforehand."

"I believe so. This is going to make things complicated for the event tomorrow."

"I'm sorry. We didn't think Ahsani would go along if we told you the police had one of our pictures."

"You're damn right he wouldn't have. I should get him to call it off now."

"Please—we're so close. After tomorrow, you'll never have to deal with us again."

"You're lucky I didn't turn you in right there. Did you read the text under her photo?"

Kasem nodded. "Wanted for involvement in a terrorist plot? I did."

"Care to explain?"

"They're just blowing smoke. What do you expect?"

"I take it you didn't see the last part." Ramshad zoomed in with his forefinger and thumb and turned the phone toward Kasem.

"Known ties to the assassin the Ahriman," Kasem read aloud.

"So how about now? Anything to add?"

"Like I said, it's smoke. They're trying to flush us out."

"If enough people see that, they could succeed. Most people aren't interested in the Wanted posters at the police office. They don't care about turning in political dissidents the cops are after. But something like this? They might."

"Ask the question."

"What question?"

Kasem raised his eyebrows. "The one you're itching to ask me."

"When I gave you the spreadsheets, I was hoping what you were doing here would be good for this country. People here, we have this fire, this spirit, you can't put it out no matter how many times the government razes us to the ground. It always comes back. But now I see this? This description of her implies you're the Ahriman. It's not true, right? It can't be."

"Do you think the Company would have brought me on if it were?"

"I don't know. If they had the right strings to pull, maybe?"

"We're not the ones who caused the attack at Suez." As Kasem said the words, he wished he believed them. He wasn't the root cause, but the attack wouldn't have happened if he hadn't been duped into setting the bombs. *I thought they were bugs.* The reminder did little to assuage his guilt, but taking out General Majed at the party, that was the answer. "General Majed was the mastermind. He covered it all up, but the Company discovered his involvement back in 2021. That's when he went into hiding."

"2021? Before the big drone strike? The one that took out the hospital?"

"Yes."

"Is that why the Americans launched the strike?"

"It is."

"I remember the footage of Suez on the news. The fires, the smoke." Ramshad looked away for several moments before meeting Kasem's gaze. "Fine. I won't stop you. Ahsani doesn't have to know, and we'll let things go forward tomorrow. But that's it. No more help, no more involvement. As far as we're concerned, you're just regular customers."

"Thank you."

"If anything goes wrong, we'll wash our hands of all of it." Ramshad polished off his drink and stood to leave, then paused. "Almost a hundred people died in the drone strike."

"I know."

"Thank you for reading us in on the target. And good luck. People like Majed—they ruined this country. They stood by and let the mullahs destroy every scrap of dignity people had left. I hope you get him," Ramshad said before he disappeared.

Once he was gone, Kasem leaned back into the plush maroon leather seat and finished his drink, lost in thought. In his time away from Iran, he had almost forgotten the fire Ramshad had referred to. The Persian pride that was engrained in so many people he had encountered when he'd lived here. He'd discounted how present it was, but he could see it in Simonyan and Ramshad. Petra had seen it in Farah. The fire was ever present, and it wasn't something to ignore.

Memories came rushing back, recollections that predated the Ahriman. His visit to Persepolis shortly after he had first moved to Tehran. The turquoise dome of the Shah Mosque in Isfahan. The rock formations in the Shahdad desert. Late nights dancing at underground parties, and the joy with which people sung and danced. The stories his parents and grandparents had recounted—stories of passion, art, and laughter.

As much as the op was for him, it was also for them. For all of them.

# Chapter 42

*Tehran, Iran*

Kasem watched the GPS from Gul's phone on his computer screen as his stomach did a series of flips. After all the preparation and anticipation, tonight was the night—they would finally have General Majed in their grasp.

Five minutes later, the dot came to a stop outside of General Majed's compound. Kasem dialed Gul's phone for a short check-in.

"I'm about to pick him up," Gul said as soon as he picked up.

"Good. Did anything feel off when you spoke earlier?"

"No more so than the fact I know you're listening."

"You'll do fine. After tonight, I'll just be a bad dream and you can get on with your life."

Gul grunted and hung up without bothering to reply.

"Sounds like he's in love with you." Petra chuckled from the front seat of the maintenance van they had parked behind the club.

"Don't worry, there's only one person for me."

She joined him in the back of the van and changed out of her jeans and T-shirt into a low-cut wraparound dress that hugged every curve of her figure.

"Seriously?" Kasem shook his head. "Why are you doing this to me? You had to change into that right here?"

"I had to make sure you can stay focused even with distraction." She tied the waist sash of the dress into a knot that allowed the ends to extend over her left hip. "How do I look?"

"It shouldn't be legal to look that good."

"I'm not sure it is here," she said as she used a handheld mirror to apply a thick line of black eyeliner. She followed the liner with several strokes of amethyst and silver eye shadow to create a smokey look around her eyes. The color of the makeup matched the sparkly tones of her dress.

Before he could reply, he heard Gul's voice over the speaker, his phone acting as a transmitter.

"*Salam, how are you?*"

"*Khoobam, very well, very well.*"

"*Are you ready to go? We're going to have a great time this evening.*"

"*Almost. Let's sneak out the back.*"

After a bit of small talk, during which Gul helped the older man locate a nice blazer, Kasem heard the two of them walk back out to the car. From what he could hear, it sounded like the general was moving a lot slower than he remembered, but it had been several years since their last encounter. He had last spoken with General Majed in person shortly before his assignment in Kuwait in 2021. The assignment had been to assassinate the Kuwaiti monarch, the Emir, but the op had derailed when he ran into Petra while he was setting a bomb at the Emir's dewaniya. Kasem shuddered at the memory from a time when he couldn't have been more entrenched in his identity as the Ahriman.

Petra squeezed his shoulder, almost as if she could read his mind. They listened to the car start and noted the movement of the red GPS locator onscreen. General Majed was on his way.

# Chapter 43

*Tehran, Iran*

Sami made his way from Roast Restaurant to the Fire and Ice club just after 10:30 p.m. He still wasn't sure precisely what he was looking for, but his gut had always served him well in the past, so he followed his instincts. He glanced around as he walked into the bar, searching for anything that smelled funny to warrant further investigation. The place was just starting to fill up; a healthy crowd, but it was still easy to move around. An emcee made an announcement the masquerade part of the evening was about to begin. Sami ignored it. He didn't have much patience for fancy dress-up.

Nothing jumped out at him. The bar seemed like any underground establishment. On speed for this party, but no different than any other he'd been to. Perhaps Gul had visited the place and left with one of the girls? That would explain his strange behavior on the day of their meeting. Still, the theory didn't sit right. Gul didn't strike him as the type to take a mistress, let alone a one-night hooker. Sami's read was that he was more of a look but don't touch kind of guy.

Sami went over to the bar and ordered a Jack and Coke and was served a Jack mixed with the Coke knockoff more easily available in Iran. He wasn't much of a drinker, but he had to look the part. He took a couple of small sips as he continued to survey the room. When he reached the end of the glass, he decided to order another and walk around, and that he'd leave when he finished the second drink.

He waved to one of the girls walking around with drink trays, clad in a skimpy nurse's outfit.

"Another Jack and Coke?" she asked.

He nodded and she switched his empty glass for a full one from her tray. Handing her a twenty-dollar bill—he had made sure to grab US dollars from his safe—he asked, "Were you working here last night?"

"I was," she said, looking at him a hint of apprehension in her eyes.

"A friend of mine was here, and he was telling me that I should come with him. I just wanted to ask you a few questions." He gave her another twenty-dollar bill, hoping the large tip in dollars rather than rials would help get her talking. "Why don't you have a seat?" He motioned to the seat across from him, glad he'd chosen a two-person high-top.

She looked at the bill, pocketed it and nodded, then took the seat. Sami pulled a picture of Gul up on his phone and showed it to her. "Do you remember him? He was here a couple of nights ago."

"Yes, I've seen him a few times."

"Do you remember who he talked to?"

"Not really. He watches the dancing and usually goes off to one of the booths for a private song. I'm only a server, I don't know anything else."

"What about last time? Did you notice anything different? Anything at all?"

She shrugged. "Not really. We've been really busy, so it was kind of a whirlwind."

"Have you had any new dancers in? Or new employees?"

"Not that I've met. They keep talking about hiring more people. We could definitely use the extra staff, but nothing ever comes of it."

"Do you remember which booth he went to?"

"I'm not sure." She pointed toward the opposite side of the dance floor. "I think it was one of the three on that side, but I could be wrong."

Sami frowned, debating what else he could ask. Before he could come up with anything, the waitress stood and glanced back at the bar. "I'm sorry. I really appreciate the tip, but I can't afford to lose this job. I have to keep serving drinks." She turned and walked off, heading toward the next high-top. Sami sighed and finished his drink before heading down the hallway to use the men's room on his way out.

Just as he was opening the door, a woman emerged from the ladies. A woman who looked uncannily familiar. He stepped into the men's room, processing what he'd seen. Was it possible he had made a mistake? There was something about her, something that made his Spidey sense tingle. He couldn't quite place her, but he knew that he recognized her.

The question was from where?

Who was she?

By the time he exited the restroom, he was sure it couldn't be a coincidence. This was what he'd been looking for. Something that didn't sit quite right. Gul's behavior, the connection to an underground club, and now her. All of it was connected, even if he had yet to figure out how.

Now he had to do figure out what to do about it. Should he let on that he'd recognized her? He could pick her up and question her, but he didn't want to tip his hand too early. She obviously wasn't the woman he knew as Lila, Kasem's girlfriend prior to his capture in 2019. So how was she linked to them?

Sami returned to his high-top and lit a cigarette. The evening show was about to commence—a special performance in honor of the club owner's son, who had just returned from Los Angeles.

The first number included ten different dancers, and Sami recognized the woman from the hallway within the group. He ignored her sensuality but watched her move, scanning his memory bank as if it were a file cabinet. Where had he seen her before?

She removed her jacket and strutted toward the opposite end of the stage. She was slim and tall, her figure accentuated by four-inch stilettos. She did a brief pirouette around the pole before swapping positions with another one of the girls. When the number concluded, she dove downward and did a hair flip, sliding to her knees.

The hair flip jogged his memory. When he had last seen her, her hair had been longer, draped over her left shoulder the way it had ended up as part of the grand finale.

His eyes widened as the realization hit him.

*The military brothel.*

# Chapter 44

*Tehran, Iran*

Petra let her headscarf fall to her shoulder once they passed from the restaurant upstairs into the downstairs club. Next to the bouncer was a table covered with an array of masks. She picked out an ornate silver and black one that covered the top half of her face and tied the attached ribbon so it was secure under her bun. Meanwhile, Kasem was vacillating on his choice of mask.

"I'll be right back," she whispered to him. She stepped into the corridor to the right of the entrance lobby and removed the knee-length cardigan she had draped over her dress. The other nights she and Kasem had visited the club, the corridor had been busy with other women using the area to hang up their coats and transition from their street-appropriate outfits to more sensual club ware. Tonight, the area was packed with three times the number of women. She had to push past a large group just to hang up her sweater and headscarf. She scanned the them quickly, but it was too dark to get a good glimpse of the various faces. A group of three were clustered around a mirror in the far corner lit by a bright LED, a set of sequined masks laid out on the table next to them. Outside the spotlight, the light was dim. Petra maneuvered her way back toward the main lobby where Kasem was waiting. Even outside the main part of the club, her head started to pound from the vibration of the techno music.

They ventured into the main bar and found the table Ramshad had reserved for them. It was on a balcony elevated slightly above the dance floor and main bar to their right, with the now-expanded stage at eye level in front of them. Petra was surprised and impressed by how much publicity Ahsani had managed to garner for the event. She had certainly never seen the club this packed, even on a busy Saturday night.

She scanned the room to get her bearings, pushing past the throbbing in her head from the music. A large group had already formed on the dance floor, and the first dance number was wrapping up on stage. Petra couldn't help but grin at the seductive hair flip Farah did as part of the finale. Whatever her reasons for taking the job, she certainly seemed at home with it. All of the women did, for that matter. They looked empowered, in touch with their sensuality in a way that was forbidden in public.

The emcee made an announcement to encourage people out onto the dance floor and handed off to the DJ, who set off a new stream of techno beats. Petra blinked several times as he turned on a traveling set of strobe lights.

"They really meant it when they said a special event," she shouted into Kasem's ear.

He nodded and said something in reply, but she couldn't hear a word. Petra leaned out over the railing and squinted to get a better gauge on the distance between them and the private booth they had reserved for General Majed. She frowned, half wishing they weren't on the balcony. To get to the booth, they would have to get through the crowd on the stairwell, across the dance floor, and past the bar. That said, their position gave them a perfect view of the whole club—far better than any they'd had when they had visited previously.

She sidled closer to Kasem and peered over his shoulder at his phone. The tracking application was open and she could see the dot indicating Gul's position creeping slowly across the city toward them.

"Looks like they ran into a lot of traffic," Kasem said, this time leaning in closer to yell over the music.

"They'll be here soon." She watched the screen for a few more seconds as the dot inched closer, then glanced over the railing once more. Her heart was racing, mixing with the vibration of the base. Soon it would all be over. One way or another.

# Chapter 45

*Tehran, Iran*

Farah finished her first number at the party and fled from the stage. She was grateful the moves were drilled into her muscle memory. Her mind was a haze and there was no way she would have been able to recall the steps if they hadn't come naturally. As soon as she was back in the dressing room, the fear returned, as if the walls were closing in on her.

*It couldn't have been him.*

No matter how many times she said it to herself, she couldn't reestablish a sense of safety. There was so much riding on what happened tonight, and with all the stress, her head had been ablaze since she had left her meet with Asma at the bathhouse earlier that week. Her mind must be playing tricks on her. She couldn't possibly have run into Sami Majed outside of the club restrooms. He'd barely looked at her, and she only caught a quick glimpse of his face, but it was enough to make her blood run cold.

*Sami Khaled Majed, the general's nephew.* She had only seen him a few times, back when she was working in the military harem. Farah crouched in the far corner of the storage area attached to the dressing room and pulled her knees into her chest, where it took several moments to stop hyperventilating.

When rational thought started to return, she began to process the possibilities. She wasn't sure she actually recalled what he looked like, just the feeling. Sami Majed had never visited her in the harem, but she remembered Afshar pointing him out once. Afshar had said he was worse than scum, as bad as General Majed—that was why his name had stuck with her so long. She had noticed him a few times after that. Sometimes he would stare at the women in the harem, but she had never seen him disappear with any of them. She'd stayed in the back, kept her distance as much as possible. Something about him had always seemed off. She was used to men objectifying her, first at the harem and now at the club, but his gaze seemed more like he was assessing them. Conducting an evaluation rather than checking them out. An appraisal of their potential value as a tool for anything but his sexual pleasure.

She let out a long exhale. Even if it had been him, what did it matter? There was no way he would recognize her in a split second after all these years. No conceivable way he could know she was involved with trying to lure his uncle out into the open. *He couldn't possibly know.* A feeling of relief washed over her.

Her primary imperative was to deal with General Majed when he arrived. The rest of the night wasn't important, so long as she completed her task. After another few seconds of hiding, she got to her feet and returned to her station to reapply her makeup. But she remained frazzled, her mind raging in the background. Should she alert Asma to what she had seen? Or had it been a trick of the light and her anxiety? She refused to do anything that could compromise the op.

Once she had finished touching up her face, she switched into her next outfit and glanced at her watch. She had about five minutes before her second number, and another forty minutes or so before she would be able to venture into the booth to spike his drink.

*I'll let her know afterward,* she decided. For now, she had to focus on the task at hand. She secured the vial into the lining of her bra and headed back toward the stage.

# Chapter 46

*Tehran, Iran*

Sami felt the vibration of his phone in his pocket and picked up.

"Ziad?" he said as he pressed the phone against his ear and covered his mouth to shield out some of the club's ambient noise.

He heard some kind of response from the other end but couldn't decipher it over the music. "I'll call you back," he shouted into the mouthpiece and hung up. He glanced around the club, searching for an alcove where he might be able to make the call, then remembered the makeshift coat check area just past the lobby. He pushed his way through the crowd as a second dance number began, but by the time he made it across the room the song was fading out. At the edge of the dance floor, a young woman in an ornate purple mask bumped into him as she was pushing into the crowd.

"Bebakshid," he said as he sidestepped her, but she got swept into the crowd and didn't reply.

Once he got to the lobby, he stepped into the coat check area and noticed a number of young women applying makeup and changing outfits for the party. A couple of them spotted him, but none seemed bothered. He stopped and watched for a moment, impressed at how one of them managed to turn a long pencil skirt into a mini dress, while another transformed a wraparound skirt into a halter dress. Both were able to execute the outfit change without undressing completely. He averted his gaze a moment later and turned toward the wall to return Ziad's call.

"Ziad? Is uncle okay?"

"That's what I was calling about, sir. He went to take a bath, but now he's disappeared. I've searched the whole grounds. He's gone."

"You lost him? Don't you remember what happened last time?"

"I know, sir. I'm very sorry. A couple of the other guards are out looking for him."

"I'll track his phone."

Sami hung up before the head of the security detail he had appointed for his uncle could reply. He stifled the urge to hurl his phone at the wall and accessed the tracking app he had installed on the general's phone after the first time he had flown the coup.

The app took a full minute to load—it always did when he needed it most urgently—but when the locator finally appeared, he almost dropped the device. Sami turned the screen horizontal to be sure he was viewing the map correctly.

*He's here?*

Sami's jaw dropped. The girl from the brothel. The connection to an underground bar. Gul's odd behavior. It was all connected, it had to be. Which meant *they* were here too. He hit a speed dial on his phone.

"I need emergency backup at Fire and Ice restaurant. The club downstairs. The foreign operatives from my bulletin are here."

# Chapter 47

*Tehran, Iran*

Kasem had just reached the coat check area—his plan being to watch Gul and General Majed from the sidelines—when he froze.

*"I need emergency backup at Fire and Ice restaurant. The club downstairs. The foreign operatives from my bulletin are here."*

Even with the interference of the music from the club, he would recognize that voice anywhere. He turned an about-face, never more grateful for the mask he had tied over his face. He headed toward the stairs leading into the lobby, mentally running through the schematic he and Petra had drawn of the club in preparation for tonight. If he remembered it right, it was halfway up the stairwell.

"We need to abort. Emergency abort," he said as he tapped on his earpiece to signal Petra. "Get out and get to the van. Now."

Kasem found the alarm station and yanked down on the lever to set off the fire alarm. A high-pitched screech filled his eardrums and overrode any echo from the club below. Sprinklers in the ceiling engaged and he wiped the water film from his forehead and made for the exits.

"Do you read me?" he asked into his comm, his head reverberating from the continued screech of the alarms.

"I read you. What happened?"

"The Watchman is here."

Kasem made it outside before a sea of people began to flood out of the club. He heard Petra utter a series of expletives over the comm.

"I have to find Farah," she said.

"Forget it. He won't be able to do anything with everyone flooding out. She'll be fine. Just get to the van."

"I have to try."

# Chapter 48

*Tehran, Iran*

When she heard the alarm go off, Farah's initial reaction was to duck under her dressing table. One of the other dancers pulled her to her feet, and they headed for the staff exit in the back hallway. The techno beats had vanished, replaced by the blaring alarm. On her way out the door, Farah managed to grab her purse off the table, along with her thigh-length cover-up and headscarf. She cursed under her breath for not sounding the alarm herself. The whole op was now impossible to salvage, and she had to wonder if she could have stopped it earlier.

*It was him.* She knew it now, deep in her bones. Whether or not he had recognized her remained to be seen, but more importantly, their best shot at General Majed had disappeared. Once they got outside to the alley, she shivered. Her skimpy clothing was soaked from the sprinklers. She felt around in her purse and grasped her phone. She typed out an emergency message and hit send.

The high-pitched screech disappeared, and her mind went blank for a second before she realized the alarm had been shut off. In the distance, she could hear sirens approaching.

She took a moment to take stock of her surroundings. Most of the party guests had exited through the main restaurant entrance, but the rest of the staff had clustered in the alley with her. Two of the servers ventured back in. She heard them saying something about grabbing their stuff before the police arrived. She considered following them, but she already had her purse and phone, so instead she headed down the alley. She cut across the next two blocks to her car and breathed a sigh of relief once she was inside. The metal structure around her made her feel secure, less vulnerable and out in the open.

She started the car and drove in the direction of her apartment. At a traffic light, she checked her phone.

*Did you pick up the groceries?* The message had arrived from Asma a minute earlier. It was code for "Are you safe?"

*Yes. On my way home.*

Over the remaining distance, Farah's head raged about what to do next. If Sami Majed had recognized her and connected her to the op, her only option was to go to ground. But if he hadn't, she would attract more attention to herself with unusual behavior.

*Let's meet at the gym tomorrow.* Farah exhaled slowly as she read the message. The reply brought her a modicum of comfort, even just to have the decision out of her hands. The message was code for lying low, a contingency they had discussed briefly during their first meeting at the bathhouse. Farah would go home, collect a few necessities, then go to a friend's place for the night, where she would stay until she received instructions the next day.

*Should I even go home?* The question surfaced in the back of her mind, but she pushed it aside.

She reached her apartment and unlocked the door, but before she could step inside, a gloved hand appeared out of nowhere, covering her mouth with a rag. Her reflexes kicked in and she wrenched her elbow backward and struggled to free herself, but her efforts were to no avail. A hard object jabbed her in the spine and a voice whispered, "Make a sound and I'll shoot you right here."

Farah's vision started to blur, and she tasted something sweet from the rag over her mouth. She sagged forward and caught sight of her attacker. She'd been so naïve to hope he hadn't recognized her. Her biggest regret as the world turned dark was that her wishful thinking had compromised the entire operation.

*I'm sorry Afshar,* she thought as the world fell away.

# Chapter 49

*Tehran, Iran*

Petra paced the length of their living room as she waited for Farah's reply. The protocol they had set up meant Farah had to confirm their meet at the gym and tell Petra she was going to get a few hours of rest before their kickboxing class the next day.

She reread the message thread three times.

*Let's meet at the gym tomorrow.* The message had been read seven minutes earlier, but no reply had arrived.

"She's fine. Just give her a few more minutes," Kasem said. His words were logical, but they didn't assuage Petra's fears. Something had gone terribly wrong tonight, and Farah would end up paying the price. That was how it always was with operations. *Collateral damage.* She had seen it more times than she could count. The need to place the greater good over any one individual—she had always struggled with that aspect of the secret world.

"I should have waited for her. I could have picked her up."

"How do you know that would have been better? Any of us could be compromised."

"But her message—the first SOS. She said she ran into Sami Majed, that he might have recognized her."

"We don't know—"

"She wasn't wearing a mask, Kasem. He's a trained intelligence operative. Of course he recognized her."

"He was never really active in the brothel, and he probably saw her for a split second at the party. We can't jump the gun here. He might not have any idea who she is."

"You could be right, but I have this feeling—"

Before she finished her thought, the phone beeped with a fresh notification.

She grabbed it off the coffee table and stared at the screen. With her free hand, she found the armrest of the couch and lowered herself onto it slowly.

"What is it?"

She gave Kasem the phone and they both reread the message. It had been sent from Farah's phone, but had clearly been written by someone else.

*I have your asset. If you want her back, meet me at your meeting place two days from now. I'll take you to where we're holding her.*

A minute later, a second message appeared. *My uncle will be there too.*

# Chapter 50

***Tehran, Iran***

"Let me get this straight. You're going to walk into the bazaar and hand yourself over to the Revolutionary Guard? Please tell me I'm about to wake up from a nightmare." Tim shook his head and continued. "I haven't had to send anyone home in a body bag since I left the force ten years ago. Please don't make me start now."

"I understand how you feel," Petra said in a quiet voice as she looked at him over the video feed. They had set up a joint video call with Rachel and Nathan, both seated at a desk in her apartment in Istanbul, and Tim and Carlos, who had set up shop at Carlos's house in New Jersey. "It's our only chance. We can't just leave Farah to die. She deserves better, and I'm not going to let that happen."

"Where do you think they're holding her?"

"According to Gul, Sami Majed has three major real estate holdings with him. The first is the apartment Farah traced the general to, the other two are houses. One is in the mountains about an hour from here, the other is in Isfahan. So, our best guess is that he's holding Farah in the mountains."

"That's probably where General Majed is too," Kasem added. "We need to move on it ASAP to get to them both."

"In that case, why not do that immediately?" Carlos asked. "Take this meet with Sami entirely out of the equation."

"There's two problems with that. Number one, we don't know for sure that's where they are, and number two, we need more time, more intel, more personnel. We can't solve the latter, but the meet with Sami at least addresses the former," Petra answered. "The one saving grace is he doesn't know Kasem's here. Just me. On top of that, he doesn't know Gul told us about the properties. We have to play that to our advantage."

Tim frowned. "What if he picks up Gul?"

"I had someone from the local station move him to a safe house. He's fine. Grumpy, but fine," Rachel replied.

"That won't help us if there's a mole, but it's the best we've got," Petra said with a shrug. "Our best option is to limit the circle—ideally just the people on this call—and move as quickly as possible."

"So your plan is to hand yourself over but have Kasem follow you and break you out?" Carlos gave them an incredulous look.

"Exactly."

"I understand the strategy, but how is Kasem going to do that on his own?" Tim asked.

"That's what we have to figure out." Petra took a deep breath and exchanged a glance with Kasem before turning back to the computer. "We need satellite coverage of the house, and we're going to try and get some backup from Ahsani," she lied. After Kasem's most recent exchange with Ramshad, they were lucky Ahsani hadn't turned them in to the cops. Kasem was hoping they could still enlist Simonyan's help, but it was a long shot. "If you have other ideas, we're open to any and all suggestions."

"Fine," Tim said with a frown. We'll come up with an infiltration plan. But I want you to get the girl and get out. All three of you. Forget General Majed."

"Is that an option?" Petra's gaze landed on the image of the Istanbul apartment. "Rachel?"

"I'm afraid not. I'm sorry. I wish I had better news. The only way we honor our original deal is if you get the general too."

"I thought as much."

"We'll get the satellite feeds," Tim interjected. He shot a look at the camera, as if to dare Rachel to disagree. "Get Ahsani on board and we'll do the rest."

# Chapter 51

*Tehran, Iran*

After dark, Kasem took three taxis as part of a surveillance detection route before he finally walked the three remaining blocks to Simonyan's house. He walked up to the boundary wall around the corner from the main gate and watched the street for a few minutes. When he was satisfied he hadn't been followed, he sent a text message from his burner phone.

*Your delivery has arrived.*

Kasem adjusted his baseball cap to stop his face from being captured by the gate cameras before he approached. It creaked as it swung open a moment later, and he walked into the front yard carrying a paper bag filled with food he'd picked up after his first taxi ride.

Simonyan beckoned to him from the front door. Once they were both inside, Kasem held his finger to his lips while he performed a quick scan for bugs.

"We're clear," he said as he put the device away.

"What are you doing here? I thought it would be risky for you to come back here after what happened."

"It is, but we don't have much choice. I had to talk to you face-to-face. I made sure I wasn't followed."

"Go on."

"General Majed's been moved. Our best guess is that he's at a house in the Alborz."

"Damn."

"There's more. His nephew grabbed one of our assets and is holding her there."

"What?" Simonyan shook his head. "Start from the beginning. As soon as I got there, I heard the fire alarms. What happened?"

"We don't know much more." Kasem explained what he and Petra had seen inside the club, and how they had received a message from Farah's phone once they were home. "Gul managed to grab a cab, and we had someone move him to a safe house. But we can't leave our asset in the cold. Asma—my wife—will meet with Sami Majed. I'll follow her to wherever he takes her."

"What do you need from me?"

"Once I have a confirmed location, I'll need help infiltrating."

"You can't be serious. If they catch me—"

"I know what I'm asking, and I'm sorry. If there was any way to do this on my own I would."

"You can't ask me to do this."

"Please. She'll be going in alone."

Simonyan grimaced. "Do you have the blueprints? Let's come up with a plan."

"Before we get to that, there's something I need you to promise me. If everything goes pear shaped, I need you to get my wife out."

"Are you saying—"

"Regardless of what that means for me."

# Chapter 52

*Alborz Mountains, Iran*

Farah opened her eyes and the room turned sideways. It took several seconds before she could identify a coffee table and armchair in front of her, and a few more tries before she could make out the rest of the room. *What happened?* she asked herself as she looked around. She crawled off of the couch, her muscles feeling as if she had been through a meat grinder. She stumbled forward after attempting to stand and made it upright on her second attempt.

Her throat constricted and she gagged, then rushed to a trash bin in the corner of the room. After her stomach had heaved its entire contents plus some, she caught her breath and collapsed onto the floor. Her memory of the night before remained absent. She had been at the club. There was a fire alarm. But what else had happened? Had someone drugged her? Why couldn't she remember?

She fumbled her way to the door and tried to open it, but the handle wouldn't budge. She banged on the door and shouted for help. "Is anyone there? Please! Someone."

She crawled back to the couch and curled into the fetal position. Her head spun, and she had flashes from the night before. The opening number at the club. She'd been waiting for General Majed. She'd gone to the restroom before her first performance.

*Sami Majed.* It all came rushing back.

Before she could process any further, the door flew open.

"You?" Her voice quaked. "What do you want from me?"

"Nothing, really." He set a tray with a bottle of water and a plate with what looked like a falafel sandwich on the coffee table. "Eat. You'll feel better."

Farah hesitated, then gulped down some of the water. She took a bite of the sandwich and repeated her question.

"I need to draw out the woman you're working with. After that, we'll see."

She munched on the sandwich, waiting for him to say more. Why wasn't he asking her any questions? Did he already know who she worked for?

He sat there in silence until she finished the sandwich, then picked up the empty plate. Without another word, he disappeared through the door. Farah heard the deadbolt click back into place. She stared at the empty room and a tear ran down her cheek. Would Asma come for her? Even if she did, they would never get out of Iran. She curled back into a ball with her head in her hands. She would gladly have given her life if it meant they had been able to capture General Majed. But she had failed, and her life as she'd known it was over.

# Chapter 53

*Tehran, Iran*

Kasem wandered through a few stalls in the Tehran Bazaar next to the entrance to the Bab Homayoun bathhouse while he waited for Petra to emerge. He pretended to be looking for a new prayer rug, checking out the stock at each of the stalls within the vicinity. Looking at the rugs helped keep him calm in addition to serving as an excuse to move around the market. Petra had gone into the bathhouse ten minutes earlier, a few minutes ahead of her scheduled meet time, after they had both scoped the area from a distance. He had contemplated going with her, but there was no possible cover in the bathhouse lobby where she would be waiting for Sami Majed. So far, they had made the best of a tough situation, but he still felt off-kilter. Their only advantage was Sami didn't know about his presence in Tehran. Everything else was in his favor.

She had her comm on, although she would certainly have to discard it once Sami showed up. At the moment, all Kasem could hear was spa music playing in the background.

"He's ten minutes late."

"I'll give him another five minutes," Petra's voice came across his earpiece.

"Sounds good."

He walked to the next stall and continued to examine the different prayer rugs and trinkets available, keeping his peripheral vision focused on the bathhouse entrance. He turned into the aisle running between the stalls and moved a little closer to one of the bazaar entrances, joining the flow of people. Given the time of day, the market wasn't as crowded as it would be a few hours later, but there were still more than enough people for him to easily disappear into the group. He paused on the opposite side of the aisle when he heard someone start chanting nearby.

"Freedom for Iranians," the voice shouted in Farsi. The chanting grew louder as others joined in. "Down with Safavi!"

Kasem moved out of the aisle as the shouting grew louder. "Political protest starting, let's get clear," he said into his comm.

"On my way."

Before Kasem could reply, he noticed something in his peripheral vision that made his blood congeal. He stepped inside the stall, ducked behind a display shelf and peered out the window to get a better look. A few seconds later, he was able to see through the crowd to another stall diagonally opposite his. "He's here. Right by the entrance. You can't miss him." Despite his preparation for the moment, Kasem shuddered. He got a glimpse of Petra at the entrance, but his view was soon blocked by a group of students joining in the protest.

"… can't hear… …" He was only able to catch a few words of her response.

"He's here," he tried to shout over the protesters.

Before he could do anything to intervene, Majed approached her from behind and the two of them vanished into the crowd. Kasem ran out of the stall, trying to keep up. He managed to keep them in sight for a minute, but two aisles over, he got stuck behind a group of protesters. By the time he got past them, Petra was gone.

# Chapter 54

### *Alborz Mountains, Iran*

Petra's head throbbed as she kept her gaze fixed on the wallpaper behind Sami Majed's head. Her heartbeat was drumming in her ears as she strained to pick up any signs of where she was. She took a few deep breaths, hoping to slow her heart rate. It only made a slight difference. A moment later, she heard the crash of thunder outside. Wherever she was, a storm was about to hit.

"Who do you work for?" he asked for at least the third time. "What are you doing here?"

"You said you already knew who I worked for," she deflected. So far, other than the blow to the head he'd given her to knock her out on the way here, Sami had been remarkably cordial. She couldn't figure out why. Everything she had read about him or heard from Kasem had made him sound like a cutthroat killer. Perhaps it was because she was a woman? Or was he trying to elicit some kind of further cooperation from her? She continued to dwell on those questions as she watched him pull up a chair and sit down across from her.

"Did you really think you could come back to Iran and no one would recognize you?"

Instead of answering, Petra merely shrugged. Until that moment, she hadn't been sure if he'd recognized her. Majed had been intimately involved in Kasem's training and transformation into the Ahriman, all of which had occurred based on a lie—that General Majed was holding her hostage in order to blackmail Kasem into cooperating. She still wasn't sure how involved Sami had been in the actual blackmailing, only that he had been central to Kasem's training. *He and Lieutenant Afshar.* She swallowed the twinge of guilt at not telling Kasem the truth about Farah's involvement with the lieutenant. Kasem had never actually told her, but Petra suspected he had been involved in Afshar's death.

"You said you were holding my asset."

"Lila Tabbas…" He shook his head and ignored her prompt. "I certainly never thought I would see you again. We never officially met since you got out of Tehran so… efficiently. Or should I say, so expediently. You've put me in a difficult position."

"I have?"

"Let me ask my earlier question a different way," he said. "Why are you here? And don't feed me some cockass story about a CIA operation to find General Majed. That may be part of why you're here, but that's not the whole story."

"It's not?" Petra kept her answers vague, intrigued at where he was going. Sami obviously thought she had other motives for returning to Iran. Whatever those potential motives were, she planned to use them to her advantage. Feeding a target information they already believed could give her the upper hand, a lesson that had been drilled into her back in Agency training. "Why do you say that?"

"You were never an operative to begin with. Just an attaché at the French embassy, maybe at most with some basic training. Now you're a spy. Which means that after you got away, you sought this life out. All of which tells me this op isn't just about following orders. Unless there's more to that story too."

"I see." Petra kept her expression neutral, but she couldn't help but be surprised Sami didn't know she had always been with the Agency. *They thought Kasem was the spy.* When they realized he wasn't, General Majed must have written them both off.

"But that means we can help each other."

"We can?"

"I'd like to make a trade."

"I'm listening."

"How do you think I knew you were here? I'm sure you saw the police bulletin that went out."

"I'd very much like to know that."

"I'm sure you would. The question is what you can offer in return."

Petra had to wonder if she was dreaming. She had surrendered herself to Sami Majed, and instead of being tortured, they were sitting face-to-face and having a conversation. "Let Farah go, and we can have this conversation."

"Not so fast, my dear."

"What do you want?"

"Did you come here alone?"

"Yes." Petra answered on instinct to protect Kasem and buy time. As soon as he investigated her cover, he would find she had arrived in Iran with her husband. Their visa applications had been kept separate, but he would figure it out soon enough.

"You stripped all identification that could have confirmed otherwise," he said with obvious skepticism. "But we can talk more about that later. I will say that you've put me in a difficult position."

"How so?"

"I went to great lengths to make it seem as if my uncle were dead, that he had died of natural causes. Since you know he's still alive, that complicates things. If you don't find him, someone else will. I know what happens to people who try to take out a man as vindictive as President Reynolds. I suppose we're lucky he hasn't sent in a massive invasion force. I don't want that to happen to my country."

"What are you saying?"

"I'll let you walk out of here—you and your asset—and in exchange, you tell them General Majed is dead. I'd like the CIA to stop hunting him."

"Why would I do that?"

"He's in his late seventies. He will be dead soon enough."

"I'm afraid that's not good enough."

"You'll see what I mean." Sami stood and removed a Swiss Army knife from his pocket. "Don't make me regret this." A few seconds later, he had cut through the zip ties securing her arms to the chair and rebound her wrists. "Come with me."

# Chapter 55

*Tehran, Iran*

Kasem navigated his way through the beginnings of a thunderstorm as he drove into the foothills outside of Tehran. According to his map software—an encrypted version of Google Maps—he was about forty minutes away from the mountain house Gul had directed them to. He was operating on autopilot, each decision more mechanical than the last, which seemed to be the only way he could process the current situation. He had hoped Petra would have activated her tracker by now so he could confirm the two locations were a match, but no such luck.

Shortly before their departure from Scotland, he and Petra had finally agreed to have trackers implanted as an emergency fail-safe. Petra had been adamant on one condition—the trackers would remain dormant unless they activated the devices themselves. Rachel had finally agreed to their terms, which meant Petra was the only one who could activate her tracker, by applying direct pressure to its subcutaneous surface for at least one full minute.

So far, there was no sign of her tracker. Which meant she hadn't been alone long enough to do so. What that meant, he wasn't sure.

*She is trained for this.* The reminder felt hollow, offering no comfort. Four hours had passed since he had watched her vanish at the bazaar. The drive from there to the mountain house would probably have taken an hour and a half, possibly longer depending on traffic, exactly when they had left, and the storm conditions. Kasem had delayed his departure in the hope of being able to follow her tracker, but after almost three hours, had been unable to wait any longer.

*The waiting.* That's what they left out of every spy movie on the planet. Waiting for a source, for the right opportunity, for daylight, for dark. Waiting, praying, hoping for a tracker to come online. No matter what, at least half of the job centered around patience.

When he stopped at a traffic light, he checked the tracking app on his phone once more. *Nothing.* He made sure for the umpteenth time it was properly linked to her tracker and was set to automatically search for its signal every five minutes. Before the light changed, he grabbed his burner phone and typed out a hurried message. A Hail Mary pass, but he had nothing to lose. The car behind him honked and he set the phone down in a hurry and sped through the green light.

Kasem thought about the document he'd read earlier that day. After much cajoling on Rachel's part, British intelligence had finally provided her with a full file on Farah. Kasem had done a half-assed job of reading it before he'd left—anything to keep from checking his phone for Petra's tracker details every thirty seconds.

What he'd read had been a gut punch. Farah had been in a relationship with Lieutenant Afshar, a fact that made him feel even more desolate. She believed General Majed had killed Afshar, but the truth was the Ahriman had wielded the knife, even if the situation had been caused and orchestrated by the general.

Which meant Kasem had wielded the knife. The memory felt as if it belonged to someone else, and in many ways it did. Yet regardless of how much work he had done to distance himself from that life, the Ahriman would follow him wherever he went.

*Petra forgave me. We're past it.*

He steadied himself against the steering wheel. Had she known about Farah's connection to Lieutenant Afshar? If she had kept it a secret, then it could only be for one reason. She suspected his involvement in Afshar's death, something he had never shared with her. He could imagine what she would say if she did know. *We can't change the past. There's no point to living in regret, not when we can work to put the future right.*

His breath steadied as he heard her voice in his head. He had made his choices, but she was right. Ultimately, General Majed was the one responsible for what had happened. For all of it. *He made this happen to me. To Afshar and everyone at the Suez.* He finally had the chance to right the scales, and Kasem clung to that reality.

The thought steadied him further, but he knew it would mean little to Farah if she were ever confronted with the truth. His guilt made him want to tell her, but it served no purpose. Petra had turned herself in to bargain for Farah's freedom, and he intended to see that through. Nothing else mattered more, not even General Majed. Still, Kasem released his right hand from the steering wheel and found the grip of his Beretta 9mm.

His phone beeped with an alert. Kasem cried out in relief as a red dot appeared on his map to indicate Petra's tracker had been activated.

In the distance, he saw a streak of lightning split the sky, followed by a crack of thunder. The rain picked up as he turned off the main road onto a steep road leading up the mountainside. He pushed down on the gas pedal as the engine revved uphill.

# Chapter 56

*Alborz Mountains, Iran*

Petra asked to stop at the restroom before following Sami through the house. After he'd made sure there was nothing threatening available, he'd stepped aside and promised her a moment of privacy.

She did a similar sweep herself and found nothing of use, but the stop did allow her to apply the deep pressure to the base of her right adductor magnus muscle needed to activate her subcutaneous tracker. Embedding the tracker so close to the knee had been painful, but she'd specifically chosen a spot she could reach easily even with her hands bound. She held on to a count of eighty just to be sure, then flushed the toilet and splashed cold water over her hands, face and neck. The skin around her wrists was raw from rubbing against the zipties, so flinched a couple of times, but the water helped ground her. The situation still felt surreal, but there was nothing to do but improvise. Improvise and trust in her instincts, her training, and her innate ability to judge other people's motivations. For now, the jury was still out on Sami Majed, but she would trust that the answer would be revealed in time. *Let's hope for sooner rather than later.*

They made their way to the other side of the house—an estate, similar in size to the house in Scotland—and he led her to a doorway at the end of a long corridor. The door opened into a suite, and they passed a kitchen and bathroom before Sami stopped when the room widened into a sitting area.

General Majed was sprawled out on the couch in the far corner as if he were the subject of a Renaissance painting. A woman was holding his left hand and appeared to be giving him a manicure, while another one was standing behind the couch and spoon feeding him from a bowl. Petra stared at the scene and blinked twice. Was she still drugged? She was no expert on medical conditions, but the man on the couch did not appear to be in his right mind. His eyes were wide and scared, darting between her and Sami and the spoon in front of his face.

How could the caricature on the sofa be the nemesis she and Kasem had upturned their lives to chase? How could he be the target of a CIA operation with an essentially unlimited budget?

She turned toward Sami and searched for the right words, but found herself unable to string them together. At the back of her mind, a reminder flashed. *This could be a trick*. "How do I know this is real?" she finally asked. In her bones, she knew the answer though. This wasn't an elaborate ruse. General Majed was alive in body, but not in mind.

"He has moments of clarity, but his condition is quite real. Talk to him yourself."

Petra took a step closer, but before she could speak, the general broke into a childish grin.

"Navid, you've brought me someone new. Thank you!"

"I wanted to make up for moving you here yesterday," Sami replied. "He thinks I'm my cousin Navid," he explained to Petra.

"Yesterday?" The General shrank back and shivered. "What happened yesterday? We didn't move."

"Actually, we did, uncle. You're at a house in the Alborz. Do you remember the fire alarms a few days ago? That's why we had to move you."

The general struggled to his feet and shoved away the two women tending to him. He limped unsteadily toward the nearest window. "Why did we come here?" He turned toward his nephew with wide eyes. "I don't like the mountains. It is always too cold."

"I turned the heat up. The ladies are here to take care of you. You have to eat so you can take your medicine."

Petra watched as Sami helped his uncle back to the couch, where he pulled a blanket up to his chin. When one of the girls reached for his hand he flinched, putting it back under the covers. "I don't want to eat anymore."

"Do you still think I'm lying?" Sami asked Petra.

"I don't know. How could he go to the club? That was just a few days ago. He's acting as if he can hardly walk."

"He can walk. When properly motivated, that is. There's nothing like a woman in a bikini to get him out of the house. It's called frontotemporal dementia. It started three years ago—a lack of impulse control, minimal social awareness. At first, I didn't think anything of it, but then he started having trouble expressing himself, finding the right words, things like that. He refused to get checked out, so I let it go. When his memory started to be affected, we finally did a CAT scan that showed atrophy in his frontal lobe."

"I'm sorry." Petra could hardly believe what she was saying.

"He's usually more lucid than this, so most people write it off as old age and poor behavior. The move really got to him; he's barely been coherent since he got here."

"Does he remember the Ahriman?"

"Ask him."

Petra approached the couch more tentatively this time.

"Join me, my dear, don't be afraid," the general said with another grin. "I don't bite. Kamila and Noor will vouch for that."

Petra sat down on the floor a few feet away, her back against the coffee table. "How are you feeling?"

"No, but I need some tea. Will you make me some?"

"I'll make some," the woman who had been feeding him answered. "I think you've had enough to eat."

"Do you recognize me, General?" Petra asked.

He tilted his head to the side and stared at her for a few seconds. "Were you at the club?"

"Do you remember the club?"

"Of course, it's right down the street. Maybe a ten-minute drive? You don't know about the club?"

"I've never seen you at the club." Petra chose her words carefully. *What is happening?* Much like the general's expression, her whole world had been tilted onto its side. She was in no way qualified to assess his dementia. If someone had told her that she would ever be inclined to believe a word that came out of Sami's mouth, she would have said they were insane. Batshit crazy.

If Sami was telling the truth, what did that mean? General Majed was still responsible for several hundred deaths at the Suez and probably countless more on operations they knew less about. She and Kasem had been sent here to do a job. Blackmailed into it. If they didn't complete it, that didn't bode well for them. Neither did trusting the CIA.

*Checkmate.*

"I want to watch television," the general said.

Petra shifted so she was no longer blocking his view.

"It's my favorite movie. I'm watching it again."

"It's a good one." She nodded as the blond-haired figure of Elsa from *Frozen* strode across the screen. She watched the character break into song, then met Sami's gaze. "I think I've seen enough. Where's Farah?"

"Not today."

Sami led her back to the opposite wing and the room where she'd awoken and secured her to the bedpost with zip ties.

*In another version of reality, this would be the start of a porno.*

On his way out, he paused at the doorway. "I have information on a mole within your organization."

"I know. How else could you have gotten my picture?"

"I was also told you were seconded from another intel organization, that you're not CIA. Do you think they'll lift a finger for you?"

"What are you getting at? Let's cut to the chase," Petra said, her patience beginning to wane.

"I thought it was obvious. I want it to be clear that I have information to trade."

*But why? You hold all the cards.* "I'm afraid I don't follow."

"I want to make that trade work."

"You'll release me and my asset, and in exchange, we tell the Company your uncle's dead. Right?"

"Not quite that simple. I do want money—a lot of money. But most importantly, this ridiculous witch hunt for my uncle has to be over. He's a pain in the ass, but he's almost gone. Leave him be. It's over."

"What about the mole?"

Sami frowned. "What about the mole?"

"Will you give him up? Or her?"

"I can't do that. If I do, it's as good as defecting."

"You said you want money. Wouldn't that make you our asset anyway?" Petra pushed back, and in doing so, took the upper hand in the conversation. She had come here to locate Farah, but the possibilities had grown. Could she turn Sami into an American asset? She would never have dreamed of it before, but he had initiated this dialogue. He obviously wanted to talk to somebody, and she intended for it to be her.

"My country is a mess. A mess because of Islamist forces within and outside the government. Western embargoes keep my people from having access to the goods they need. Those embargoes keep them from earning a fair wage. The clerics in power use religion to manipulate everyone and everything. Why should we waste our resources on a nuclear program when people are starving on the streets? Why do we even care about destroying Israel? I have no love for the Zionists, but they exist. Who cares? I just want to live my life."

He kicked at the doorframe. "When I first started in intelligence, it was all about power. The West was the enemy, especially America. That was certainly the case for my uncle. And can you blame us after what your CIA did in the 50s? We were far from perfect, but we were strong and growing. We were making improvements to an oppressive system—granting women more rights, improving civil liberties. Maybe one day we could even have had a safe environment for a gay man. All of that gone, lost with the Shah's Secret Police—"

"Aren't you part of the Secret Police?"

"I do not serve the Shah. I have served my country. My service shouldn't be dictated by the people in power. I am a patriot."

Petra waited for him to keep going. She could sense he was on the cusp of giving in, and she didn't want to do anything to disrupt it.

"All of that Iran versus the West, where did it get us? We have no allies, not even amongst our neighbors. Russia and their czar would no sooner lift a finger for us. Instead, this government ties us to bombmakers in Hezbollah and people who hang young kids on the streets. Nothing has changed. In fact, it's gotten worse. It keeps getting worse. Something has to change."

Petra nodded as she processed everything he had said. "Perhaps you and I aren't as different as I thought. I love this country. My father is from here. The man I loved came from here too." She was careful to use past tense when it came to mentioning Kasem. "You're right, something has to change. You can help make that happen."

"I'm a patriot." He met her gaze in silence for a protracted moment. Without another word, he switched off the overhead light and vanished out the door. Petra heard the click of a deadbolt and she was alone, her mind a myriad of questions. One in particular kept repeating in her head. What had happened to make Sami cross over? And if this wasn't all an elaborate ruse, how had she and the entire team completely missed it?

She looked to her left and could see a glimpse of the mountainside through the closest windows. The sky was a mottled pattern of gray clouds, one that was incredibly beautiful.

She fought to stay awake, considering everything that had happened in the last twenty-four hours. Had she activated her tracker earlier? Or had she dreamed it? As far as she could tell, they were at the address Gul had given them, which meant Kasem would be moving on the location later that night.

And when he did, she was no longer sure he should kill Sami, or even General Majed. The exhaustion of the day and the weeks preceding it caught up with her, and she couldn't help but close her eyes, wondering how she could convince Kasem.

She choked back a laugh as sleep overtook her. *I must still be stoned.*

# Chapter 57

### *New York, United States*

"All right, Kasem, are you ready?" Tim said as he stared at the set of projections on the conference table in front of him. Rachel had now involved the Istanbul office of the Agency—the independent intel organization Petra and Carlos had both worked for previously. As part of that arrangement, Time and Carlos had relocated to their offices in New York. There were three different feeds. Two from the cameras attached to Kasem's pack, one on the left front strap and the other on the back. The remaining feed was an infrared satellite feed overlayed onto a map with the location of Petra's tracker. They could see a light heat signature that lined up to her position.

Rachel was monitoring both of their vital signs on a tablet from Istanbul station, but for the moment, Tim was more concerned about their locations than detailed readouts of their heart rates and blood pressures.

*Alive and functional, that's all I need.*

The line crackled as Kasem's voice came over the speakers embedded in the table. "If I manage to get out of here, I'll have to kill you for choosing this approach. But yeah, ready as a rookie climber can be."

"You've got this," Rachel piped up in a tone that sounded more terrified than convincing.

"Here goes nothing." The sound of Kasem's voice was replaced by the muffled sound of movement as he placed his first climbing anchor and prepared to descend the hundred feet of cliff face to the riverbank that would lead him to the mountain house where Petra was being held.

Tim shot Rachel a look and selectively muted his transmission to Kasem. "Sound like you mean it or don't say it."

He would normally have been more diplomatic, but this op had pushed his patience to the limit. This approach would have been difficult even for a four-person SEAL team, but because of the mission's sensitivity, Kasem was undertaking it without backup. After reviewing the various possibilities for Kasem's approach to the house, he and Carlos had told Kasem not to take the route through the woods he had originally identified. Without an existing trail, his presence would be obvious to any guards with even minimal tracking experience. By rappelling down to the riverbed, Kasem could walk through the water to hide his tracks and emerge closer to the house without leaving much of a trace. Even with the climb, Tim was confident this way offered him the best shot at survival.

*Still wouldn't put it at over ten percent.* Tim exchanged a glance with Carlos as they watched Kasem's front feed. With only the moonlight and the camera's limited visibility, they couldn't see much detail of the rock, just a hazy surface with Kasem's hands moving in and out of the picture.

"Laying my first anchor." The corner of a spring-loaded camming device appeared on the front feed along with both of Kasem's hands. A moment later, the snap of the springs engaging inside the rock face echoed over the speakers.

Rachel looked as if she were about to say something, but Tim shut her down. "The kid doesn't need to be micromanaged."

"Testing it now." Kasem tugged on the end of the active pro before attaching his first sling and carabiner. He gradually applied more force to the rope on the carabiner before leaning his weight into it. "Starting my descent now."

The next twenty minutes dragged as Kasem rappelled slowly down the rock face. With each anchor that he set, the process moved a little faster as he got more comfortable. "Too bad you aren't here, Mary Poppins," he said, using Petra's nickname for Carlos, an old joke to refer to the fact he seemed to have an unlimited set of gear hidden in his jacket whenever he was out an op. "I could use some of your gadgets."

"Better step it up or I might die of old age before you get to the bottom."

"Don't get snippy, old man. I'm the one doing the hard work."

Carlos chuckled. "I bet Petra could climb better than that blindfolded. Actually, you know, I think she did. *During rookie training.*"

"Doesn't surprise me. But I have to wonder—did *you?*"

"I'm going to plead the fifth on that one."

"Mary Poppins was a decent climber, if I remember right," Tim interjected. "It's the lockpick he struggles with—always carrying the kit around, never able to use it properly."

"That was our secret!"

"Don't worry, Agent Puppy, your secret's safe with me." Before the banter continued, Kasem added, "I'm only a few feet from the bottom now. One, maybe two more anchors."

"Take your time, no rush," Tim said in his most reassuring tone.

Five minutes later, Kasem was safely on the riverbank. He let out a sigh of obvious relief. "Tim, please don't make me do anything like that again."

"Only once more, when you and your chérie do it on your way out. But yes, after that, I promise. You can sit back and watch the feed. I'll do all the climbing."

"I look forward to it."

"It ain't no picnic up here, let me tell you. First, I have to deal with this *old man* sitting next to me hogging all the guac, and I've got to take care of your pretty ass."

"Thanks, man. I knew you were checking out my ass. It is pretty, isn't it? Too bad neither of these cameras have the best view."

"It might get Carlos's attention long enough for me to get some guac." Tim reached over to the side table and grabbed a tortilla chip, but turned around only to find that Carlos was hugging the bowl of guacamole.

"It's mine, all mine," he snickered.

"Petra will kill you if you eat all the guac," Kasem said. "Save some for me. I'm the one out here doing all the heavy lifting."

"Boys, can we focus?" Rachel interjected.

"So sorry to offend your delicate sensibilities, my lady. I hear and obey." Kasem continued to move forward, the feed catching bits of the riverbank and surrounding trees. The mix of shades of gray and shadow were hard to make out, but Tim could see his location was moving closer to the house. Kasem's heat signature, marked by a green dot to indicate his tracker, was making fast progress through the river.

"I can see the house now." The video feed lurched as Kasem hauled himself out of the water. "I'm going to climb this tree and see if I can get a better perimeter view. Standby." Kasem stopped moving and Tim exhaled slowly. The first major hurdle was complete, which put his chance of success at just a smidge above Tim's earlier estimate of ten percent. Now all the kid had to do was infiltrate the property, find and exfil Petra and the asset, neutralize General Majed, and get out alive. Tim took another guzzle from the glass of tonic he had poured himself. He didn't drink on the job, but the tonic tasted close enough to a G&T. It was going to be a long day.

# Chapter 58

*Alborz Mountains, Iran*

Kasem selected a well-developed juniper tree and ducked behind it to do a quick survey on the property. He removed the back camera from his pack and snapped it into the receptacle on his night-vision goggles, then scanned the area. Dropping the pack on the ground, he pulled himself up onto a wide branch about five feet above him and took another look at the property, shifting from side to side before he found a decent view through the trees ahead of him. The forest density thinned out within another thirty feet, transforming into a lawn that framed the mountain property.

"I see three perimeter guards on this side of the grounds, fairly spread out. Lighting is dim." He glanced at the tracker app on his phone but it wasn't clear enough to decipher which side of the property Petra's marker was on. "Any pointers on Petra?"

"East side, second floor," Rachel replied over his comm.

"Tim, how much would I have to pay to get you and all your guys down here like we did back in Burundi? You too, Mary Poppins—can't go without that jacket."

"We're all there in spirit, kid," Tim said. "It's just like the simulation back in Scotland. Take it in steps—get across the grounds, neutralize the guards, get inside."

"I'm tacking the rear camera to one of the branches and will move to the east side of the property along the tree line. Let me know if the west guards move." Kasem didn't wait for a reply, removing the camera from his goggles. After checking the viewscreen in a couple of spots to ensure the best vantage point of the property, he used some duct tape from his pack to attach it to the most appropriate branch.

"Moving now."

\*\*\*\*\*\*

Kasem made it to eastern edge of the property within a couple of minutes, then scanned the site one more time. He switched on the heat sensors in his goggles and took another look. "Two guards ahead, but one's at the corner, so he probably won't see me. Eight heat signatures inside, one on the second floor—must be Petra."

*Now or never.*

He was closer to the deck lights on this side, so he pushed his goggles on top of his head and waited a few seconds for his vision to adjust. From inside the pack, he retrieved a Kalashnikov out-the-front switchblade and tested the blade. He'd always felt most comfortable using this type of knife for close combat. The grip was familiar—more familiar than he liked to admit. He closed it back up and tucked it into a holster at his waist.

*The Ahriman's favorite knife.*

His jaw clenched. If he needed to be the Ahriman to free Petra, then that's exactly who he would be. He refused to let her die at Sami Majed's mercy because he was too much of a wimp to lean into his killer instincts. She had accepted all of him, including the darkest parts of his past. Now he had to accept them for himself.

He removed a tranq gun and lined it up, taking aim in the direction of the guard. With this lighting, he was unlikely to hit the target—not in the dark without a sniper rifle. His plan was to distract him long enough to cover the three-hundred feet between them before the guard realized what was happening. Kasem inhaled slowly, using a box breathing technique to steady himself. The mental clarity that came with an operation, especially one of this urgency, was refreshing. A level of sureness that would have normally eluded him.

*Whatever I have to do.* The Ahriman had indeed returned.

He exhaled and squeezed the trigger.

# Chapter 59

*Alborz Mountains, Iran*

Petra awoke about an hour after Sami left, according to the bright red numerals on the digital clock mounted on the wall. She attempted to roll onto her right side. The sharp jab of the zip ties that secured her left arm cut through her grogginess. She recalled how quickly she had drifted earlier and grimaced. Whatever drug Sami had given her, it was most definitely still working its way through her system. She squeezed both her hands into fists, digging her fingernails into the bed of her palms.

Through the window she could see bits of the moonlit mountainside. Kasem must be on his way now, as it had been several hours since she had activated her tracker. Which meant she had to find a way out of her current predicament. Decisions about whether or not to kill the general and his nephew would come later.

Both of her wrists were secured separately to each side of the headboard, her chest facing toward the ceiling. Her best chance was to access the underwire blade she had hidden in her bra, but to do that she had to be able to reach it with her hands. It was more like a curved nail file than an actual knife, but it would do the job. The hard surface of the file was palpable through the recycled polyester and elastane mix of her T-shirt and sports bra. Since it had been hidden against her actual underwire, she had hoped he wouldn't find it in a normal search and had been proved correct. After meeting him in person, she had an inkling that he took no pleasure in such a search. *I bet he'd be more interested in Kasem.*

Not that it mattered.

Or maybe it did. She couldn't imagine having to suppress such a central facet of her identity. It didn't excuse everything he had done to Kasem, but she couldn't deny that it added perspective.

She only knew a snippet of what he had gone through as the general's prisoner, but the little he had recounted was bad enough. Shackled to the ceiling in a basement cell. Alone for days. *Nothing could excuse that.* And General Majed. He'd been the one who had informed Kasem that she'd been taken prisoner.

Kasem had traded his service for her freedom. Could she have made the same choice? Would she? Petra shuddered and brought her focus back to the underwire file. After a couple of tries, she managed to slide the right tie along the bedframe about an inch. A few more attempts and it was only a foot away from her other wrist. With a deep breath, she twisted her torso to the left and flipped over bringing her knees into her chest. She threaded her head and neck through the gap between her arms. Her wrists were still crossed, but she could now maneuver her chest close enough to her hands. It took a little more twisting to get her right hand through the bottom of her shirt, but she could finally feel the cool metal directly against her thumb and index finger.

She slid it out slowly, careful not to drop it as she maneuvered it under her bra, past her stomach, and out of her shirt. Once it was free, she levered the file underneath the zip tie on her wrist. Luckily the plastic wasn't that strong—probably a result of production with the embargo—and she was able to work the sharp edge through to break it with minimal effort. Once that wrist was free, she made fast work of the remaining zip tie.

*Thank God for all that yoga.* If they made it out of here, she would never skip another class. In general, she favored more high intensity interval training, along with heavy weights, but over the last year, she had been forcing herself to do yoga to help with muscle fatigue and recovery. *And apparently, contortionist bondage.* A grin flashed across her face. Something she and Kasem could have some fun with when they finally got out of here.

She placed her feet slowly on the floor and padded toward the door. A few steps away, she tripped and almost fell forward. She fumbled at her feet to figure out what had tripped her and found the trainers she'd been wearing when Majed had picked her up at the bazaar.

*Guess I don't have to walk around barefoot like I'm Bruce Willis.*

She slipped her shoes on, taking a moment to double knot the laces, then crept to the door. As expected, the door was locked.

Petra fiddled briefly with the file, then shoved it into her pocket. She moved to the windows closest to her. A quick check was disappointing—the window joint wasn't wide enough for her to squeeze through, so she didn't risk opening it. On the other side of the corner room, the window looked more promising. It didn't extend all the way to the floor but was at least three feet wide. It had an angle joint to limit how far it would swing open, but she might get lucky. She squinted toward the garden below. There were at least two guards stationed at the edges of the perimeter—she could make out their shadows against the dim exterior lights. Because of the mountain slope, the ground was an extra story below, about three total. She could use a spider drop onto the yard to reduce the height, but she'd never been that great at them. If she angled her descent, she might be able drop down onto the parapet over the deck first, then lower herself to the deck railing and onto the grass. That way would take longer though, which would make it more likely that one of the guards would spot her.

It was probably the best option available. Or maybe the least-worst option. Provided she could make it out the window in the first place.

After another semi-contortionist feat, Petra stepped out onto the window ledge, grateful that part of the roof was in the shadow of the perimeter lighting. Being careful to keep a solid hold on the window frame, she moved away from the angled glass toward the parapet. The ledge only gave her a couple of baby steps, but every bit would count. She lowered her center of gravity slowly, still maintaining a grip on the frame, then brought herself into a crouch. Reaching across her body with her left hand, she released the opposite hand to turn around. For a moment, she thought she was about to fall off the balance beam, a childhood memory from gymnastics class, but her muscles prevailed long enough to pivot her feet around so her back was now against the wall.

Keeping up her grip with her left hand, she leaned away from it and swung her left leg to create some momentum. The parapet wasn't far, but depth perception at night was tricky.

*Three, two, one.* At the top of her leg's swing, she pushed off. She hit the smooth slope of the parapet with a soft thump, her head ricocheting against the taut canvas. She grappled for anything to catch hold of, but was unable to find a grip. She spread her legs out to create as much friction as possible and slid down the surface, still groping for the smallest fingerhold. Her feet found air and she slipped over the edge, bracing herself to try to the catch the ledge. The ledge eluded her left hand, but her right closed on the support bar and she hung there, suspended by one arm. She swayed sideways to avoid the deck railing; she wouldn't be able to drop onto it clean as she had hoped. When her swing had slowed a bit, she released her grip and let go.

Her knees buckled when she touched the ground, turning her vertical momentum horizontal as she rolled onto her side. Her left shoulder and arm slammed into the side of the deck and she cringed. She crouched in the grass, her breathing rapid, and simultaneously assessed two things. The fall hadn't resulted in any sharp pains, so she had likely gotten through it without serious injury. The more important question was, where was the nearest guard? She could have sworn she had seen a shadow on the other side of the deck, and there was no way her descent could have gone unnoticed at that distance. So where was he?

She was about to go check it out when a hand clasped over her mouth.

# Chapter 60

*Alborz Mountains, Iran*

Petra didn't hesitate for a second. She slammed her right elbow backward and stepped diagonally. If her assailant had a gun, a solid elbow to the gut was usually enough to throw off the aim. The hand over her mouth broke away, but both arms came around her, trapping her in a bear hug. She crouched down and shoved both of her arms outward to break the grip. It gave slightly and she took advantage of the reprieve to repeat the motion even harder. Her attacker stumbled and fell to the ground.

She was about to kick at him when he started waving at her with both hands. She leaned closer and realized that her ears were filled with a thick hum.

"Petra, it's me. Can you hear me?"

She could just make out the words as she crumpled onto the grass beside him. Her head spun and the house turned sideways and the ground came rushing up to her.

# Chapter 61

*Alborz Mountains, Iran*

By the time she came to, Petra's head felt like she'd been hit by a rockslide. The right side of her head throbbed as if her heart was beating against the side of her skull. She looked around. She was leaning against a wide juniper tree, and she could see numerous shadows cast by the dense forest around her.

A forest? Why was she in a forest? Her eyes widened as the events of the last day came flooding back.

Her capture at the bazaar. The most surreal conversation imaginable with Sami Majed. The sliver of sympathy she had begun to feel for him. She shut her eyes for a second, recalling the jump out of the window.

*I must have hit the parapet harder than I thought.*

She touched her head with her right hand and found a mix of damp blood congealed at her hairline. But how had she ended up here? She turned her head slowly and her vision turned forty-five degrees. She shivered, moving her hand from the front of her hairline toward her right ear. The side of her head was sticky, especially the base of her ear.

*I guess this is what it's like to fall off the balance beam as an adult.*

She used the tree trunk to help her stand and steadied herself as she took mini steps to turn around. Leaning against the trunk, she could see the house behind her. The house itself was still dark, so most likely they hadn't set off any alarms. She strained to see the corners of the garden—the places where she remembered seeing shadows—but couldn't make anything out.

She took a step forward and the ringing in her ears threatened to overwhelm her again. She fought to maintain consciousness, keeping hold of the nearest tree branch for support.

There was no sign of Kasem.

Her throat constricted. Where was he?

# Chapter 62

*Alborz Mountains, Iran*

Kasem took out the last guard with two tranq darts and pulled his unconscious form across the grass into the nearest part of the woods. He had used two darts on each guard to ensure they would be out long enough for him to do what he had to do. Thunder cracked in the distance, this time closer than the last. The storm was coming at the perfect time for his work. He glanced at the sky and whispered a 'thank you' to the universe for holding off until his feet were firmly on solid ground. The climb down the rock face had been treacherous enough, but he could handle the rain at this point.

With Petra essentially out of commission, the rest of the operation was up to him. When she was coming in and out of consciousness, she'd told him General Majed was inside the house, probably in one of the first-floor bedrooms. She had also said something about the general having severe dementia, but he couldn't quite make sense of it.

*No one with dementia goes to a strip club.* At least, he didn't think so. It sounded like a trick. Had Petra seen the general with her own eyes, or was she just communicating what Sami Majed had told her? Unfortunately, he didn't have time to clarify, certainly not with her in that state.

Even if it were true, he wasn't sure how much he cared. They had a job to do. The to-do list had grown now that he had to exfil Farah as well, but the original remit hadn't changed. Locate and neutralize General Majed. Full stop. Especially now that Petra was safe.

The fact she couldn't hear was bad, but the wound wasn't deep. She probably had a mild concussion, but he doubted it was anything severe. She wasn't throwing up or nauseated, which eliminated the symptoms of the most serious concussions.

His main concern was that with her balance as off as it currently was there was no way she could scale the rock face to get to his car. Their best option now was to steal a car from the property rather than forcing her to climb. And even if Petra could handle the climb because of her previous training, the chance Farah could make it was slim to none.

*Maybe Simonyan will come through.* He didn't dare to hope for it. Kasem had sent him a text on his way out of the city, but he hadn't received a reply. Regular cell service was limited in the mountains—the Agency tracker app worked over satellite—so it was possible Simonyan had responded and his reply just hadn't come through. Part of him was glad. Having both him and Farah, two people who had directly suffered from the Ahriman's actions, in the same place might be too much to handle.

Or so he was telling himself. A voice in the back of his mind questioned his motives. Was Petra right about the dementia? If it were true, could he really go through with the op? Was this about justice… or revenge?

He shoved the worry aside. Whatever the answer was, he didn't have time for it right now. He'd made a decision and now he had to live with it.

Kasem made a beeline for the house. He kept to the shadows, unsure whether there were any hidden security cameras. When he reached the side of the house, he pressed his back against the wall. He switched out his tranq gun for the Glock inside his pack and attached a silencer. From there, he aimed at the exterior lights and took out the two lampposts nearest to him. He turned the next corner and took out the remaining two.

With the inside of the house dark and the garden lights out of commission, he now had the advantage. He pulled on his night-vision goggles and walked toward the side door. Instead of approaching it directly, he leveled the gun at the corners of the doorframe to set off the alarm.

Within a second, a siren began to blare. He grinned, then moved quickly toward the other side of the house. Since he'd compromised the lights, his best chance was to draw all the guards outside. He only wished he'd been able to lay some of his explosives at the tree line to help amplify the show. The guards were probably just hired hands, maybe even ex-military Sami Majed had hired as private security. Kasem bore them no ill will. The further they were from the bombs that were about to go off, the better.

# Chapter 63

*New York, United States*

"Are you sure this is a good idea, bud?" Carlos couldn't help but ask as he watched the video feed of Kasem turning his Glock on the side door. A second later, the alarm went off and he sighed. Whatever the kid was doing, he wasn't listening to them anymore. In fact, he hadn't responded to any of their prompts for a while—not since he had deposited an unconscious Petra at the edge of the property. "Is his comm even working?"

"I doubt it," Nathan said with a grimace. "He's stopped giving us regular updates. I'm not sure when we last got one. Besides, the alarm sounds too far away."

"If he did, it wasn't an accident. Can you run a locator on the earpiece?"

"Sure, but we have his tracker so—"

"Just do it." Carlos caught himself. He shouldn't take his tension out on the tech geek. Still, he couldn't help be annoyed to have to deal with another rookie who'd once made googly eyes at Petra. Tech geeks were a necessary annoyance in the field, and because of his relationship with Rachel, Nathan was someone they could trust. That said, Carlos's level of confidence with their type of desk jockey was just about nil. During an op in Madagascar, Nathan had messed up a hack of the security system that had led to Carlos being captured. Needless to say, Carlos had had trouble trusting his competence since. The most annoying tech geek Carlos had ever dealt with was Grant, Petra's ex-boyfriend, the one who had turned Kasem in as the Ahriman and committed numerous other faux-pas all in the name of love. Carlos steeled his frustration and prayed that he would never have to deal with another Agency tech geek or rookie. *They're all basically kryptonite.*

A second alarm came over the speaker. *You'd better have a good plan,* Carlos imagined himself saying to Kasem.

"Adding it to the feed now," Nathan said in a meek voice.

A blue dot appeared on the project map of the property. While it appeared to be in general proximity with the dot that marked Kasem's location, the two dots weren't overlapping.

"Zoom in," Carlos said. "There—he doesn't have the comm anymore. It looks like it's next to Petra." He leaned forward toward the microphone. "Petra, kid, do you read me?"

"Nate, can you engage the LED on the comm from here?" Tim asked. "She might not realize she has it."

A few seconds later, the speaker crackled with Petra's voice. "Homebase, do you read me? Hearing compromised but slowly recovering."

"We've got you, Lockjaw," Carlos replied, using Petra's old Agency code name. A wave of relief flooded over him. Kasem might have gone batshit crazy setting off all the alarms—a third siren sounded on cue, further justifying Carlos's concerns—but at least he'd had enough clarity to leave a commlink with Petra.

Tim hit the mute button on their end. "What the hell is the kid doing? Is he trying to get himself killed?"

*Doesn't mean he's not off his rocker.* Carlos unmuted and spoke into the mic. "Lockjaw, this is home base, do you read me?"

"It's coming in and out. Do you have a location on Kasem? I can hear alarms at the house."

"He's on the west side of the house, opposite where you exited." Carlos glanced back at Kasem's front feed. "Actually, scratch that, he's on the east side now. How's your head? Your boy toy said it didn't look that bad."

"I've had better days, but I'll be fine."

Carlos heard the grit in her voice and tried to preempt her. "Just stay put, kiddo. You're in no condition to go charging back in there."

"He set off all the alarms, which means he's trying to draw out the internal guards. He'll need backup."

"Hold fast. We sent an emergency signal to Farah's handler."

"You know Six isn't going to lift a finger for us. Rachel, tell me I'm wrong."

"They said they'll consider it and get back to me with options. They don't want to compromise any of their in-country assets."

"But *she's* one of their assets."

"They think it's too high risk. I guess she doesn't know that many operational details."

"That means our best option is to take out the target, then you finish it with the Predator drone."

Carlos noticed the steadiness returning to her tone. Her hearing was returning, along with her partner's recklessness. *Don't do it.* "You don't even have a weapon, kiddo."

"I'm moving in now."

# Chapter 64

*Alborz Mountains, Iran*

Petra's balance was still off as she made it across the yard to the house, but it had improved considerably. Since the perimeter guards had all been neutralized, she didn't bother remaining concealed, just made a beeline for the deck. Without night-vision goggles, combined with the onslaught of rain, that was the only feature of the house she could make out clearly. The alarms still sounded far off, but they were getting louder, so her hearing was continuing to improve. She had to hope that wasn't wishful thinking.

She reached the deck railing and took shelter under the parapet. "Homebase, do you have a twenty on Kasem? I'm at the deck entrance now."

"Looks like he's east of your position, possibly at the side door."

"Got it."

Petra felt around for the sliding door entrance to the house and her hand touched broken glass. She pulled it back; luckily it was just a scrape. Kasem had shot through the door to trigger one of the alarms. She pulled off her soaked T-shirt, wrapped it around her left hand and found the door handle, still intact. The tread was still operational and she stepped through the opening, broken glass crunching under her shoes. *Straight out of Die Hard. Thankfully, I'm not barefoot.*

She took a few steps and cursed as her shin collided with the sharp corner of what felt like a marble coffee table. Clearly, Sami hadn't spared any expense in setting up this safe house, although that shouldn't surprise her. Proceeding more carefully, she made her way through the sitting room toward the hallway that led in the direction of General Majed's suite. Regardless of where Kasem was at the moment, he would be heading there.

She groped her way forward and was tempted to turn on the lights but decided against it. With alarms going off for the last few minutes, the interior guards would have dispersed outside to neutralize the threat. If Kasem hadn't taken care of them yet, the lights would only attract their attention back into the house. Moving slowly to prevent any more collisions, she found her way to the kitchen counter, catching herself before she tripped over a stool.

Her vision was starting to adjust, and she could see the hallway ahead more clearly. She shook off her shoes to leave as much glass behind as possible and continued ahead. She grabbed a chef's knife from the counter, but it was too heavy and unwieldy, so she exchanged it for a smaller serrated one.

Bracing herself, she couldn't help but think, *I would trade these shoes and the knife for a gun.*

# Chapter 65

*Alborz Mountains, Iran*

Sami Majed slammed on his breaks and sprinted toward the house. After depositing Lila back in the locked room, he had started driving back to the city. He was almost all the way back when his phone had alerted him the silent alarms had gone off at the mountain property. It had taken him over an hour to drive back through the storm, and the last ten minutes had been one alert after another as each perimeter alarm sounded.

*I should have known she would find a way to call for backup.*

Rain enveloped him, a wall he had to push through to move forward. The beam from his headlamps could hardly cut through the thick mist. Between the alarms blaring incessantly and thunder overhead, he could scarcely think straight.

Obviously, he had misread the situation when he had captured the CIA agent—Lila or whatever her name was. He had scanned her for any trackers shortly after administering the drug that had knocked her out and there had been nothing. Which meant he'd missed something, or she had managed to escape. Either way, it was a solid screwup.

*Time to clean it up.* He had to wonder if the girl had even considered his offer. If she hadn't, he would have to find a way to up the stakes, a way to convince her. The possibility had only occurred to him when he'd first received her file. He knew in his gut he wasn't wrong about this. He was certain they could reach a deal of some sort. He wanted out, and he was going to find a way to make it happen.

He reached the top of the driveway and almost dropped the keys as he tried to open the door. Whatever was happening, no one had taken out the front door. That didn't surprise him. The house was far more vulnerable from the mountain side. A quick upward glance before he stepped inside confirmed the front cameras had been taken out. He could only hope the internal cameras remained functional.

Sami pulled the door shut behind him, welcoming his exit from the downpour. He groped for the mudroom lights and covered the few steps toward the hidden security console. Swiping his right hand over his soaked T-shirt did little to dry his right hand enough for the console palm scan. He scrambled for a towel in the hall bathroom, then accessed the console with his handprint. A moment later, the sound of the alarms was replaced by a resounding silence, one that seemed even more threatening.

He removed his gun from its shoulder holster and slid the towel over it, then ejected and reinserted the magazine after drying it off as well. He'd never had a gun jam because it was damp, but in his experience, caution was never overrated.

With gun ready, he bolted down the corridor toward his uncle's suite. Would the general have had the mental clarity to head to the safe room as soon as the first alarm was triggered? He'd moved his uncle and the associated posse here in such a hurry earlier that week, he hadn't even gone over all the basic safety protocols with them. He'd been too wrapped up in setting up his plan. Perhaps it had even been a Freudian slip—he was so tired of being his uncle's caretaker.

That mistake would now bite him in the ass. Or worse, an invalid old man would be the one who paid for it.

# Chapter 66

*Alborz Mountains, Iran*

Kasem waited for any remaining security personnel by the east side door. After taking out most of the exterior cameras and alarm triggers—all except the front door—he'd returned to this spot. By sending a couple more shots into the doorframe, his plan was to draw all the remaining guards there while he waited comfortably concealed thirty feet away at the base of an evergreen. With his night-vision goggles on he had decent visibility, and the breadth of the tree kept the worst of the rain off him. He was still soaked, but by luring the guards out he retained more control of the situation.

That plan had served him well so far. He'd been able to tranq three more guards—two who had emerged directly out of the side door and one who had come around the back of the house, probably from the deck.

He tapped his ear, only to remember he had left his comm with Petra. In the rush to pursue her up the mountain, he had neglected to bring some essential items. An extra commlink would have been useful, especially if the team had managed to get real-time imaging set up. Rachel had been working on it, but it involved re-tasking an Agency satellite, so he doubted she would succeed. Getting coverage over the mountains in Iran without compromising them seemed like a tall order.

He looked back at the house for heat signatures once more and frowned. Through the walls, the heat readings had questionable reliability. They were better than nothing, but what worried him now was the personnel count. Before Petra had escaped, he had seen three guards clustered on the north side of the house, one upstairs, and four more scattered around the first floor. Yet he had only taken out three guards from the interior of the house. On top of that, the three clustered on the first floor had disappeared. The house had no heat signatures now that he could detect.

Even with the rain and the alarms, Kasem was dead certain he would have heard or seen something if that group had escaped by car. He couldn't have missed something that big. Which could only mean one thing—the house was equipped with some kind of safe room. Kasem kicked himself for not thinking of it before. Of course, Sami Majed would have made sure such a provision was built into the property. It was so obvious, Kasem could hardly believe his own hubris. He'd been so caught up in the opportunity to complete the op, as soon as Petra was free, he had gone in guns blazing.

Kasem was in the process of assessing what to do when he noticed a new image appear on the deck. *The last guard?* He turned back to look across the garden toward the spot where he had deposited Petra, but the goggles' heat sensor had a maximum range of sixty or so yards. Kicking himself for not having brought an extra comm, he moved quietly toward the house.

He had just reached the side door when he froze with one foot just inside the doorframe. A light on the front side of the house had just come on.

# Chapter 67

*Alborz Mountains, Iran*

Petra stopped mid step as a light came on down the hallway by the front door. She stepped into the nearest doorway and peered around the corner. From where she stood, the entrance was too far away to get a clear look, but she could see a shadow moving. Even without being able to see, she had a pretty good guess as to who it was. A second later, the alarms stopped.

"I think Sami Majed just got here," she whispered into her comm. "Any updates on the team from Six?"

"They said they would have a couple of people available," Rachel answered. "Thirty minutes out, but they won't deploy without confirmation their asset is alive. Predator drone is on route."

*Thirty minutes too many.* Petra grimaced. She glanced in the opposite direction to gauge how far she was from the east side suite where General Majed had been staying. Taking the gamble, she sped in that direction, turning the corner in three steps so she would be out of Sami's line of site from the mudroom.

By the time she reached the general's bedroom, she knew the effort was futile. There was no one there. The sound of footsteps just outside the suite gave her barely enough time to dive into the space between the bed and the wall alongside it.

Stars flashed in her vision and she pinched her cheek hard—the pain helped to keep her conscious and awake. The descent to the ground had been far from graceful. Despite her best efforts, she had probably made quite a sound, although she hadn't heard much more than a soft thud as her shoulder hit the thick carpet.

The bedroom door swung wider, and she saw a pair of black leather shoes as the lights came on. The figure stood for a moment, then turned around and she heard footsteps going back out to the hallway.

Petra pushed herself to her feet. Wherever the footsteps were going was likely to be where General Majed had hidden. She had no choice but to follow. Kasem would catch up, but in the meantime, she had a job to do.

She rounded the corner and saw a shadow using a touchscreen panel on the wall and then disappear around the corner. Petra crept slowly up to the panel and tapped on it—the device was her best shot for locating Farah—but it remained dark. She thought quickly back to her walk through the house earlier with Sami and the blueprints Rachel had obtained. If she had to guess, he would have avoided taking her on a route that passed the room where he was holding Farah. The chance she would make a noise when they were on route was too high. Which left the opposite wing of the house.

Instead of continuing to follow the figure, she ventured back down the hallway toward the adjoining wing, which was designed as a smaller standalone apartment tacked onto the main house. She checked two doors and found an empty storeroom and a restroom. On the third try, she found a locked door and tapped on it, but couldn't make anything out. Since her head was still filled with an incessant buzz from her earlier concussion, she decided to check the room. The deadbolt released easily, but there was an additional flap latch secured by a combination padlock. She fiddled with the hasp and used the knife she had picked up in the kitchen as a chisel to loosen the screws fastening the plate to the door frame. Luckily the screws were old, worn and rusted, so with a few additional tugs, she was able to release the hasp from the frame.

When the door swung open, she found a bound and gagged Farah struggling against her restraints on a mattress by the wall. Petra crossed the room and released her.

"Thank you for coming," Farah said quietly.

"Follow me."

They backtracked down the hallway, and Petra opened the door to the storeroom she had checked earlier. "I want you to stay here." She pointed toward the area behind the two sets of shelving.

"But I want to help you—"

"The best way to help is by making sure you don't get caught again."

"Fine."

Petra scanned the shelves for anything useful, but nothing stuck out. She rotated the shelves slightly to provide additional concealment for Farah. "I'll be back as soon as I can."

She peered back into the hallway and froze when she saw a shadow moving at the end of the hall, turning onto the stairs leading toward the basement. She remained out of sight and knocked the side of her head in an attempt to reduce the buzzing, to no avail. She was about to follow when a second figure appeared in her frame of vision.

"Stop right there," Kasem said as he pointed his Glock at Sami Majed. "Give me one reason I shouldn't take you out right now."

# Chapter 68

*Alborz Mountains, Iran*

Farah shuddered in the darkness of the storeroom. As soon as Asma had vanished into the hallway, the walls had begun to close in on her. She pushed back—she was still alive and kicking, and her rage started to overcome the fear. She had initiated this entire op for a reason, and she wasn't about to forget it now. *General Majed.* Nothing else mattered, not even her own survival. He had to die for what he'd done to Afshar. For the atrocities he had committed. But more importantly, for what he'd done to her, snatching away the life she and Afshar could have had together.

Her jaw set as she recalled the rumors of Afshar's death. She had refused to believe it, but after three days of rumors and his absence, she'd ventured to his apartment. All the while, she begged Allah and any God out there to set the rumors straight. Since their relationship was taboo, she was never supposed to visit during the day; if it got out that he was seeing a girl from the brothel at home, it could compromise his position in the military. But she'd had no choice.

*He can't be dead.* She remembered reciting that to herself on her way up the stairs. When she had run into his cousin in the hallway—they were there to collect his things—she had realized it was true. She'd turned away in a pretense that she'd come to the wrong place. The next day, the death announcement had appeared in the paper. Apparently, he'd been mugged on the street. Farah had never believed it—she knew exactly who was responsible.

She shifted her position and her shoulder knocked into one of the boxes on the shelf. She unlatched the lid and couldn't believe her luck. Paydirt. The purse she'd had with her when she left the club was inside. She reached for it, found her phone, and once it had booted up, sent an emergency message to her MI6 handler. Digging further, she found the gun she had obtained on the black market several months earlier. Within a couple days of sighting General Majed at the club, she had asked one of the bouncers at the club to get her one. She'd blamed it on a few handsy patrons. "There was one who even followed me to my car," she had explained. Before her next shift, he had pulled her aside and handed it to her. Since then, she had kept it hidden inside a planter in her apartment, too scared to carry it around with her. That night at the club had been different though. She had missed one chance at the general, and she wasn't about to let another one pass her by.

She removed the gun from her purse. She'd taken a few shooting lessons and wasn't a terrible shot, but was far from comfortable with the weight in her hand. The recoil was tremendously painful on her shoulder, and she'd been surprised how much force was required to pull the trigger. Still, the 9mm sub-compact pistol—apparently a knockoff of the Kahr PM9 according to the bouncer, not that she had a clue what that meant—was comforting.

Drawing a deep breath, she slid the shelves aside and moved quietly to the door. Too much of this operation had already happened outside of her control. She refused to leave any more to chance. With gun in hand, she headed out into the hallway.

# Chapter 69

*Alborz Mountains, Iran*

Simonyan ran past the front door of the house and turned left toward the side abutting the mountain slope. Based on Kasem's messages about the location, he'd been able to obtain blueprints. Although the house had been purchased privately three years earlier, it had previously been used as a small military training facility. Or maybe a spy school. He didn't know or care. All he knew was the situation was an emergency. He didn't have the details—Kasem had only told him the coordinates and begged for his help.

Simonyan swiped his hand across his face, his vision impaired by the rain. According to the blueprints, this side of the house had a small window that led directly to the basement. It was probably alarmed, but at this point that hardly mattered. Kasem had already told him that he planned to trigger the alarms. Simonyan had attempted to intercept the response from law enforcement by calling in the alarm as part of a training drill, but he'd passed into the no-service zone before getting confirmation the message had been received. Which meant at any minute a squad of police cars could show up. Kasem's last message had mentioned something about another backup team, but it was also up in the air.

Between the police and any security provisions Sami Majed would have called in, the situation could easily turn into a massive firefight. Simonyan intended to make his exit before that happened. He refused to let his daughter become an orphan, but he would do everything in his power to extract Kasem and his team before it came to that.

Based on the blueprints, securing this side window was the most viable option. It would be large enough for him to get through, and because of its position, he doubted there would be any cameras in the vicinity, making it their best possible escape route as well.

Simonyan stopped when he saw the appropriate projection from the house. The window was on the opposite side of the projection. He tapped the button on his headlamp to increase the illumination, but the beam barely penetrated the thick screen of rain ahead of him. He scrambled across the projected surface and dropped down to the other side. A moment later, he found the window. He removed a mini crowbar from his pack and aimed it at the bottom left corner of the pane. A few targeted blows made quick work of it. He was grateful for the storm, as it disguised the sound of the breaking glass. As he'd suspected, the window wasn't alarmed, probably because it was well hidden.

Shining the headlamp through he scanned the inside of the basement. To the right he could see a closed off room, and the rest of the basement looked like a hoarder's paradise.

*A safe room?*

If it was indeed that, this had to be where General Majed was hiding. He thought quickly about what he had in his pack—two cubes of Semtex, but they'd have to be specially placed to breach the room. Even then, it would only work depending on what the structure was made of. Simonyan grimaced. He was no explosives expert. While he wanted the general to pay for his crimes, he wasn't in the habit of committing murder. Perhaps the threat of the explosives would be enough to get the general to open the door?

He decided not to dwell on it any longer. His primary goal was to try and get his people out safely before the whole place turned into a firefight. He gauged the distance from the window to the floor. It was only a few feet below but there was barely room between the piles of stacked junk. The rain was already starting to leak in, so he assumed that would continue to help muffle any noise he made. He pulled the sleeves of his jacket over his fingers to protect his hands and lowered himself down.

# Chapter 70

*Alborz Mountains, Iran*

"On your knees." Kasem motioned with his pistol. He kept his grip steady and watched as Sami Majed lowered his gun to the floor and then put his hands in the air. "Kick it toward me."

"I never thought I'd see you again."

"Lucky you."

"We figured you must be dead when the Russians couldn't find you. They said someone even tried to impersonate the Ahriman, that's why their op went off the rails. I assume that was you?"

"Does it matter?"

"Just curious."

"I'll be the one asking questions."

"I'm sorry for what we did to you, but I'm not your enemy. Your wife, girlfriend, whatever—she knows. We were going to work out a deal. One that gets you out of Iran alive. My uncle isn't worth your life."

"Forgive me, but I already sold my soul to you once. I'm not planning to do it again."

"The only way you get out of Iran alive is with my help." Sami paused. "I bet you know that, and maybe you don't care, but the same goes for her too. Is that what you want for her? History would beg to differ."

"What I want is for your uncle to pay for what he did. You too."

"Right, because you never had an opportunity to get out. I gift wrapped Suez to you on a platter. You were already out of the country. Why didn't you run when you had a chance? You came back of your own volition. I don't know what story you fed yourself, but you were addicted to being the Ahriman. To the power and all the importance that came with it."

Kasem tamped down on his memory of that night at the Suez Canal. The night he had planted bombs when he thought they were simply a sophisticated bug system. A system the man in front of him had supplied. "You tricked me into what I did. I've been clawing my way back ever since."

"Keep telling yourself that. That you don't see that commander's family in the warehouse. Or Lieutenant Afshar's blood on your—"

"Enough." Kasem stared at his old trainer, one of the men who had molded him into the Ahriman. Who had demolished his identity as Kasem Ismaili with a sledgehammer. Who had duped him into believing he had to do so, that it was the price for Petra's freedom. "You manipulated me into killing over three hundred people that night."

He bridged the distance between them and pressed the muzzle of his pistol against Sami's head. "This ends now."

# Chapter 71

*Alborz Mountains, Iran*

"Kasem, stop," Petra cried out from the end of the hallway. She had been watching the exchange between them in silence, transfixed. Seeing her fiancé holding a gun at Sami Majed's head execution style had finally snapped her out of it. Kasem deserved his confrontation, deserved justice for everything Sami and General Majed had done to him, but killing Sami in cold blood? That went too far.

She knew Kasem had done terrible things during his time as the Ahriman. In the time since he had reappeared in her life, she had dealt with her feelings about those atrocities. She no longer felt he needed to redeem himself. The past was gone and buried. But committing murder today would cost him his soul.

"I don't know what he told you, but you can't trust him. It's time to end this. First him, then his uncle."

"I'm not saying we should trust him." Petra approached slowly. "But we can hear him out. At least use him to find the general."

"He's downstairs in the safe room. His nurse took him down there as soon as the silent alarm went off."

Kasem kept the gun at Sami's head. "How do we get him out?"

"It's a manual release, can only be opened from the inside."

"Fine, so we blow the room. Problem solved."

"You still need my help to get out of Iran. Or maybe for you both to disappear…"

Petra stepped closer to her fiancé. She could see his tranq gun holstered in his belt. In one quick step, she grabbed it and stepped around him to point it at Sami. Without hesitation, she squeezed the trigger.

# Chapter 72

*Alborz Mountains, Iran*

Sami Majed slumped forward.

"Whatever we decide to do, he's not worth your soul," Petra said, reaching out to grab Kasem's hand. "Come on, let's get to the safe room."

"I already set two charges at the door joint."

Kasem turned toward the voice. Simonyan was standing a few feet down the hall. Kasem looked at his face and could tell immediately that he had overheard what Majed had said.

*That you don't see that commander's family in the warehouse.*

"Thank you for coming," Kasem said in a quiet voice. He wanted to ask how much Simonyan had put together. He wanted to contradict Majed's accusation, to make sure Simonyan knew he hadn't been the one to give the order.

*But I did follow it.*

"We don't have much time. The police and whatever military backup he had on call must be on their way here. Let's get moving." Simonyan glanced at Petra. "I don't believe we've had the pleasure."

"I'm his partner."

"Secure him and follow me." They took a few minutes to strip Sami of his weapons and hog-tie him securely, then left him on the floor where he was. Simonyan led them down the hallway and turned right into the north wing of the house. From there, he headed through the corridor toward a narrow staircase that led downstairs.

On their way, Petra handed Kasem back the earpiece.

"Are you sure?"

"You need to hear it more than I do."

Her statement landed with multiple meanings, but he disregarded all of them and squeezed it back into his ear. "Heading to the safe room."

"Acknowledged," Carlos replied.

Kasem's head churned until they reached the safe room. Simonyan banged on the door and stepped in front of what looked like a peephole camera.

"I'm Captain Davit Simonyan. Your guards have been neutralized. Open the door and we won't hurt you."

*Like hell we won't.* Kasem counted to ten in his head, then did a quick check of the Semtex charges Simonyan had laid. "The charges look good."

"If you don't open the door in one minute, we're going to blow the hinges." Simonyan waved at the peephole once more. When the room remained silent, he nodded and the three of them retreated to the crawl space underneath the staircase.

*Three, two, one.* Simonyan pressed a key on his phone to trigger the explosive.

# Chapter 73

*Alborz Mountains, Iran*

Farah felt the floor shake beneath her.
*Lieutenant Afshar's blood on your hands.*
She'd heard it right, that was what Sami Majed had said. Did that mean what she thought? Could that man be responsible for Afshar's death? The man Asma had just helped? The man she'd called her partner? The possibility was a nonstarter.

*It can't be.* She focused on that, clung to it. General Majed had been the one who'd had Afshar executed. It had to be. There was no way she could have worked with—worked for—the woman who was so clearly in a relationship with Afshar's killer. She refused to believe it. If Asma was helping him, then she was as guilty as he was.

She couldn't have let that happen. She hadn't let it happen.
*I won't.*
Farah steadied her grip on the pistol and adjusted her hiding spot. Eventually, they would emerge from the basement with General Majed. And when they did, she would be waiting.

# Chapter 74

*Alborz Mountains, Iran*

Kasem wiped his sleeve over his face. The pale blue fabric was hardly visible anymore, coated with a mix of grays and browns, a product of his trek through the forest. That and the explosion itself. Soot hung like a haze in the air, and he coughed, tasting ash. He hadn't been this close to a bomb site in a while. He had forgotten the smell, the burnt essence that landed on his skin and hair, that stung his eyes.

The basement disappeared, and he was back in his cell the day after he'd been captured. Hanging by his wrists. Dust and grime coated every surface of his body.

He blinked and the image vanished.

Getting to his feet, he motioned to Simonyan and Petra behind him. They had just begun to stir. A soft buzz filled his ears, but he knew it would clear within a few minutes.

The mass of items lined up in rows that filled the cellar had toppled over. His boots crunched over bits of dust and glass and who knew what else.

"I guess we solved the hoarding problem. They won't need anyone to go through all this junk." He looked at Petra. He'd forgotten about her head wound and hoped the explosion hadn't caused her any more damage. "How's your ear?" He pointed to it at the same time in case she couldn't hear him.

"Still humming, but it's getting better not worse."

"Good." He was relieved she could at least hear him. Perhaps that was the first good omen of the evening. After the nightmare climb down the mountain, her injury, and now the fact Simonyan knew he had been involved in his brother-in-law's death, they were due for an uptick. Something. Anything.

All that started now. Petra might have stopped him from executing Sami, but General Majed was a different story. Everything that had gone wrong in his life started with that man. Today, he would right that balance.

\*\*\*\*\*\*

Kasem rounded the staircase and took in the remnants of the door to the safe room. Their calculations had been reasonably correct. The door seam had blown open, and it was hanging off what looked like one hinge at the top right corner.

"Is everyone okay? Can you hear us?" Simonyan said from his left.

A flash of green appeared in the gap between the door and its blown seam. The corner of a woman's face appeared in the vicinity, followed by more as Kasem spotted her tunic. The brilliant green was muddied by gray bits of concrete and red blood. "We're here. I don't know if he can get up."

"Help us," a childlike lilt said from behind her.

Kasem froze. Despite the tone, it was a voice he would never forget. The voice that had convinced him Petra was being held hostage. The voice that had first referred to him as the Ahriman.

General Majed.

# Chapter 75

*Alborz Mountains, Iran*

General Majed. Except it wasn't.

Kasem moved toward the voice on autopilot. Everything rode on what was just ahead. The object of this mission. The person who had occupied his nightmares for almost a decade. He felt as if he were floating overhead watching the scene from a helicopter, even down to the hum of the chopper blades.

He wasn't sure how, but a moment later, he had heaved the general from the wreckage and tossed him onto his shoulder. The corpulent form might as well have been a feather. Kasem only spent a second looking for where to put the dribbling man in his grasp.

"I didn't do anything," he kept saying. "Ali, why are you hurting me? I didn't steal your toy, I promise. I didn't take it."

None of the words registered in Kasem's head until he had thrown General Majed onto the rug in the hallway upstairs. The general turned and saw his nephew unconscious next to him and screamed, trying to scramble away from Kasem.

"Ali, why did you do this to him? I'm sorry, I shouldn't have taken it. I wish I could give it back but it broke. Don't do that to me, please!"

*Ali.* For the first time since the general had called him that, the name began to sink in. The General Majed Kasem had known had never mentioned that name, but Rachel's background file had. General Majed had had a brother named Ali. A brother who had passed when he was young.

"Don't you know who I am?"

"Why are you doing this? I'm sorry about your toy, so sorry. Please don't be angry. I'll tell Mamani and Baba everything."

Kasem took a step back from the sobbing general and pulled his Glock from his holster. He glanced over at Sami on the floor, then looked back at the general.

"I am the Ahriman, your vision, your creation," he whispered. "The Ahriman has come for you. Finally." The words felt right, justified. General Majed had named him for the Persian spirit of destruction, a character from Zoroastrian mythology. It didn't matter that the man at his feet had no idea who he was or what he had done.

"Ali, I'm sorry! I'll never steal your toys again."

"It's time to pay the piper, General. You made the Ahriman. Did you never think the spirit would return for you? The monster always returns to his creator."

"Don't hurt me. I'm sorry. I'll never do it again."

Kasem ignored his pleas and pointed the gun at the general's head. His mind spun as he relived his memories once more. The hopelessness of his imprisonment. The stench of human excrement that never abated. The helplessness, especially once he'd been told Petra had also been taken prisoner.

The warehouse going up in flames.

Radio reports of the bombs at Suez.

He could rebalance it all right now. A lifetime's worth of rage and revenge.

Except the man at his feet wasn't who he remembered. The child begging for reprieve wasn't the one who had turned him. He wasn't the one who had molded the Ahriman from the remnants of Kasem Ismaili's decimated identity.

All that was left was exactly that—a child.

Kasem shut his eyes and tried to banish the memories. There was no way to put them right. Petra had said killing Sami Majed in cold blood would cost him his soul. What would killing this shadow of a man do? Someone who had no recollection of the monster he had created?

He relaxed his grip on the trigger and lowered the gun. He didn't know the true path to redemption, but it was something he'd sought for the last several years. A path that had led him to propose to Petra at a restaurant in Montmartre a year earlier. A path he hoped would one day lead him to marriage and a life together.

Despite all of his worst acts, he'd been able to become Kasem Ismaili once again. If only in her eyes, that was enough. The pain of his lost years haunted him. His time as the Ahriman, as a puppet, as a slave to this man. But the man who had enslaved him was now dead. And that time was already lost.

# Chapter 76

*Alborz Mountains, Iran*

Petra raced up the stairs, desperately trying to shake off the fog that encompassed her head. She and Simonyan had pulled the woman from the wreckage of the safe room, but before he had lowered her to the cellar floor—a mean feat amongst all of the half-destroyed junk—she had realized Kasem was gone. Half a second earlier he'd pulled a blubbing General Majed from the debris, but now he had disappeared.

Despite her shaky sense of balance, she hung on to the railing and took the stairs two at a time. Why were there so many of them? And what had the general been whimpering when Kasem had pulled him out? *Ali? Something about Ali?* The name rang a bell. She had seen it in his file, but the details eluded her.

By the time she reached the top of the stairwell, she finally understood. She had wanted to verify the general's condition with a doctor, but now there was no need. After the explosion, there was no way he could be faking it. General Majed obviously thought Kasem was his late brother. Whatever she had feared Kasem was about to do to Sami Majed, that was nothing in comparison to what he might do to the man who almost destroyed his life.

She willed her legs to move faster, using the walls for balance as she rushed down the hallway. She would get there in time. She had to, there was no other choice. Their life together had only just begun, and she refused to have it end here in Iran all over again. To have him hand over his soul once more.

The loud crack of a bullet pierced the air.

She was too late.

\*\*\*\*\*\*

She covered the remaining distance in a few seconds, a cloud of despair threatening to smother her. Sami had been right—they needed his help to get out of Tehran. Or at least they needed someone's. After what Simonyan had just heard, she wasn't sure why he was still there. They had no backup, and to call the operation a shitshow was being charitable. The CIA would tout the victory of General Majed's death, but they had barely bothered to provide her and Kasem with support during the op. Would they lift a finger for their extraction? Would the Agency? Rachel and the team would do everything they could, but without the Company's resources, they would be out of luck. If this weren't Tehran, she could have counted on Carlos and Tim to move mountains, even to show up themselves, but she would be deluding herself if she believed it were that easy to set up an extraction team here. Not within Iranian borders. They weren't cavalier enough to risk an international incident without CIA backing. Especially not with a mole in the mix.

The thought of the CIA's likely betrayal made her blood curdle. Why did she keep falling into their traps? Or the Agency's? Each organization had proven time and again they weren't to be trusted. They made every promise and then hung their people out to dry.

*I'll make them pay.* Kasem might trace the root of their problems back to General Majed, but the truth was it went back further than that. To the lies the Agency had fed her when they recruited her.

*The greater good.* The biggest piece of crap she'd ever heard. The ultimate excuse, meant to justify every deviation from the values they flaunted.

She buried her feelings as far as they could go and turned the corner into the hallway.

Kasem was kneeling over General Majed's body putting pressure on a wound to his abdomen. About ten feet beyond them, Farah was leaning with her left shoulder propped against the wall, her right arm outstretched, gun in hand.

A gun pointed straight at Kasem.

"Farah, I need you to put the gun down." Petra took a step forward, tranq gun in hand.

*I'll make them pay for this disaster.* That resolution echoed through her head as she wondered how on earth they had believed this op could end any different.

# Chapter 77

*Alborz Mountains, Iran*

"Tell me what happened to Afshar." Farah's hand shook. She could scarcely keep her grip on the pistol steady.

"I need you to put the gun down," Petra repeated.

"Don't come any closer. I'll shoot him, I will."

"I'll stay right here. But you still need to put the gun down."

"What happened to Afshar? What did you do to him?"

"Nothing you do here today will bring him back."

"I don't care. I need answers."

"You already shot the man responsible." Petra hadn't seen it, but she didn't need to see it to ascertain what had happened. Despite the general's dementia, she felt no remorse, only a sense of justice. In fact, she was grateful to Farah for taking that decision out of Kasem's hands. Regardless of what he decided, it would have haunted him forever.

"The guards will be here any second," Petra added.

Kasem shook his head. "They're all tranqed."

"Is he dead?"

"No, but he will be if we can't stop the bleeding," he answered.

Petra glanced at him, but he had a faraway look in his eyes. As if he wasn't really there with them. "Let me see." She put her arms overhead and let the tranq gun pivot over her right index finger. In a slow, deliberate motion, she set it onto the floor. She didn't think Farah would shoot her, but all bets were off when it came to Kasem. She stepped closer to the general and checked for a pulse.

There was nothing.

She looked at the wound Kasem was putting pressure on. He still seemed in a daze, but there was no blood pouring out of it, just a congealed mess. The window for intervention that could have saved General Majed had passed.

"He's gone," she whispered. She reached across the body and squeezed Kasem's hand, then turned to Farah. "The man who took Afshar from you is dead."

"He said Afshar's blood was on your hands."

"It—" Kasem started to reply.

Sami Majed grunted, struggling against the rope that bound him. "It was always my uncle. The Ahriman was his creation. You wielded the knife for him many times, but it was all because of him. His plan, his ideas, his manipulation... maybe even mine."

Tears were pouring down Farah's cheeks. Her entire body was quaking now. Petra braced herself and moved toward her.

"Don't come any closer."

The air shook as Farah fired a warning shot, the bullet landing in the drywall behind Petra.

"Nothing you do now will bring him back." Petra stepped closer. She could see the corridor behind Farah now. Simonyan was moving quietly through the living room in their direction. In his right hand, he held a pistol. With his left, he motioned for her to keep Farah's attention.

"The man responsible for his death is gone," she continued.

Was she trying to convince Farah?

Simonyan?

Kasem?

Perhaps even herself?

She repeated a variation of the words, and each time fortified her belief. What had started only as an attempt to get Farah to relinquish the gun had become a way to process her own feelings. The General Majed she had met this day was a far cry from the military strategist who had created the Ahriman or orchestrated one of the biggest terrorist attacks in history. His body had died moments earlier, but his mind had disappeared long before that.

The dead man at their feet was just a child who had stolen his big brother's toy.

Even as a child, the general had manipulated people to shine the spotlight on himself. Whatever lesson there was in that, General Majed was gone.

Petra stopped in front of Farah, only a couple of inches in front of the gun. "Everyone in this room bears some responsibility for what happened to Afshar. There's more than enough blame to go around. But killing us will not bring you peace."

Simonyan was only a few feet away now. She had successfully kept Farah's focus so that she had no idea of his approach. He signaled toward her again—he could neutralize Farah easily—but Petra made a slight gesture with her right hand. Farah wasn't a target, just a grieving woman. Petra didn't want her to die, even if that meant risking her own life.

She raised her hands and placed them both around the barrel of the gun. The metal was warm to the touch, but not scalding. "And it won't bring him back." She pushed down on the gun and Farah released it. It hit the ceramic tile with a double clang.

Farah fell forward into her arms, her body convulsed by sobs.

A siren outside broke the tension, followed by several car doors slamming.

Simonyan gestured in the direction of the basement. "Go now, while you still can. The window downstairs."

# Chapter 78

*Alborz Mountains, Iran*

Kasem hesitated for a second, then met Petra's gaze and nodded. "We'll give you fifteen minutes to get everyone clear. The guards are out in the woods, but we've got Farah, Sami, and the two nurses," he said to Simonyan.

Kasem jumped to his feet, but before sprinting back toward the staircase, he looked at Simonyan. There was a lot he wanted to say. He wanted to thank him for giving them a window to escape. For internalizing all that Petra had said. The Ahriman had taken most of his wife's family, but it was General Majed who had given the order. General Majed who was responsible.

General Majed who was dead.

Kasem wished there was something he could say or do to make amends. He had kept Simonyan in the dark, and in the midst of their relationship as asset and handler, they had formed a bond. Simonyan had risked everything to help them. Sami Majed had said they needed his help to get out of Iran alive. That might still be true, but he wasn't going to wait to find out. More than Sami, they needed Simonyan.

"Let me know when you get clear," he said as he began to run down the hallway. Petra was ahead of him, although he made up the distance quickly. Normally, she was way faster than him, but her balance had taken a solid hit because of her head wound. At least her hearing seemed to be more or less back.

When they reached the basement, they dodged the debris from the explosion and made for the window. Petra tripped over a crate of what looked like old board games and LEGO. The lid of a box marked "Monop" fell to the side as she caught herself.

"Ow, those damned little pieces." She got to her feet and paused, fiddling with something on her wrist.

"We have to go." Kasem beckoned from below the windowsill. "You first."

"You go ahead; the first one will have to help pull the other up."

She gave him a leg up and he caught the edge of the sill, heaving himself through with a muscle-up. He lay in the brush for half a second to catch his breath, then flipped over and pivoted to anchor his feet against the spot where the house outcropping met the ground. He would have preferred a better anchor point, but there was little chance of finding one quickly enough. Especially in the dark. Wedging his boots at the joint as best as possible, he leaned his torso forward through the open window. He winced as bits of broken glass cut into the gap between his shirt and pants. His gloves had protected his hands on the way up.

Petra swung her arms back and forth a couple of times, then leaped toward him. Her grip slipped as she grasped for his arms, but he managed to catch hold of her elbows, giving her the extra second for her hands to take hold.

She looked up at him. "On three."

He swayed back and forth. "One, two, three." He put as much force into the direction of his swing as he could muster, and her hands closed around the sill.

She yelled several curse words as the glass cut into her hands but maintained her grip. A second later, he helped hoist her out of the window.

The rain was still coming down but had slowed from an impenetrable wall into a steady mist. They ran toward the east side of the house, the opposite direction from the driveway. Kasem strained his ears to hear what was going on behind them, but he couldn't make out much from that direction. Just a few muffled voices. Or perhaps his mind was playing tricks on him.

They got to the yard and made it into the tree cover, but Kasem didn't pause to look back. Once they got to the riverbed, they would be far enough away for him to signal.

Petra stumbled to the ground at the riverbank, and he finally stopped to glance behind. All he could hear was raindrops pattering into the branches that surrounded them. They were clear of the house, the worst of the commotion behind them.

"It's time," Petra said.

He checked his phone and nodded, but the moment felt incomplete. It was time, but they would pay the price.

She spoke into the comm. "Tim, go for it."

"But your tracker—"

"We have to wipe all traces."

"Are you sure?"

"We'll find another way. Do it, now."

Petra removed the SIM cards from her CIA-connected phone, then Kasem's, and stamped on both with her foot. She grabbed Kasem's hand and the two of them looked in the direction of the house. For a couple of minutes nothing changed. Then a spot in the distance flashed, turning into a combo of red and yellow as the Predator drone obliterated the house.

And along with it, the body of General Majed.

# Chapter 79

*Alborz Mountains, Iran*

Petra and Kasem took shelter under an outcropping of rock to wait out the worst of the storm, which had regained its intensity. When they finally began the climb, her head had stopped pounding and her balance had stabilized. She proceeded with caution a couple of feet behind Kasem. Each time he clipped into a subsequent anchor, he tested it, but she still used a secondary test as she attached to each one. Under normal circumstances, she was a reasonably skilled climber, but she'd never had to scale a mountain face within a few hours of a head injury. At the top of the cliff, she almost collapsed in the car. Her body and mind threatened to succumb to the exhaustion, but she pinched herself and pulled down hard on each ear lobe—anything to keep herself awake. They were clear of the house, but a far cry from safe until they could find a place to lie low.

Kasem glanced at her from the driver's seat. "You okay?"

"I'll be fine."

"Did you get sick earlier? You might have a concussion."

"No vomiting—so if I do, it's a mild one."

"We should still get you checked out."

"As soon as we get to the safe house," Petra agreed. She wished she felt more confident in the arrangement they had made, but there was no way around it. Kasem had made contact with Tanya Mir, the shifty former French asset Gaston had provided them. Three sizeable deposits later, she'd set up a small apartment for them on the outskirts of the city—a place that was off CIA and Agency radar. Tanya was willing to provide them with passage out of the country, but neither of them were particularly confident in her ability to deliver.

*Beggars can't be choosers.* Petra sighed and watched the mountainside as they descended the switchbacks. Moonlight had turned to dawn and she could see the outline of the city in the distance. "Whatever happens next, that's some view," she whispered.

"No one I'd rather share it with."

After a pit stop at a gas station en route, they made it to the safe house three hours later. That afternoon, news circulated online about a gas fire that had killed an elderly man at a house in the Alborz Mountains. No other casualties were reported.

"Looks like Simonyan got everyone clear," Petra said as she looked up from the article.

"I knew he would."

"When you're ready to talk about any of it, I'm here."

"I know."

Although she was tempted to press him further, Petra decided against it. Kasem deserved to process everything that had happened at his own pace. She could only imagine how difficult it all was—the confrontation with General Majed alone would have been more than enough. With her interactions with Sami Majed, Farah's relationship with Lieutenant Afshar, and the fact Simonyan now knew about Kasem's involvement in his brother-in-law's death on top of that, it was a miracle he was still mentally functional.

Petra napped on and off during the first day at the safe house. They kept watch in shifts, on constant alert for any police activity. The next morning, Kasem checked his burner phone and gasped.

"What is it?"

Kasem looked up from typing a reply. "Ramshad. He saw the news coverage and put two and two together. Petra, he says he'll help."

"I thought he was done."

"So did I."

Petra squeezed his hand. She knew how much Ramshad's help meant to him. They would probably never see each other again, but he and Kasem had formed a real friendship despite all the cloak and dagger tactics of the op.

After another fitful night, Kasem woke her at three in the morning. Ramshad had arranged for transport in a cargo truck to the town of Rasht. They hid in a compartment under the back seat in the cab. The ride back through the Alborz was bumpy but uneventful. From there, they transferred to a rental car—two local tourists on their way to Bandar Anzali on the Caspian coast. They left the car in an empty lot near a coastal alcove on the outskirts of the town per Ramshad's instructions. On foot, they made their way to the beach, where they would board a boat that would take them to Azerbaijan.

Petra laid down with her head in Kasem's lap and watched their last Iranian sunset. Despite the continuing danger, it reminded her of a night they had spent together on Kish Island. "Do you remember watching the sunset like this?"

"I'll never forget."

"Simpler times?"

"Beautiful memories." He smiled at her. "I wouldn't trade it for where we are now though. We deserve to know all of who we are, not just the easy parts. I still choose you."

"I love you too. And yes, I choose you too."

Dusk turned to dark, and they waited for the signal from the arriving boat. Shortly after midnight, Kasem motioned out toward the water. "There it is." When it was closer, they rose to make their way down the beach.

A car flashed its lights from the parking lot behind them and Kasem squeezed her hand. "Go, I'll go check it out."

"I won't go without you."

The moonlight was dim, but she could see him struggling with what to do. Finally, he said, "Stay here in the shadows."

Petra pretended to agree but followed a few steps behind.

# Chapter 80

*Bandar Anzali, Iran*

Kasem approached the headlights with caution. *It's probably nothing*, he told himself, yet he couldn't ignore the foreboding in his gut. It was time for the Ahriman to pay the piper.

The driver's door opened, and he squinted at the shadow that emerged. The giant shadow.

"Kasem? Did I get here in time?"

Kasem recognized his friend's voice and jogged forward, throwing caution to the wind. "It's good to see you."

"I wanted to say goodbye." Ramshad held out his hand and Kasem shook it.

"Thank you for coming, my friend."

"Good luck to both of you. I hope we can meet again some time."

"I'll find a way to let you know that we're safe."

"Too bad we can't have a drink together out here."

"Another time."

"Insha'Allah," Ramshad agreed. "Now go. It's time."

Kasem glanced out at the water. The lights from the boat were closer. "Thank you for everything. Before I go, there's something I want to tell you."

"Go on."

"My real name is Kasem Ismaili."

"I won't forget it."

Kasem headed back down to the beach, and Petra joined him within a few steps. An inflatable raft approached, and they waded into the water to board it.

A few minutes later, they climbed a ladder onto the larger craft. Once they were aboard, he looked back and watched Ramshad's headlights disappear.
*Always forward, never back.*

# Chapter 81

*Astara, Azerbaijan*

The night their boat docked in Azerbaijan, Petra slept for the first time. Real deep sleep, uninterrupted by ongoing fear or a need to keep watch.

When she rose the next morning, she could hardly believe where she was. Each step through the new safe house felt like it was straight out of a dream.

She made it to the kitchen and fiddled with the espresso maker. "Do you want some coffee? Do you know how to work this thing?"

"Not really. I just pushed the big silver button, and an espresso came out."

Petra glanced over her shoulder, about to chastise him for not making a second cup. Kasem was seated by the floor-to-ceiling windows at the far side of the living room. He was deeply engrossed in *Oath of Loyalty,* a Mitch Rapp novel by Kyle Mills that he'd picked out from the bookcase down the hall. Next to him, the side table had an empty plate of whatever he had eaten for breakfast along with a mug of what had to be coffee. She paused for a second to stare at the picture. All thought of reprimanding him had vanished. It was so foreign to see him seated that way, doing something so normal.

"What's wrong?"

"Nothing. I, I don't think I've seen you reading like that in a long time."

*A really long time.* The last time she had seen him that relaxed was back in their Machiya house in Kyoto, three years earlier. That time had been a honeymoon period for them, shortly after she had decided to give their relationship another shot.

250

*No, not even there.* She blinked away a stray tear. Her last memory of him being fully relaxed was from ten years earlier, when they first got together in Tehran.
*Before the Ahriman ever existed.*

Petra looked away quickly, turning her attention back to the machine. She had to pour out a couple of muddy espressos before she figured out the water supply had run low. A few minutes later, she sat down in the armchair opposite Kasem, curled up against the backrest with her knees to her chest. The early morning air coming through the screen door was chilly and she shivered, then pulled a throw draped over the armrest up to her chin.

Petra savored the sip. The first beam of dawn had just appeared over the horizon. The east view off the patio was nothing short of spectacular. She planned to spend most of the afternoon seated outside staring out at the Caspian Sea, cold be damned.

The loudspeaker from a minaret in the Caucasus Mountains behind the villa sputtered. A moment later, the dawn namaz prayer began, echoing through the living room. Petra leaned back into the armchair. She had never been religious, but she'd grown up hearing the muezzin's call in Kuwait. It had often awoken her in the middle of the night, but today she found it strangely comforting—a return to a time when things were simpler. In Tehran, she had become so used to it that she had stopped listening. Being able to take it in now, in this moment, felt like a gift.

*We're free.*

She thought back to the trick she had pulled, something that had started when they were still at the estate in Scotland. Once she and Kasem had decided to run as soon as the operation was over, she knew she needed to do something to set the plan in motion. With Tim's help, she had learned how to remove her embedded tracker, and before her jump from the window of the room she was held in, she had attached it to her watch.

Before they fled the mountain house, she had deposited the watch in the basement amongst the debris of half-destroyed junk. When Tim had engaged the drones, he hadn't known if they were clear of the strike zone. The night before, Kasem had used a one-time phone to let the team know they were safe. He'd also sent one final message to Ramshad before destroying the SIM card and battery. Petra had also taken the opportunity to remove and destroy Kasem's tracker, just in case it could be activated remotely.

The official CIA story was that they had neutralized General Majed and been killed trying to escape the police. It was a risk to let the team know they were alive, but one they had decided to take. Only their immediate family and a select group of friends would know they had survived. Both she and Kasem preferred an existence where they had people they could rely on, not only those they had to run from. They would maintain an additional phone, one without GPS, for emergency contact in the future, but other than that, they planned to disappear.

Their last nights in Iran felt like they had happened to other people. The ride in the cargo truck and journey from the beach were all a haze. Perhaps they were still stuck in that dream. Petra kept expecting to wake up.

The villa was an old French intelligence safe house that was now rarely used, but Gaston had made the arrangements. He had aptly referred to it as *la maison du paradis*. Petra couldn't think of a better name for it.

She finished her first cup and returned to the kitchen for a second, then went back to her spot by the window.

Most of the day passed in a similar state of relaxation. Petra took advantage of some fleeting early afternoon sunshine to do a calisthenics workout on the patio. As soon as she was done, she rushed inside and held her fingers over the gas fireplace for several minutes to thaw out. Momentum had carried her through eight sets of box-up burpees, but each time she had placed her hands on the deck, they had started to ache progressively from the frost.

After a long soak in the tub, she had even taken a nap. She awoke snuggled under the covers when Kasem beckoned her to the living room.

"Hurry, the press conference is about to start."

She rubbed the grogginess out of her eyes and sidled onto the couch next to him.

The president appeared onscreen a moment later. "Good morning. Today I can report to the American people and to everyone worldwide that the United States conducted a targeted operation that killed General Majed, a former Iranian military official turned terrorist who was responsible for the murder of over three hundred people at the Suez Canal. None of us will ever forget the largest attack in over a decade, one that sparked enormous backlash in cities worldwide."

Kasem gripped her hand tightly as the president continued, describing the aftermath of the attack at Suez and how they had initially believed the Ahriman was responsible, only to discover General Majed's culpability three years later. The president went on to detail the official parameters of the operation, how he had commissioned a small team to locate and neutralize the general while limiting civilian casualties.

"While the team ensured that no civilians were harmed, the firefight that ensued and killed General Majed did result in the death of two American team members. Their identities will remain classified for the foreseeable future. We will honor their sacrifice in the years going forward. General Majed's death marks the most significant achievement in our nation's ongoing battle against terrorism since the death of Osama bin Laden in 2011."

*The death of two team members.*

Petra felt a wave of emotion slam into her. With that statement, they were free. There would be no more operations. No more supposedly last forays back into the business. No more grappling with questions about the greater good.

Kasem turned toward her. His eyes looked almost as watery as hers felt.

"We're free," he whispered, as if saying the words any louder might compromise their new reality.

She leaned over and kissed him, then met his gaze once more. "Yes. We're free."

"Do you know what this means?"

"What?"

He gestured toward the patio. "I think this is the perfect wedding venue."

# Chapter 82

*One week later – Istanbul, Turkey*

Rachel handed the list over to her boss. "I think you can see where the leak came from. You showed the file I gave you to three team leads. I conducted confidential interviews with two team members associated with each. Only one lead handed out the document in its entirety. Including the exact picture that showed up on the police bulletin in Tehran. The resulting conclusion is fairly obvious—the leak had to come from him or someone on his team."

"Devon? Come on. That's not possible."

"You have my report. If there's grounds to disagree, I'll leave that to you."

"Why don't we look into the team further before we run this up the flagpole?"

"I already dropped all of this off with Conway earlier today."

James frowned. "Very well. Do you think it was an intentional breach?"

"I'd rather not speculate. I'd look pretty closely at who he's had contact with."

"Let me know what you need to dig deeper. You have my full support."

"I'm afraid you'll have to run your own investigating. That said, I'll be available for testimony when you decide to move forward."

"Are you saying…"

"I'll be joining Alex Mittal's team over at the Agency. Smaller place, less red tape. Seems like a better fit for me than the CIA. Don't worry, you still get credit for taking out General Majed."

Rachel left without bothering to wait for a reply. There wasn't more to be said.

# Chapter 83

*Istanbul, Turkey*

Rachel glanced at the caller ID and frowned. "What can I do for you, Conway?"

"I know we left things on shaky ground, but I'd like you to be in charge of a new operation."

"Excuse me?"

"Before you turn me down, let me explain. First, you can run this from the Agency. I'm not asking you to come back—I know that ship has sailed. More importantly, I believe this will be very cathartic for you."

"Can't say I'm not intrigued."

"We need to monitor Devon's movements. Trace all of his contacts. Figure out how this breach happened."

"What about damage control?"

"The good news is that it's contained. There are only two ops he could have compromised, besides yours," Conway continued.

"That's three too many."

"I agree. Which is why I'd like to right the scale. I want you to run a counterintel op to nail his ass to the wall, as well as anyone he's been working with. Based on your report on General Majed, we might even collect a defector in the bargain."

"Sami Majed," Rachel said.

"Exactly. I know he might have been blowing smoke, but I doubt it. If you agree, you can follow this from both sides and see where it leads."

"I'll think about it."

"Alex is already on board, but he said it's your call. Let me know what you decide."

"Will do."

# Chapter 84

*Two weeks later – Astara, Azerbaijan*

Petra surveyed herself in the mirror and smoothed the front of the silver A-line dress she had picked out for the wedding. *Kasem and I are getting married.* The thought still seemed like fiction. A version of the future she had hardly dared hope for after his arrest a few months earlier.

"You look beautiful," her mom, Danielle, said quietly behind her, her eyes watery. "The dress, your hair, everything—it's perfect. I'm so happy for you. I only wish you didn't have to leave so soon."

Blinking away her own tears, Petra turned to embrace her mom. The two weeks since they had made it out of Iran had passed like a whirlwind. Carlos was the one who had suggested it—a last hurrah before they headed off into new lives and identities. He'd arranged for her parents to come out, and for Kasem's as well.

The reunion had been full of tears. They wouldn't be able to visit for a long time, and only on occasion after that. But now that no one would be hunting for them, in time, the world would once again be open. Both sets of parents had struggled with the planned arrangement, as had Kasem's sister, but eventually they had convinced them.

Despite working as an intelligence agent since she graduated from undergrad, Petra had never read her parents in on the type of work she did, instead maintaining a cover of consulting and international teaching work that required extensive travel. During those days spent looking out at the Caspian, she had finally worked up the courage to tell them. She wanted them to at least understand why they would have to disappear for a while.

"I'll find a way to stay in touch, but we won't be able to see each other for some time."

They had protested at first, but finally her dad had met her gaze with a bittersweet smile. "So long as you are doing what you think is right, we are with you, always, Jaleela joon," he said, using her middle name, Jaleela, and the suffix joon, a Persian term of deep endearment. "We love you and support you, no matter what."

That moment replayed in Petra's head as she stepped back from her mom, waving her right hand in front of her face so as not to ruin her makeup. Her mom had been unusually quiet as she got dressed, watching her apply her makeup in silence. "I love you, Mom," she whispered.

Looking back at the mirror, at her mom standing behind her, Petra felt a wave of sadness wash over her. She would miss them, but she drew comfort from the fact that in time they would be able to see each other again.

"He makes you happy, right? This is what you want?" Danielle asked.

"He does. I only wish we had more time for you to get to know him better."

"Me too." Danielle gave her a quick nod. "I'll be right back." She disappeared in the direction of the bathroom. When she returned a few minutes later, she spoke in an unsteady voice. "I think it's time, my dear."

Petra followed her mom toward the patio. Kasem and the few guests who had been able to make it were already seated outside; they had only been able to invite their closest friends and family members. They reached the living room and Petra smiled at her dad, who was fidgeting on the couch while he waited for them. His face lit up. "I thought you were going to be late, Jaleela," he said softly. "You both look stunning."

"Not so bad yourself." Danielle took his hand.

Petra was a few steps behind her and gave her father a bear hug as soon as she reached him. "I love you both so much."

"Let's not keep everybody waiting," he said in a somewhat gruff tone, obviously an attempt to stave off his emotions.

"All right, Dad." Petra linked one arm with each of her parents and they stepped out into the backyard together. She breathed deep and drank in the sunshine. The air was warm with the midday sun, but not too hot. The smell of the sea greeted her, along with a few birds chirping in the distance.

The three of them walked out slowly, stepping carefully onto the stone patio leading out to the archway. Petra's gaze skimmed the two rows on each side of the aisle they had set up. Chris and Rachel were both to her right, along with Carlos's wife, Diane. Gaston and Tim were seated on her left, next to Kasem's parents and sister. Petra locked eyes with Kasem, standing at the front next to Carlos, who they had asked to officiate. At one point, when she thought her parents might not be able to attend, she had asked him to give her away, but asking him to officiate made so much more sense. He'd been a huge piece of her journey since graduating from college—a mentor and close friend, and for the most part had been supportive of their relationship, even developing his own friendship with Kasem.

When Petra and her parents reached the small platform they were using as a makeshift altar, she gave each of them another hug and they retreated to the first row. Stepping up to Kasem, she took his hands and they beamed at each other.

"We're here... finally," she whispered.

"Best day of my life."

"Friends, family, we're here to celebrate Petra and Kasem, two people who found each other against all odds," Carlos started off. "I first met Petra, or kid sister, as I like to call her now, through work, where we quickly went from colleagues, to mentor and mentee, to close friends, and finally became family. I've seen these two go through thick and thin, and I have to admit I wasn't always sure where they would end up. Now that we're here, I think I speak for all of us when I say how delighted we are they made it to today. Marriage is a journey that takes us through countless ups and downs, bringing us more joy than we could possibly imagine, especially on a day like today. But also, at times, pushing us to the brink with sadness, frustration, sometimes even anger. During those dark times, we come back to the partnership that we chose, and the memories that built it. That recollection grounds us and reminds us of what we're fighting for, and *why*. In that spirit, I've chosen an excerpt from the poem 'On Marriage' by Kahlil Gibran that I believe describes it best.

> *You shall be together when the white wings of death scatter your days.*
> *Ay, you shall be together even in the silent memory of God.*
> *But let there be spaces in your togetherness,*
> *And let the winds of the heavens dance between you.*
>
> *Love one another, but make not a bond of love:*
> *Let it rather be a moving sea between the shores of your souls.*
> *Fill each other's cup but drink not from one cup.*
> *Sing and dance together and be joyous, but let each one of you be alone,*
> *Even as the strings of a lute are alone though they quiver with the same music.*
>
> *Give your hearts, but not into each other's keeping.*
> *For only the hand of Life can contain your hearts.*
> *And stand together yet not too near together:*
> *For the pillars of the temple stand apart,*
> *And the oak tree and the cypress grow not in each other's shadow.*

Carlos paused as he reached the end of the poem. "I believe these verses to be one of the best representations of a successful marriage, something to always strive for and work toward—to love and give to one another, while letting your partner flourish as an individual. Petra and Kasem, I wish you both a long, wonderful life together with everything that makes you sing, dance, and be joyous together. So, without further ado, let's get to the main event." His voice quavered, then steadied as he took them through the ring exchange and prompted them to say their vows.

Petra choked up as she ran through the vows she and Kasem had written together their last night in Tehran—the night before she had gone to the bathhouse to meet with Sami Majed.

"Kasem, I promise to be your champion, to support you in all the traits that make you who you are. I promise to be real with you, to celebrate your victories, remind you that failures are simply temporary roadblocks we will overcome together, and be strong in the face of whatever life throws at us. I promise to love you and to laugh with you, to sing and dance, and try not to take myself too seriously. Above all, I promise to be your partner, to make all the big decisions together, and to make my journey alongside yours."

Kasem repeated the same vows, and when he reached the end, Carlos took over again. "You kids are going to make me cry. Now, in front of your family and friends, I pronounce you husband and wife. Hurry up and kiss so we can all go eat and party."

Kasem drew her close. "I love you, wife," he whispered and kissed her.

"I love you, husband."

### THE END

Dear Reader,

I'm so excited that you read my book. It still feels kind of surreal, that I have readers who actually read my books! Thank you so much.

I would love to hear what you thought of *Battle for the Veiled City*. Would you mind posting a review on Amazon, Goodreads, or Bookbub?

Word of mouth and reviews are critical for any author to succeed. I would be so grateful if you would post a review! Even if it's only a line or two, it would be a tremendous help.

If you'd like to stay in touch, sign up for my mailing list here: **http://smarturl.it/PujaList**

I'll let you know about new releases, contests, and more!

Thank you again!

With all my best,

Puja Guha

# About the Author

Puja Guha grew up and has worked all over the world, something which she channels into her writing, incorporating settings from New York to Madagascar to Iran. So far, she has published four spy thrillers, an international family drama and a psychological thriller. Her spy thriller series *The Ahriman Legacy* is an Amazon international bestseller and has been recommended by the US Review of Books. The series follows a former spy and assassin on their adventures together all over the world, from Kuwait to Paris, Madagascar, and finally to Iran. Her recent psychological thriller *Sirens of Memory* was named one of the best crime fiction books of 2021 by Diverse Voices Book Review.

# Connect with Puja Guha

Email: pujaguha@pujaguha.com
Follow me on Twitter: http://twitter.com/guhapuja
Friend me on Facebook: http://facebook.com/puja.guha
Google plus: https://plus.google.com/106961837703326951468
Connect with me on Goodreads:
http://www.goodreads.com/user/show/21394716-puja-guha
Connect with me on Linkedin:
http://www.linkedin.com/in/pujaguha
Webpage: www.pujaguha.com

Made in United States
Troutdale, OR
04/10/2025